"Hellboy!" Abe snapped.

Hellboy twisted around, even as he drew the pistol, to see the face of Jangbu changing, flesh changing texture, jaw protruding. His eyes began to burn, fire licking up from the edges.

"Him? This old guy was your guy?" he shouted to Anastasia.

"No. It wasn't him," she said, her voice curiously lifeless.

Which was when Hellboy noticed that it wasn't just Jangbu. The villagers were all changing, skin turning to rough, scaly hide, fangs protruding, eyes on fire. Jangbu hissed and started toward them.

They were all shape-shifters. Or, at least, all subhuman. From the look of them, they were part human, and part dragon.

Abe squeezed the trigger on the Uzi. Bullets dug up earth just a few feet in front of the dragon-men. They paused. But the others, the ones who were changing even as they lunged at the helicopter, didn't slow down.

The chopper blades whirred, and Redfield took her up. The helicopter rose quickly, one of the dragon-men hanging from the left skid. He let go and fell thirty feet to the ground, landing on his feet without any injury at all.

"Stupid git, where's he going?" Anastasia snapped, drawing her pistol and waving it around to help keep the villagers back.

"Standard operating procedure," Hellboy said. "We don't have another chopper. If there's trouble, orders are to dust off, get help."

Abe swung the barrel of the Uzi around. "Help isn't coming before we run out of bullets."

"Guess not," Hellboy replied, turning quickly, long coat whipping around his tail behind him. "So we do what we came here for."

Other HELLBOY titles available from Pocket Books

The Lost Army by Christopher Golden
The Bones of Giants by Christopher Golden
On Earth As It Is In Hell by Brian Hodge
Unnatural Selection by Tim Lebbon
The God Machine by Thomas E. Sniegoski

THE DRAGON POOL

CHRISTOPHER GOLDEN

POCKET **STAR** BOOKS

New York London Toronto Sydney

An *Original* Publication of POCKET BOOKS

A Pocket Star Book published by
POCKET BOOKS, a division of Simon & Schuster, Inc.
1230 Avenue of the Americas, New York, NY 10020

For information address Pocket Books, 1230 Avenue of the Americas, New York, NY 10020

ISBN-13: 978-1-4165-0785-7
ISBN-10: 1-4165-0785-X

This Pocket Books paperback edition April 2007

10 9 8 7 6 5 4 3 2 1

Cover art by Mike Mignola

Manufactured in the United States of America

For information regarding special discounts for bulk purchases, please contact Simon & Schuster Special Sales at 1-800-456-6798 or business@simonandschuster.com.

For David Kraus.
Here there be dragons.

Acknowledgments

The author would like to thank editor Jennifer Heddle and deal maker Scott Shannon for thowing the party, Tom Sniegoski, Tim Lebbon, and Brian Hodge for making it a blast, and especially Mike Mignola for bringing the dancing girls. Special thanks are also due to Jason Hall for the history lesson, and LeeAnne Sniegoski for her eagle eye.

THE DRAGON POOL

Prologue

1991

The surface of Lake Tashi rippled with the cool breeze that swept down from the snowcapped mountains of the Nyenchen Tanghla range. Anastasia Bransfield gazed out across sapphire water that gleamed in golden sunlight, and knew that she stood at the edge of the world, at a place where gods and legends seemed not so very far away and never forgotten.

At forty-two, she had spent half her life as an archaeologist, preeminent in her field, and her work had taken her to some of the most remote and exotic locations in the world—not to mention some of the most dangerous. Yet never had she visited a place more beautiful than this Tibetan mountain range. Lake Tashi stretched across a plateau fifteen thousand feet above sea level. The air carried the chill from the mountains, yet it was clean and crisp and made her feel more alive than she had ever felt before.

On the hillside above the lake, gusts of wind swirled small clouds of dirt up and away, as her team excavated an ancient village where a mountain king was rumored to have lived. The British Museum had launched this dig as a joint venture with the Archaeological Council of Tibet. The region was controlled by the Chinese government, which was usually resistant to the idea of digging up the past, particularly sites that might be considered holy—but Anastasia had received the blessing of both parties to lead the expedition. Her reputation had won over the Chinese, something the museum people had counted on when they hired her.

She stood at the base of the hill, taking her first official break of the day. The excavation had been going quite well thus far. They had exposed one structure that appeared to be a fairly large, communal building that would be quite uncharacteristic for a mountain village thousands of years old—unless it was a palace. It seemed they had found preliminary evidence that the theories behind the expedition were sound.

Anastasia cared not at all.

Only a few members of her team knew it, but she hadn't come up here looking for the palace of any mountain king. Or, more accurately, it wasn't all she'd come for. If her own research held up, there was a reason none of the legends and stories about the village ever gave the same name for the king, or his people. There was a reason the breathtaking landscape around Lake Tashi was inhabited only by nomadic herders. And although there was a small village not far to the northwest, and a monastery on a mountainside to the east, there was a reason that no one had ever settled on the hills above the lake or on its shores.

There were secrets here. And there were those who did not want the dig to continue for fear of those secrets being unearthed. In the fifteen weeks since they had begun, equipment had been sabotaged or stolen, excavation sites had caved in even though she herself had seen to their safety and stability, and strange figures had been spotted sneaking around the encampment after dark. Her top engineer, Frank Danovich, had admitted to her that he'd gotten a quick glimpse of an intruder by flashlight on the night of a cave-in, and said the bastard was so ugly he was monstrous.

Anastasia had asked him to elaborate, but Danovich had just knocked back a shot of rum and turned away. She hadn't prodded him further. Anastasia had dealt with her share of monsters. As far as the rest of the world was concerned, she'd even been in love with one once upon a time.

"What's your secret?" she whispered, gazing out across the brilliant blue water of Lake Tashi. The wind whistled down off the mountains, but carried no answer.

Yet she had her suspicions.

"Dr. Bransfield!" a voice called from behind her.

She turned and squinted. With the angle of the sun coming over the hill, even the brim of her New York Yankees cap was not enough to keep the glare from her eyes. She held up a hand to shade her face, and at last she could make out the figure hurrying down the rough path they had worn up the hillside to the dig site. Rafe Mattei was a twenty-two-year-old archaeology student, one of a group that was having its first real field exposure on this expedition. For a kid—at forty-two, she figured she'd earned the right to call him that—Rafe was a handsome man, tall and thin, with rich chocolate eyes.

Anastasia tried not to think about him that way. It helped that he called her Dr. Bransfield; it reminded her that she herself wasn't a kid anymore.

"Dr. Bransfield!" he called again.

Rafe nearly tripped as he reached the bottom of the hill. His eyes were wide with excitement, and he was flushed from having run all the way down to fetch her.

"What've we got, Rafe?" she asked, striding past him and starting up the hill along the same path he had descended.

He fell into step beside her without complaint. "Professor Kyichu sent me to bring you back. We found it, Dr. Bransfield. The temple."

Anastasia stopped and turned to him. Rafe searched her eyes, enthusiastic but still not quite sure what the significance of it all was. How could he be? None of the students knew what she was really looking for—but Kyichu did. A Tibetan who'd been living and teaching in London for years, Kyichu was the one who had convinced the Chinese government to cooperate. The widower had even brought his eleven-year-old daughter, Kora, along as an unofficial member of the team. Anastasia had shared with him her true goal, but only after he had begun to guess at her purpose. He thought her a dreamer, thought she put too much stock in legends, but Anastasia had insisted that every legend grew from a seed of truth, and that was what she sought on the shore of Lake Tashi.

"Is it part of the palace?" she asked.

Rafe shook his head. "Just next to it. All they've excavated so far is the door. There's writing on it, though. A lot of writing."

Anastasia laughed softly. She took off her Yankees cap and shook out her long, strawberry blond hair, feeling strangely freed by this news. With a grin she grabbed Rafe's head in both hands, pulled him forward, and kissed his forehead.

"That's the best news I've had in a year."

Shaking her head at her own caprice, she hurried up the hill, baseball cap crushed in her grip. In truth, until she knew what was written on that door, this discovery could be either good news, or a frustrating disappointment. But at least she would have the beginnings of the answers she sought.

Together they hurried up the hillside. Though she was in excellent physical condition, by the time they reached the excavation site, Anastasia was huffing and had to stop to catch her breath. She told herself it was the elevation and was pleased to see that Rafe seemed equally winded. Dust from the dig swirled away in the chill mountain breeze, but she tugged on the neck of her thick sweater, overheated from the climb.

Students and other archaeologists on the team hovered around her as she made a beeline for the place Rafe indicated. They barraged her with questions, but she ignored them, her focus entirely on the opening in the hillside ahead. Equipment had been pulled back, and diggers stood around, waiting for instructions.

On the edge of the newly excavated hole, she fell to her knees. The hole sloped down at a forty-five-degree angle. The ladders had been laid down more as steps than to be used for climbing. Professor Kyichu stood in front of a stone door with one of the students. Etched in the door were lines of characters from the ancient language of this land.

"Han," Anastasia said.

He turned and smiled up at her. "That was fast."

"What does it say?"

Professor Kyichu nodded, his expression turning solemn. "You were right, Dr. Bransfield. I am sorry for doubting it. We have found the legend that we sought.

"We have found the Dragon King Pool."

On her knees, there in the dirt, Yankees cap still clutched in her hand, Anastasia could only grin. She shook her head in amazement. Moments like this—they made all of the tedium worthwhile.

"Have you translated the—" she began.

A shout interrupted her, a voice calling her name. Hers and Han Kyichu's.

Anastasia turned, half-rising, to see Ellie Morris running toward her. Others gave way as Ellie raced to the edge of the hole, panic in her eyes, chest heaving with exertion.

"Ellie, what is it, love?"

Anastasia reached for her, but the woman threw her hands up, shaking her head. Her eyes were damp with nascent tears.

"Professor," Ellie said, staring down into the hole, not even noticing the remarkable temple door they had discovered. "Han . . . I'm sorry, we've searched everywhere, but . . ."

The woman bit her lip, a tear tracing through the dirt on her face. She clapped a hand over her mouth, and now the tears fell in earnest.

"Please, Eleanor," Professor Kyichu said, "what has happened?"

Ellie hugged herself, glanced at Anastasia, then back at Han Kyichu. "It's your daughter, Professor. It's Kora. We can't find her anywhere.

"She's gone."

Chapter 1

Hellboy barreled down the mountain trail, breaking a new path through the trees. Branches slapped at him, scratching his face and generally pissing him off. He let out a thunderous shout of frustration and annoyance as he hurtled between a pair of tall trees. The space was too narrow, and his shoulders scraped the trunks, tearing off bark. His hooves pounded the hard earth beneath him, maneuvering over rocks and upraised roots, sliding in moss.

I came to Chile for this? he thought. *Coulda gone to Rio, watching some half-naked girls on parade.*

He came to the edge of a ravine, but his momentum was too great. No way could he stop. Instead he leaped, throwing himself toward the opposite side. His arms pinwheeled, and he pulled his legs up, sure he would make it . . . then sure he would not.

"Ah, crap." He crashed into the wall of the ravine, a few feet shy of the top. Vines hung down, and he tried to get his hands tangled in them, tried to get ahold of something, but it was too late.

He landed in a heap at the base of the ravine, legs buckling beneath him, and sprawled across the richly smelling earth. Something ripped, and he hoped it was the tear in his jacket getting worse and not the seat of his pants. This whole mission was humiliating enough already.

Hellboy stood, bones aching from the sprinting he'd done, and brushed leaves and moss off of his long, brown jacket and shorts. He pulled some kind of weird fuzz off of his cheek, where it had stuck to his bristly stubble.

"This was a stupid plan," he muttered, even as he warily looked up at the edge of the ravine twenty feet above him.

A shape darted into view, dark against the gloom of the forest, wings beating the air as it circled above him. In the shadows, it could have passed for an owl. But he wasn't that lucky.

The thing let out a flesh-prickling cry and began to circle faster. *Calling all its little buddies,* Hellboy thought. *Fantastic. All according to plan. Use the big, indestructible guy as bait.*

Even as the thought went through his head, he saw other shadows flitting out of the trees, wings fluttering as they joined the first, gliding above him like vultures.

"All right, buzzards. Just had to catch my breath."

With a sigh, he drew his gun, a huge, heavy pistol with a barrel four times the width of any ordinary handgun. Growing up, training with the BPRD, his marksmanship scores had never risen above pitiful. But if he got close enough, and with a gun this big, he could hit just about anything.

They dived toward him, dropping out of the sky, wings pinned as they came in for the kill. Hellboy took aim, squeezed the trigger, and one of them exploded into gristle and red mist. Then the others were swarming around him, and Hellboy gritted his teeth in disgust.

Flying heads, he thought. *That's what my life has come to? Flying heads?*

They had a name, he knew. The locals—the Araucanian people of Chile—called them Chonchonyi, but Hellboy couldn't take the damn things seriously. They were huge, monstrous heads with hideous, elongated faces. Their narrow fangs jutted up from black, ropy lips, and black, ridged wings stuck out from the sides of the heads like grotesque ears. Despite their ridiculous appearance, they were as vicious as any other strain of vampire, feasting on the old and infirm and relishing the blood and flesh of small children best of all. They never would have come after Hellboy . . . but he'd gone after them first.

"It's nothing personal," he said. He leveled the massive pistol again and pulled the trigger. The bullet tore a wing off one of the bloodthirsty heads, and it fell to the ground, convulsing. "It's my job."

Hell of a way to make a living.

They swarmed him. Hellboy swatted at them with

his huge, stone hand. One of the Chonchonyi landed on his left shoulder, fangs tearing through his jacket, sinking deep into his flesh. He cried out in pain, swore loudly, then slammed purposefully into a tree, scraping the thing off on the rough bark. It left a stinking, bloody smear and released a stench like skunk cabbage. He knew he'd never get the smell out of his coat.

Another bit into his tail, and he whipped the appendage up, tossing the bloodsucking predator into a tangle of bushes.

"That's it," he muttered. "The tail's off-limits."

He ran again, wondering why he'd stopped. Sure, the fall down the ravine had slowed him down, but trying to make a stand against a swarm of ravenous, flesh-eating, flying heads was just stupid. He had crap aim and not enough bullets, and anyway, that wasn't the plan.

Stick to the plan, he told himself.

He ran, hooves punching through soft soil now, years of detritus that had built up at the base of the ravine. When he emerged, he spared a quick glance upward and gauged his direction by the location of the sun. Typical vampires didn't come out until after dark, but the BPRD records included dozens of offshoot breeds or related species, and they all had their own rules. These things preferred the dark and the damp, but they'd go where the food was if necessary. Or if someone had stirred up their nest with a thermite charge and burned down a couple of acres of Chilean forest.

Whatever worked.

"Come on, come on," he muttered as he ran. The gun felt heavy in his hand. Several of the disgusting things flapped around his head, trying to take a bite of him, but they couldn't latch on while he was in motion. One snapped its jaws at his right temple, and its fangs struck the filed stumps of his horns, raising sparks. Hellboy slapped it away with the barrel of his gun.

Annoyed, he got off another shot, but the bullet plunged harmlessly into the forest. He had a hard enough time hitting a target when they were both standing still. With both him and the target in motion, the idea was absurd. He fired another bullet, just because it made him feel good to get out some of his frustration. The things were like giant vampire mosquitoes, and they were annoying the crap out of him.

Not for much longer.

His chest started to burn. Exercise was his friend and all, but this was ridiculous. His hooves pounded the earth, and he was practically in free fall, whipping down the mountainside, dodging through trees. He holstered the pistol on the run and stumbled over a rock, nearly falling. The heads started to shriek, calling to one another again, and he thought he knew what that meant. It was a good sign.

Until they started suicide runs. One of them slammed into him, fangs tearing the sleeve of his jacket before it fell, and he trampled it underhoof. Another came at his face, and Hellboy raised his ancient, massive left hand and punched it without slowing down. It spattered his face and body like a bug on a windshield, that skunk stink all over him now.

"Oh, great. That's just freakin' great," he shouted at the forest around him.

One got its fangs into his right thigh before he swatted it away. Two more were trampled. They were frenzied, now, as they tried to stop him from reaching open ground.

Then it was too late. Hellboy burst from the woods with the Chonchonyi darting all around him, their dark wings slapping the air, jaws gnashing, shrieking in fury and alarm.

The village lay ahead, a pretty little settlement on a lake. But the dwellings were quiet, empty. The villagers had other plans today. As Hellboy tromped into the clearing with the leeches flying around him, chanting filled the air. The words were an ancient spell, passed down through generations of Araucanians. Hellboy kept running until he'd passed the Seal of Solomon that he and the village elders had drawn in the dirt in the middle of the clearing.

The chant grew louder. The creatures began to falter in the air, flying in strange, wandering patterns, disoriented by the spell; then one by one they flew shakily toward the Seal of Solomon. Several fell to the ground and had to flop there, dragging themselves toward the

Seal, scuttling like crabs on the ridges of their wings.

The villagers looked on in amazement and horror. One little boy screamed, and his mother covered his eyes. Several other children turned and fled toward their homes. But most of the people remained, mesmerized by the sight, chanting and watching as the malevolent, bloodthirsty things that had preyed upon them throughout the ages gathered in the air and on the ground above the Seal of Solomon.

Hellboy looked around for the rest of his team, two professorial types and a pretty, red-haired young woman with her arms crossed and a look of defiance etched upon her features.

"Liz," he said, "come on. It's time."

"You know I can't do this," she said, with an insouciant toss of her hair, glaring at him as though damning him for his expectations. "Did you not notice the village, all the people, and oh, maybe the nice, flammable *forest?*"

Hellboy stretched, bones popping. His shins ached. He yawned as he plucked leaves from his jacket.

"You're fine," he replied. "We're in a clearing, hundreds of yards from the village. All the people are behind you, out of the way. Scorched earth policy, Liz. You don't have to control the power of the burn, only direction."

Something in her face gave way, and he saw in her again the little girl she'd been when they'd first met—the little firestarter who'd accidentally roasted her family and neighbors alive. The tough façade was gone, and all that remained was the fear of the fire inside her. It'd been years since the last time the flames had gotten the better of her, burning uncontrollably, but she could never forget. The fire was the enemy, even when she needed it—especially when she needed it. He hoped she'd make peace with it someday, but for now—

"Liz . . ."

She tucked a lock of red hair behind her ear and peered past him at the abhorrent, absurd creatures flying in drunken circles above the Seal of Solomon. More of them were dragging themselves on the ground; they would remain disoriented as long as the villagers continued their chant.

Gnawing her upper lip, Liz raised her right hand. White flames danced on her fingers and began to spread to her wrist. The fire blossomed from her hand, a churning inferno that rolled across the ground and engulfed the creatures.

The chant grew louder, so that the villagers could hear one another over the roar of the fire and the screaming of the burning demons. Liz closed her hand, snuffing the flames on her fingers and palm, then put her hands over her ears. Hellboy turned her around and led her back toward the village, wishing he had never come to Chile.

"Flying heads," he muttered. "My life's a circus."

Professor Trevor Bruttenholm sat at his enormous cherrywood desk among shelves upon shelves of scrolls and manuscripts and leather-bound tomes of arcane lore. Most of the books ought to have been stored in the archives of the Bureau for Paranormal Research and Defense, along with the artifacts and magical talismans that lay on his desk and on the mantel of the fireplace, gathering dust. But Bruttenholm had been one of the founders of the BPRD, and spent fifteen years as its director. Even the parade of bureaucrats who had headed up the Bureau after he'd resigned that position understood that the man deserved a bit of indulgence.

No one disturbed Professor Bruttenholm's office. Every artifact and manuscript existed as a mystery he had yet to solve. Some of them might take him years to decipher, and others he might never figure out, but he never stopped. Each of these he considered open cases, and they never remained far out of his mind, or out of reach.

This morning he sat in the high-backed chair behind his desk and smoked his pipe, the air redolent with the sweetness of his Turkish tobacco, and leafed through the pages of a German text he'd had in his possession since the Second World War. He easily translated the words, the strange prophecies, within, but had never been able to make sense of them. In almost fifty years, not a single prophecy from the book had come true. Every other agent or researcher in the employ of the BPRD he'd consulted over the years had presumed it must be a fraud, but something about it troubled him.

Trevor Bruttenholm trusted his instincts. Everything in his office held secrets yet to be unlocked. That was why he had given up the position of director so many years ago, and why, though he was an old man, he still functioned as a field agent for the BPRD. Life was brief, and he hadn't time to waste on the sort of politics that the director's job required.

Dust motes swirled in the morning light that crept across the room through the trio of tall windows on the eastern wall. Bruttenholm had never been a sound sleeper, and age had only exacerbated the problem. This morning he had come into his office just after four o'clock, long before dawn. Such hours were not uncommon for him. He rubbed his eyes and went back to deciphering German prophecies. The lamp on his desk was still on, but the morning sunlight had faded it to a dull glow.

There was a knock at the door, and Bruttenholm raised a bushy, white eyebrow as he glanced up. He slipped a finger into the book to mark his page.

"Come in."

The door opened immediately, and Dr. Tom Manning took a single step into the room, one hand on the knob. In his other hand, the BPRD's Director of Field Operations held a case folder. The man's pallid complexion seemed almost jaundiced in the morning light.

"Why is it always so dark in here?" Dr. Manning asked.

"I have a predilection for dark wood and heavy

drapes, Tom. You know this. It's very British of me, or so you've told me a dozen times."

Manning actually smiled, not a common occurrence. His hair was thinning, and the twenty-five extra pounds he carried around depressed him almost as much as the bureaucracy he had to deal with every day. One day, he would make a fine old curmudgeon, if a heart attack did not take him first. In truth, Bruttenholm thought that one day, Tom Manning would make a fine director for the Bureau—far better than the politicians who had served in the role for so long. He had a "buck stops here" mentality that was more than necessary for such a job, and for the Field Operations post he currently held.

"Good morning, Professor," Dr. Manning said, beginning again.

"And to you, Tom. To what do I owe the pleasure?"

"I have a field assignment that I'd like you to take the lead on."

Bruttenholm raised both eyebrows this time. The BPRD usually tried to discourage his work as a field agent these days, putting his value as a researcher and occult expert far above his value as an active agent.

"Go on."

Dr. Manning stepped farther into the room and handed him the case file. "We've received a joint request from the British and Chinese governments to conduct an investigation in Tibet. The British ambassador describes the situation as 'urgent.'"

"And the Chinese?" Bruttenholm asked, taking the proffered file.

"You know the Chinese government," Manning replied. "They've signed off on the formal request, but they act as though they're doing it as a favor to London. They'd never admit they need our help."

"Why is London involved at all?"

Manning sighed impatiently. "It's all in the file, Professor. Hellboy and Agent Sherman are due back in a few hours. We'll have a briefing this afternoon, and you'll leave tomorrow."

Curious, Bruttenholm opened the folder and glanced at the first couple of pages, smoothing his white goatee. Dr. Manning hesitated a moment, then turned to go.

"Tom," the professor said. "Stop."

Manning froze in the doorway and turned back to face him with obvious reluctance.

Bruttenholm stared at him. Dr. Manning might have been the Director of Field Operations and, thus, his superior, but they both knew the BPRD would not have existed without Bruttenholm and Hellboy, whom he called his son. Most of the time, the professor allowed Manning the illusion that he was in charge.

"It's an archaeological dig," Bruttenholm said.

"Yes."

"Run by the British Museum."

"Yes."

"And they've specifically requested Hellboy?"

Dr. Manning shrugged. "You know how highly the Brits regard him, particularly since the Egyptian incident in '86."

"One Brit in particular."

"As it may be," Manning replied, opening his hands in surrender. "Trevor, they think they've unearthed part of something called the Dragon King's temple, which is associated with just the sort of legend that has a tendency to cause trouble when the past is disturbed. There's been sabotage at the dig, and sightings of individuals who might not be entirely human. There's also the matter of a missing child, the eleven-year-old daughter of one of the archaeologists."

Bruttenholm shook his head. "We don't know there's anything supernatural involved here at all."

Manning crossed his arms. "What do your instincts tell you?"

The professor sighed. He ran his hands through his unruly white hair, understanding, now, why Tom Manning had wanted him to lead the investigation. He wanted to make sure that whoever was doing the thinking for the BPRD in the field had his head in the game.

"You already know what the project's leader thinks," Manning said. "She's had more than a few brushes with our sort of business over the years, as you know. Her instincts have always proved reliable."

Professor Bruttenholm returned his attention to the contents of the folder. It was precisely the sort of incident that the BPRD had been created to investigate. Research and defense were the stated purposes of the group, but the defense element often meant attempting to prevent supernatural forces from wreaking havoc upon the world. Such prevention did not need to be global to warrant their attention. When evil made its presence known, they had a duty to extinguish it. And, in this case, with a formal request from the British and Chinese governments, they couldn't refuse without creating a diplomatic incident. No matter what Bruttenholm would have preferred.

"It isn't Dr. Bransfield's instincts that concern me," the professor said, without looking up. "Hellboy claims his feelings for her are a thing of the past, but you saw how distracted he was the last time their paths crossed. For weeks, his mind was somewhere else. It isn't healthy for him."

Manning cocked his head. "It happens to the best of us, Professor."

Bruttenholm blinked and looked up, wondering if Manning understood what he'd just said. Love. The frailty of the heart. It happened to everyone at some point in their lives, if they were fortunate. It was human. If the bittersweet distraction of a former love was part of being human, what right did he have to prevent it?

Again, he stroked his goatee, staring at Anastasia Bransfield's signature on the documents in the folder. He was an old man who only wanted to save his son from heartache, as any parent would. But Hellboy hadn't been a child for a very long time. And Bruttenholm knew that his son would want to see Anastasia, now that the invitation had come.

But the professor didn't have to like it.

He'd set his pipe down, and now he picked it up again. He relit the pipe and drew in a lungful of sweet smoke.

"You know, you're really not supposed to smoke in here," Manning said.

Bruttenholm tapped the folder on his desk. "Tibet it is, then."

Hellboy always liked coming home to the BPRD headquarters. It was tucked away on a hillside in Fairfield, Connecticut, up a wooded, winding drive. The building was all glass and concrete, and yet its designer had created it to become a part of the landscape. It was built partially into the hillside and surrounded with trees and shrubs that seemed to bring life to the place. Hellboy had lived in far less pleasant circumstances. Despite the politicians and scientists who passed through its corridors every day, it still felt like home to him most of the time.

Of course, he knew that was due in large part to the fact that Liz Sherman and Abe Sapien, his closest friends, lived there. Their world existed, like his, within that glass-and-concrete building. And, of course, the man Hellboy thought of as his father was there as well.

On a day like today, when he was numbed by the journey from Chile to the United States, BPRD headquarters seemed particularly welcoming. He sat in the backseat of a truck and looked out the window as they emerged from the trees and the building came in sight. The engine rumbled as the vehicle labored up the hill. Liz had balled up her jacket and lay sleeping with her head upon his lap. The woman could sleep anywhere, especially if she'd recently summoned fire.

The truck shuddered to a stop at the entrance.

"Liz," Hellboy said, giving her a gentle shake. "We're home."

Her eyes fluttered open. "Home," she repeated.

The word didn't mean the same thing to her. Since the fire had first manifested in her at eleven years old, burning her life and family down around her, the BPRD had been more like self-imposed prison for her. She was not a captive, of course. She had run away many times as a child, and since she had reached adulthood and joined the Bureau as a field agent, she'd quit more than a few times. Abe and Hellboy were comfortable living in a place where they weren't constantly reminded how different they were. Liz was the opposite. She looked ordinary—even pretty—on the outside, but living at BPRD headquarters was a daily admission that she wasn't like other people, that she was a danger to them all, a freak.

It got under her skin.

Liz sat up, reached into the back of the truck for

her duffel bag, and popped open the door. She slid out, then paused to glance back at Hellboy.

"Going back to sleep. Thanks for watching my back."

Hellboy nodded. "Sleep well."

Liz shut the door and headed for the building entrance without waiting for him. As tired as she was, he wouldn't have expected it. Tonight, or maybe tomorrow, they'd all sit in his room and watch a movie and eat bad Chinese food and everything would be fine. Liz just needed some down time.

Hellboy grabbed his own duffel and disembarked. He tapped the truck's roof with his left hand.

"Thanks for the pickup."

The driver waved out the window and pulled away, and the truck returned down the road, where the driver would leave it in the garage near the front gates. Hellboy shouldered his bag and went inside. By the time he stepped through the entrance and into the buzz of the Bureau offices, Liz was nowhere to be seen. Agents and researchers and coffee-carrying assistants moved through the corridors. Phones rang. Hellboy waved to several people as he strode through the midst of the BPRD's operations. It always fascinated him, the spectrum of reactions he got from people—even those he worked with on a regular basis. Some of them treated him like a celebrity, others like a monster. The ones he liked the best treated him like just another coworker, or somebody to talk movies with over a beer.

When he entered the residential wing of the complex, and the door closed behind him, he exhaled. It had been nice to come home, but now he could truly relax, maybe make up a batch of nachos with all the fixings, guacamole and all.

He passed Abe's door. As usual, he could hear music from within. Abe would be curled up with a book, or sitting on the floor surrounded by piles of books like Burgess Meredith in that classic *Twilight Zone* episode. But, always, there was the music. Today it was *The Notting Hillbillies,* a quirky little album if ever there was one. Not Hellboy's thing, but Abe had forced him to listen one day while they were playing Scrabble.

When he unlocked the door to his own room and pushed it open, the first thing he saw was the manila envelope that lay on the floor just inside. Someone had slid it under the door. Interoffice mail. But this one had a red CONFIDENTIAL stamp on it, so it wasn't a memo about Bureau staffers wasting too many paper clips or budget cuts forcing them to take the free coffee out of the break rooms.

"This can't be anything good," Hellboy said.

He closed the door behind him and dumped the duffel bag to one side. As he went into his apartment, listening to the comforting hum of the refrigerator and gazing lovingly at the huge sofa that sprawled in front of the television, he tried to ignore the manila envelope. He went to the fridge and stood in the open door, drinking a quart of orange juice right from the carton. When he closed the refrigerator, he glanced at the envelope, as though it might have done him the favor of vanishing.

Lamenting the nachos he'd promised himself, Hellboy grumbled as he crossed the room and snatched the envelope off the floor. He tore it open, ignoring the PLEASE RECYCLE message printed on the front, and slipped out the memo.

TO: Prof. T. Bruttenholm, Abraham Sapien, Hellboy
FR: Dr. Thomas Manning, Dir. Field Ops
RE: Dragon Pool

Gentlemen, please convene in my office at 3 pm today to discuss Dragon Pool investigation. Due to the urgent nature of this case, the team will depart BPRD HQ for air transport at 9:20 pm.

Hellboy glanced at the clock on the wall. It was a quarter after two already. He crumpled the memo in his fist and went back out into the corridor, leaving his door open. Still grumbling, he went down and knocked on Abe's door, his massive right fist shaking the wood in its frame. Normally he showed more courtesy, but he wasn't in a courteous mood.

The music paused, and a moment later, the door swung inward. Abe stood just inside, a kind of dim golden light filling his living room. His vision was extraordinary, and he favored gloom over brightness, even when reading. All that time underwater, Hellboy figured.

"Welcome home," Abe said, but his words had an inquisitive tone. There was very little that looked human about the amphibious man's appearance. His mottled, greenish skin had dark markings that only increased his resemblance to many forms of ocean life, not to mention the gills and finlike ridges. But his mannerisms were almost entirely human.

Hellboy held the crumpled memo out to him. "Yeah. Some welcome. I was going to make nachos. You know anything about this?"

Abe cocked his head to one side. "If that's the note from Dr. Manning about our three o'clock briefing, then, yes."

Hellboy waited, but Abe did not continue.

"Okay," he prodded. "Are you going to make me play twenty questions?"

"Of course not. I'd been thinking about charades, though," Abe said straight-faced.

Hellboy shook his head, unable to keep up the intensity of his annoyance with Manning when Abe was cracking wise.

"Are you trying to be funny?"

"Succeeding, actually," Abe replied.

"Says who?"

"Well, I can't expect you to be an unbiased judge. You'd have to have a sense of humor."

Hellboy glared. "I've got a great sense of humor."

Abe pointed at him. "See how I just did that again? I've been practicing."

Unable to help himself, Hellboy laughed softly. He reached up to fiddle with the little knot of hair at the back of his head.

"You're a riot, Abe. Seriously. But, the memo?"

"Yes. The Dragon Pool. A mythological site discovered in Tibet. There's been trouble, apparently caused by something inhuman. A girl's gone missing."

Hellboy straightened up, filling the doorway of Abe's apartment. "All right. I get the urgency. Why isn't Liz on the team?"

The amphibian shifted with agitation. Most people would never have noticed, but Hellboy knew him too well.

"She didn't tell you?" Abe asked.

"Tell me what?" Hellboy growled.

"She's taking a leave of absence. Several weeks, I think."

Hellboy leaned against the doorframe, disappointment spreading through him. "Why? And how come she told you but not me? I just spent a week with her in Chile. You'd think she'd mention something like that."

Abe shrugged. "Maybe she thought you'd be annoyed and didn't want to have to discuss it with you. As for why she's going, I can only guess she's gotten claustrophobic here again. To be honest, I thought it was an improvement. At least it's an officially sanctioned leave of absence and not another resignation."

"There's that," Hellboy allowed. He threw up his hands in surrender. "Okay, so, any idea what the case is about? What's in Tibet, aside from llamas?"

Dark eyes wide, Abe cocked his head like a curious bird.

"Anastasia Bransfield."

All of the frustration and cantankerousness left Hellboy at the utterance of her name. A myriad of reactions swept through him, but all he could do was blink and stare at Abe.

"Oh."

Chapter 2

Anastasia woke with a start. A sound echoed in her mind—a loud, abrupt noise—but she wasn't certain if it had been real or a dream.

When the second gunshot came, she had her answer.

"Bloody hell," she whispered, climbing from her bedroll. She'd been raised a proper English girl with a disdain for guns, but that hadn't stopped her from learning how to use one. Quick as she could, she slipped on her boots. Given the events of the past thirty-six hours, she'd slept in her jeans and tank top, just in case. Day before yesterday, they'd spent hours scouring the lakeshore and the mountainside and every part of the dig—every ditch and dirt pile—searching for Kora Kyichu. Then, last night, the entrance to the Dragon King's temple had been caved in and the saboteur chased from the camp.

Frank Danovich and Ellie Morris had both gotten a half-decent look at the culprit in the moonlight, and what they described was a nightmare. Leathery face, protruding jaw, long teeth, and eyes that flickered with weird light when they'd cornered him. Danovich had been the one to call it "weird light," actually.

Ellie had said he had fire leaking from his eyes.

This confirmed the basic description Anastasia had gotten from Xin, who supervised the project's diggers. By then, she'd already used the wireless to call in her report and demand they contact the BPRD. Apparently her request had been passed along the appropriate channels, but there was no telling how long it would take to reach the Bureau or when help might be forthcoming.

For now, they were on their own.

At sunrise yesterday, half the camp had been put to work on the careful reexcavation of the entrance to the temple, and the rest of them had broadened their search for Kora. Kyichu had lost his wife a number of years before, and though he kept his wits about him as he directed the search, Anastasia had seen the haunted look in his eyes. His gaze strayed again and again toward the lake. His thoughts obviously mirrored her own. If the girl had wandered off, and they hadn't found her in a day and a half, the most likely solution was that she had somehow swum too far out into the lake and drowned.

Perhaps under other circumstances, they would have assumed that was precisely what had happened and simply mourned the girl. But there was at least one mysterious saboteur plaguing the dig, and the thought that he might be responsible weighed heavily on them all.

Tonight, Anastasia had posted guards around the camp, and at the entrance to the temple, which had been freshly cleared just before sundown. In the morning, she'd planned to take a small detachment from the camp and travel to the nearby village to see if the locals could tell them anything about who might want to sabotage their dig and find out what they knew about a little girl gone missing.

But morning hadn't arrived yet. Gunshots could only mean one thing: The saboteur had returned.

She slid her pistol from the holster she'd hung on a hook jutting from the tent pole and stepped out into the chilly night air, the gun's weight a comfort in her hand. The crescent moon cast an otherworldly glow upon the land, and the surface of the lake glinted with a million points of light. The mountain loomed to her right, cranes and pulleys silhouetted mantislike against the night sky. For a moment, she heard nothing but the wind.

Then another shot came, the crack of a rifle. Anastasia bolted in the direction of the shooter, boots kicking up dirt. She didn't want to end up with a bullet in the face, but if the bastard who'd been causing them so much trouble was in her camp, she wasn't going to hide from him.

Voices carried on the wind ahead of her. Someone was shouting.

"That way!" she heard. "Son of a bitch went that way!"

Danovich. Chances were he was the shooter as

well. Frank was a dead shot with a rifle. Other people had begun to emerge from their tents at the base of the mountain, but she ignored them, starting up the slope, pistol clutched in her right hand. The dig sprawled across the face of the mountain just above her, excavations gaping shadowlike craters on the moon. None of the machinery ran. Not a single engine rumbled. There wasn't even the sound of buckets being filled, shovels turning soil, or pulleys turning. That was to be expected in the middle of the night, but with the knowledge that someone or something prowled the abandoned dig site, looking to do them harm, the quiet made her shiver.

Her grip on the gun tightened.

More shouts sounded. She heard boots pounding dirt and saw several figures crest an outcropping of rock above her. They were familiar shadows, and one of them could only have been Han Kyichu. The moonlight made a halo of his white hair, though the rest of him was in darkness.

"Han!" Anastasia shouted, more to make sure that Danovich didn't shoot her than anything else.

"Dr. Bransfield!" Kyichu called down to her. "He's there with you! We just saw him!"

Anastasia stopped and lowered herself into a half crouch. She gripped the pistol in both hands and spun around, scanning the slope around her. Shadows loomed beneath jagged outcroppings and behind rows of low, stunted bushes. Nothing moved. From up on the ridge she heard the cocking of a rifle and knew Danovich must have run up to join the others. A spark of panic ignited in her.

Her chest rose and fell, and she could feel the throb of her pulse in her temple. Anastasia listened to the wind and her own breath, and she hated this silent, invisible figure more than she'd ever hated anyone in her life. She hated him for making her afraid, and she hated him for the way her finger tightened even further on the trigger, for making her willing to shoot him.

"Stacie, there!" Danovich shouted from above.

The rifle cracked. A divot of earth erupted twenty feet to her right, behind a scree of low, tangled brush. A shadow lunged away. The moonlight seemed to slip around him, as though he existed just beyond its reach, but the silhouette was real enough. His running footfalls were heavy on dirt and stone—as though his weight was far greater than the thin, wiry figure ought to have carried. Again, Danovich took a shot, and again, the bullet struck the rocky slope.

Fast, Anastasia thought. *The bastard's fast.*

But he wasn't heading for camp. Why would he? Too many people, too much attention. Sabotage was about sneaking around. He'd been trying to ruin the dig, not kill the archaeological team.

Anastasia took off after him. The terrain was rough, and she nearly stumbled but gave herself over to the downhill momentum of the slope. The shore of the lake was below. The water rippled in the moonlight, giving her an even better silhouette of the slender intruder. He ran so quickly that it was breathtaking to see, but it also meant there was no way in hell she was going to catch up to him.

No way.

She stopped, leveled the pistol in her right hand, sighted on his retreating back as he crossed the last few yards toward the water, and pulled the trigger. The gun bucked in her hand. The saboteur grunted as the bullet punched through his upper right shoulder, spinning him around. For just an instant she caught a glimpse of his face—of teeth like diamond shards and eyes that flickered with flames—then his momentum carried him into the lake. He hit the water in a tangle of limbs and went under.

"Oh, well done, Stasia," she whispered to herself, staring at the water as it closed over him. "Silly sod."

The gun did not waver as she raced down to the water's edge. Behind her, she could hear Danovich cheering for her and other voices calling out in alarm or triumph. People ran up toward her from camp and down from the mountain ridge, but Anastasia paid them no attention. Her entire focus was on the water. A dark spot formed on the water, then dissipated, and she figured it was blood. But the bullet had only struck him in the shoulder. So where was he? Why wasn't he coming up?

"Dr. Bransfield?" a voice said behind her. "Stacie?"

A hand touched her shoulder, and she shook it off.

Weren't these people paying attention? Didn't they understand that this wasn't some local trying to drive them off or a rival hoping to scare them so he could move in and claim their work for himself?

Of course they didn't. They hadn't lived through the things she'd lived through. To read about the supernatural in the newspaper was a far different thing from experiencing it firsthand. Half of them probably still thought Hellboy was an urban legend, even though he'd been on magazine covers and the evening news.

Frank Danovich came up beside her, rifle clutched in his hands.

"Nice shooting, Doc," the engineer said.

Anastasia still felt the ache of the gun's recoil, and it made her want to throw up. Danovich's lightheartedness did nothing to soothe her, nor did the knowledge that the man she'd shot might not be human. She hated guns and hated even more how often in her life they had been necessary.

She did not look up at Danovich, instead continuing to watch the surface of the lake. The concentric ripples of the saboteur's plunge had smoothed.

"What are you staring at?" the engineer asked.

"Bubbles."

Danovich cleared his throat. "No offense, Stacie, but what the hell are you talking about?"

At last she tore her gaze away. She glanced around and saw clusters of diggers and techs and specialists whispering among themselves. Ellie Morris stood by

Professor Kyichu, one hand on the back of his neck, sorrow and sympathy on her face. Ellie was a medical doctor, so perhaps she was just expressing an interest in the man's health, but Anastasia wondered if there was more than a collegial relationship between them. For Han Kyichu's sake, she hoped so.

Professor Kyichu stared at the gun in her hand. Unsettled, Anastasia clicked on the safety and slipped it into the rear waistband of her jeans as she walked toward him. Danovich dogged her steps.

"Stacie," he said in a bad stage whisper.

She frowned and looked at him. The wind whipped her hair across her face, and she put up a hand to push it aside. The late-September night was frigid, and she shivered.

"What is it?" Danovich asked. "What were you looking at in the water?"

Anastasia didn't want to speak of it with so many people around, but she understood the fear in Professor Kyichu's eyes. If this man had been both saboteur and kidnapper, if he had Kora trapped in a cave or hut somewhere—and Anastasia had just shot him—then the girl was as good as dead.

Danovich stayed beside her as she went up to Ellie and Professor Kyichu. The four of them huddled together, and though other members of the team were milling around, the chatter was enough to distract most of them from a few quiet words.

"I don't know if Kora was abducted or not," she

whispered, gaze locked with Kyichu's. "But she's a smart girl, Han, so—like you—I can't believe she just drowned. We also don't know if the man I just shot was her kidnapper."

"And now we'll never know," Ellie said, despair in her voice.

"We will," Anastasia replied sharply. "I hit him. He's bleeding. But he's alive. I saw air bubbles on the surface and tracked him as far as I could. He swam out about fifty yards and turned east."

Professor Kyichu stared at her. Their friendship was strained by his fear for his daughter. She could not hold that against him, and yet the grim doubt in his eyes and his voice hurt her.

"Nobody can hold their breath for that long," Kyichu said.

Anastasia held his gaze. "Nobody human."

Professor Kyichu nodded. They'd all heard Xin and the others who'd seen the saboteur describe him.

"You got a good look?" Ellie asked.

"Good enough. Did he do any damage?"

Danovich slung his rifle over his shoulder. "Not this time. I spotted him as he was slinking up toward the temple entrance excavation. He took off at the first shot. Can't believe I missed him. It's not like me."

"He's damned quick," Ellie said.

None of them wanted to follow that train of thought. At length, Danovich spoke again. "So, what now?"

Anastasia turned to look out over the lake. "Help is

on the way, I hope. Meanwhile, we keep one team working while the rest of us search for Kora. In the morning, we head for the village, just as we planned. And we stay on guard."

A shout of alarm came from behind her, and she heard the sound of boots pounding the rocky ground. Anastasia turned, snatching the gun from the small of her back at the same time. Before she could even raise the pistol to take aim, she saw lanky, handsome Rafe Mattei running toward them. Several people moved aside to let him pass. One of the other students on the dig tried to reach for him, but Rafe shook his head and kept moving until he stood in front of the half circle made by Anastasia, Professor Kyichu, Danovich, and Ellie Morris. Others gathered around, now, all of them doubtless fearing the worst.

Rafe had confusion in his eyes.

"What's wrong?" Anastasia demanded. "More sabotage? Did he cave in one of the digs?"

The young man struggled to catch his breath, but shook his head. "No, no. Nothing like that."

"What is it, then?" Professor Kyichu asked. "Kora?"

The apology in Rafe's eyes was enough to dispel that hope. Again he shook his head, and then he turned to Anastasia.

"Dr. Bransfield, you asked us to keep working once the temple entrance was cleared," he said. "We've been at it all night."

"All night," Anastasia said, frowning. "I never asked anyone to—"

"No, you didn't. Dr. Conrad did. We've been photographing and cataloging everything *in situ,* while he's been translating the paintings and writing on the walls and the objects in the foyer room."

A flicker of anger went through her. A specialist in ancient languages—among other things—Mark Conrad was essentially her second-in-command on this project, but not by her choice. He was talented and knowledgeable, but also an arrogant brown noser who pandered to their employers at the British Museum and romanced government ministers at museum events, jockeying for her position. Anastasia might be a hero to some in the British archaeological community, but some of the older, more proper members of the museum's board did not like the publicity she'd received over the years; they found it unseemly. On the other hand, they received all sorts of outside funding because of Anastasia's reputation, public image, and connections. So, while there were those who disliked her maverick nature, no one was willing to hand Mark Conrad her job just yet.

The problem with Dr. Conrad was that he was more than willing to wait and be a sneering little wanker about it in the meantime. Handsome and slick, with his shoulder-length blond hair, he reminded her of an oily James Bond villain.

But he was annoyingly good at his job.

"Conrad found something?"

Rafe glanced around at the others, blinking uncertainly. "Translated something, actually. There's some writing, but mostly it's pictographs."

Anastasia sighed in frustration. "Out with it, Rafe. What in hell are you talking about?"

"The temple, Dr. Bransfield," he said. "It's . . . well, it's not a temple. That's the thing. Professor Kyichu was right that the temple's here somewhere, or it was, once. But what we've found is not the temple. It's some kind of preparatory chamber."

Han Kyichu moved in closer, almost cutting Ellie and Danovich out, so now it was just him, Anastasia, and Rafe in a tight circle.

"Preparing for what?" the professor asked.

Rafe looked pale in the moonlight. "Sacrifice, sir. Human, child sacrifice."

The thrum of the plane's engines had lulled him to sleep, but Hellboy could not get comfortable in the chair. It had more legroom by far than a typical commercial airliner, but still was not made for someone of his size. Nothing was, really. So he tried his best to stay asleep, even though every few minutes his head bobbed, and he snapped upward, blinking muzzily. He shifted constantly in the chair, like a dog turning in circles in search of a comfortable spot. The filed-down stumps of his horns whacked the window a couple of times, so he tried to keep his head in the other direction, or his chin down on his chest. Breaking the glass at 30,000 feet was a terrible idea.

A couple of times, he caught himself snorting loudly, and finally he forced his eyes to stay open. Hellboy blinked and took a deep breath, shaking his head. No more sleeping.

He felt a bit of drool on his chin and wiped it away. Embarrassed, he glanced around, but nobody was paying attention. Professor Bruttenholm was in the sleeping compartment at the back of the plane. Hellboy would've been much more comfortable back there, but there wasn't room for both of them, and the professor was an old man. He slept little but needed what rest he could get.

Aside from the flight crew, the only other people on the BPRD transport plane were Abe, the chopper pilot, Redfield, and a trio of field agents Manning had insisted on sending along. They were more brawn than investigative brain, but Manning didn't like the idea of sending only three agents and a pilot halfway around the world without any backup. One of them, the thin, pixieish blond girl was called Sarah. A weapons expert and their medic, she didn't look as though she could hurt anyone. Hellboy knew better. She was a pro. And if Sarah Rhys-Hughes vouched for the two men she sat with now, playing poker at the front of the compartment, that was enough for Hellboy. The orange-haired, thick-necked guy had the unlikely name of

Meaney, and the soft-spoken, dark-skinned Londoner was called Neil.

Across the aisle, Abe wore his CD Walkman and nodded almost imperceptibly to the music while he read. It was a paperback of a novel by John Irving aptly titled *The Water-Method Man*. Abe read all sorts of things, but whenever they flew, it was paperback fiction.

The amphibious man noticed Hellboy's scrutiny and lowered his book, then slipped off his headphones. "You can't sleep?"

Hellboy took a deep breath and let it out, settling deeper into his chair, straining his seat belt. "Can't get comfortable."

Most people had a hard time deciphering when Abe was smiling. Hellboy understood. The same thing was true of him. If someone didn't know him, they were more likely to think he was scowling at them. With Abe, a smile was little more than a strange parting of the lips. It wasn't pretty. They knew each other well enough to know the difference.

"What's funny?" Hellboy asked.

Abe tilted his head. "It isn't the chair that has you distracted."

"I'm not distracted."

Abe nodded, as though allowing for the possibility that this was the truth. He started to put his headphones back on, then paused.

"You never told me the story, you know."

Hellboy glanced out the window, wondering where they were. Their destination was twelve hours ahead of Connecticut on the international time chart. The plane had taken off at a quarter past ten in the evening. That meant it was already morning in Tibet. It would take them thirty-three hours to reach the landing strip and several hours more to unload and travel to the site of the archaeological dig.

A day and a half. And Anastasia was waiting.

"What story?"

"You know," Abe said. "All you've ever said was that you and Anastasia met while you were on a case. Why haven't you ever told me the story?"

Hellboy glanced at him. "Liz hasn't told you?"

"You told Liz, but not me?" Abe said, obviously a bit irked.

"Yeah. And she told you she was taking a leave of absence, but not me. We're all such fickle friends."

Abe stared at him, wide eyes almost hypnotic. "You're avoiding the subject."

"You think, Dr. Freud?"

"I'm not going to analyze you. I'm just curious. Never mind. I didn't mean to pry."

And that was it, precisely. Hellboy did not mind talking about Stasia, and some of the digs they went on together during the year and a half that he had traipsed around the world with her playing Indiana Jones, and falling in love. Gloriously, stupidly in love.

But the things that were intimate, that were shared only by the two of them, he'd always held close.

But Stasia was just an ex, now, an old flame, and Abe was one of his closest friends.

"I met her in a pub," he said.

Abe perked up. "A pub? You're not serious."

Hellboy gave him an impatient stare.

"Okay, a pub," Abe relented. "But you said you'd met her on a case."

"I did. The case just happens to end with the opening line of a bad joke. 'These two goblins walked into a bar. . . .'"

London, England, 10 June, 1979

Hellboy didn't care much for punk, but there were times he could relate to the directionless anger and frustration that churned in all that sound and fury. For the pissed off youth of England, though, punk had been Camelot—a brief and shining moment. But it was late spring of '79, and Hellboy knew the moment was over. Punk was dead. How else to explain walking into a dark, smoky pub just down from Great Russell Street full of old-timers and museum curators and hearing The Sex Pistols on the little stereo behind the bar?

The ripple of its effects was still expanding, but that was just echoes.

Rain dripped from his trench coat as he entered the

pub, carrying a small vacuum cleaner by its handle. The smell of damp metal filled his nostrils, along with smoke and stale beer. With the rain and fog and the lateness of the hour, it was black as pitch outside, but it was hardly any brighter in the pub. He ran his left hand—his ordinary hand—over the stubble on his head, wiping the beads of water away. Then he patted the pockets to make sure he had the little silver box.

The smoke was nearly as thick as the fog had been outside. He started across the pub, the wooden beams of the floor creaking under his hooves. He kept his tail low, though he knew there weren't a lot of ways to make himself inconspicuous. Several of the old duffers at the bar tapped one another and gestured in his direction, and conversation began to diminish as he made his way through the pub. The tables on his left were jammed with university students and professorial types from the museum. One young redheaded woman cocked her head and raised an eyebrow as she watched him pass by, smoke ringlets drifting past her face like clouds across the moon. Her companion, a fiftyish man with a thick beard, knocked back a shot of whiskey. Several people—closest to the door—closed their gaping mouths long enough to stand up and bolt from the pub.

That was fine with Hellboy. He wasn't here for them.

The bartender saw him. Eyes wide, the thick-mustached man bent to reach under the bar—probably for a club or ax handle or something that would hurt if it connected with his skull. Hellboy could see his own reflection in the mirror behind the man and tried to put on as stern a face as possible. His eyes gleamed yellow in the gloom. He figured the cigarette smoke had something to do with that.

Hellboy didn't bother to raise his massive right hand, which held the vacuum cleaner. Instead, he used his gloved left hand to twitch back his trench coat to reveal the huge pistol holstered there. No way would he draw the gun with all of these people around, but all the bartender needed to do was keep his mouth shut for a few more seconds.

A burst of ugly laughter came from the back of the pub. A row of booths ran along the wall at a weird angle so that you had to be almost right on top of their occupants before you could see who was sitting there. Privacy effort or bad floor plan, he'd never know. Despite the fact that the pub was packed, the booths were all empty, except for the last one, the farthest from the door, the one deepest in shadow and wreathed in smoke.

The laughter came again, a deep, snorting, obnoxious amusement that made the hair on the back of his neck stand on end and made him flex his left hand like he was getting ready to hit someone. Much as he'd like to, he was actually hoping to avoid beating the crap out of anyone tonight. Things would get broken. The Bureau might have to pay for that. And some innocent bystander was likely to get hurt.

The vacuum cleaner would be much safer than the gun.

Hellboy strode toward the booth, trying to be as stealthy as someone his size, and with hooves, could be. The snorting laughter continued, now punctuated by slurring voices.

"S'got to be the sweetest score yet," said a gravelly voice. "Didja see the look on that one bloke's face?"

The reply came in a reedy, high, old man's voice. "Silly sod, he was. But, look here, Vaughan, you really think we can get 20 million for them trinkets?"

The low, rasping voice returned. "Oh, we'll get it, Burch. Count on it, mate."

The laughter came again. Hellboy figured it had to belong to the one called Burch. No way was that insinuating giggle coming from the same throat as the deep rumble Vaughan spoke with.

He paused just out of view from the booth and unspooled the cord from the vacuum. The bartender had both hands on the bar, gripping it with white knuckles while he waited to see what was going to happen. Hellboy beckoned him over. The man paled. With his face so white and the sheen of sweat on him, he looked as though he'd eaten bad fish. Most of the regulars had remained silent, drinking their pints and whiskeys and watching him with open curiosity. Some conversation came from the students and curators, but that didn't surprise him. Certain kinds of people just couldn't stop talking. He didn't mind. The talking was good, white noise. Less chance Vaughan and his partner would notice the lull in the room. Not that they were likely to anyway, as drunk as they were.

The bartender started slowly toward him, and Hellboy gave him an exasperated look. The man hurried. Hellboy handed him the end of the vacuum cord and pointed behind the bar.

"Plug it in, will ya?" he asked, keeping his tone low and conversational.

The man nodded. Hellboy waited until he'd done it, then unsnapped the vacuum hose, holding its suction head down by his side. Then he took the last few steps over to the booth, emerging from the fog of cigarette smoke to stand menacingly over the two laughing thieves.

They stopped laughing.

The skinny little old man on the right of the booth was called Blue Burches. He had a piggish snout and tiny upturned tusks that jutted up from his lower jaw. His blue jacket and bright blue trousers had spots on them from the lager he'd already spilled on himself. His companion loomed on the left side of the booth, broad and ugly. Black Vaughan was the brains of the partnership, according to what Hellboy had learned from pressuring a water bogey called Shellycoat down at the docks. The morons had stolen a shipment of mystically active Egyptian relics being returned to the British Museum after an exhibition tour.

"Evening, boys," Hellboy said.

Vaughan shook his head and sneered at Burch. "Stupid git. You were followed."

"Like hell I was," Burch replied, crossing his arms like a petulant child.

Black Vaughan turned and glared up at Hellboy from beneath his prominent brow. "How'd you find us?"

Hellboy shrugged. "No offense. It wasn't hard. You guys aren't the sharpest knives in the drawer. First mistake was trying to sell the relics you stole back to the museum. Some private buyer would've paid you pretty much whatever you want, and wouldn't have called in help."

Vindicated, Burch gave a superior sniff and picked up his pint of lager. His head swayed a bit, and he had trouble finding his mouth with the glass. Drunken goblins looked like fools, but they weren't any more compliant than the sober kind.

"Think you're so bloody clever," Vaughan sneered. "I know who you are."

"Yeah," Hellboy replied with a sigh. "Fame's a bitch."

Burch lurched to his feet and cocked the glass back, spilling golden lager across the table. Drunk as he was, he telegraphed the move badly, and Hellboy grabbed his wrist before the blow could land. The glass fell from his grip and shattered on the table. Whimpering in pain, putting his all into the old, helpless man act, Blue Burches slid back into the booth, shaking as he began to sob.

Then he snarled, baring fangs and those little curved tusks. He slid as far back into the booth as he could, and began to vanish, dissipating into a swirl of blue smoke like some stage magician's bad illusion. In seconds, he'd mix with the cigarette fog and be gone.

Hellboy flicked the switch on the vacuum and it moaned to life, droning loudly. Then he reached out with the vacuum hose and sucked that blue smoke into the canister, before flicking the power off and turning to set the vacuum on a barstool.

"One down," he said, giving Black Vaughan a hard look.

The brawny goblin laughed, and that low rasp insinuated itself under Hellboy's skin, actually gave him a shiver. The goblin shook his head as though in disdain, but as he did, his flesh changed. With the sound of his skull cracking, two enormous horns burst from the side of his head, then his face elongated painfully, so that now he looked like a bull—or at least like the Minotaur.

The goblin-thing erupted from his seat with such force that the table shattered into half a dozen long shards. Black Vaughan started to bellow some threat or another, but Hellboy had lost patience.

"Sit down!" he shouted, and he brought the stone fist of his colossal right hand down on Vaughan's head, snapping one of the bull's horns.

The blow hammered the goblin back into his seat, and, with his left hand, Hellboy drew the heavy cannon from its holster and pointed it at the creature's skull.

"No, no, wait," Vaughan said, wheezing as he tried to calm himself. He held up both hands in surrender. "I can tell you where we've got the stash. All the stuff we nicked. Not a piece missing."

Hellboy holstered the gun. "Found it already. We've got one of those psychics who can touch stuff and learn from it, track it. Psychometry, it's called. Comes in handy. No pun intended."

Vaughan stared at him. "You already have the relics?"

"Yeah."

The look of sadness on the goblin's face would have been heartbreaking if Hellboy didn't still want to beat the crap out of him for being such a cocky bastard.

"What do you want with us, then?"

Hellboy stared at him. "We want you not to give us trouble in the future. Your pal Burch is out of the game. Now it's your turn."

He reached into his pocket. Vaughan shrank away from him, but he was trapped by the back wall of the pub and the bench he was sitting on. There was nowhere for him to go as Hellboy drew the silver snuffbox out of his pocket. A groan of utter despair escaped the goblin's throat when he saw the pretty little box. He'd spent centuries trapped in that little box thanks to an occultist in Herefordshire and had escaped only twice. The last time had been twenty-seven years before.

"How did you find it?" the goblin asked in a very small voice.

"Private collector. He loaned it to us on condition that we give it back, with its original occupant inside."

Terror in his eyes, the goblin looked up at him. "It was just a bit of mischief. You're a bloke's got up to some mischief, I'm sure. You don't know what it's like, trapped in there. Drove me mad. Never a moment of comfort. We didn't harm a soul."

Hellboy blinked. "Other than the three people you gutted on the docks when you were stealing all of this. Not to mention the thousands that might have died if you'd unleashed the spells in some of those relics."

"This is a bit of a laugh for you, is it? You find all this funny?" Vaughan demanded.

Shifting guiltily, Hellboy took the cover off the silver snuffbox.

"A little," he confessed, as Black Vaughan's essence was drawn, screaming, into the box, his body deflating as he was sucked in. The goblin's clothes were left behind on the bench in the wrecked booth.

Hellboy took out a small silver key, locked the snuffbox, and slipped it back into his coat pocket. Then he picked up the vacuum and turned away from the ruin of the booth, trying to ignore the eyes of every patron in the pub. The old-timers who were regulars wore bemused expressions. This wasn't the weirdest thing they'd seen in this place. But the students and museum people gaped wider than ever.

"Oy!" the bartender shouted as he walked by. "Who's going to pay for the damage?"

Hellboy shot him a hard look, but on this subject, the bartender wasn't nearly as easily cowed. "British Museum. Ask for Dr. Paul Campbell."

"I'm just supposed to take your word on that, let you walk out of here?"

Not sure he'd heard the man properly, and giving the bartender a moment to rethink his wording, Hellboy turned to face him. But before either of them could speak again, Hellboy saw the reflection in the mirror of the redheaded woman he'd noticed earlier. She had risen from her table, to the panicked whispers of her friends, and was walking toward him.

"Hellboy?" she ventured.

He loved the lilt in her voice. Before he turned, he examined her in the mirror. Young, maybe late twenties, with the most perfect skin he had ever seen and straight, dark red hair that she tied back without bow or ribbon. Nothing fancy about her. Just porcelain features and bright, intelligent eyes, not to mention the confidence to approach him.

When he turned, she smiled, and when she spoke, her hands fluttered around like birds. "Hi. Right, hello. I'm Anastasia Bransfield. I work with Dr. Campbell. Well, sort of. I'm an archaeologist with the . . . never mind."

She offered a self-deprecating grin at her fumbling. "I'm not very good at this," Anastasia said, before looking past him at the bartender. "Martin, don't get your knickers in a twist, mate. The museum's just across the street. We're in here all the time, yeah? I'll vouch for Hellboy, and if Dr. Campbell won't replace that table from his budget, I'll cover it myself. No worries, all right?"

Soothed by her voice and mere presence, Martin gave a small shrug. "Just don't like trouble in 'ere, Stacie. You know that."

"Bollocks," Anastasia said, grinning. "You just don't like trouble you didn't start."

"Cheeky thing," the bartender said.

But by then Anastasia's attention was on Hellboy again. She gestured to the vacuum cleaner full of Blue Burches. "You in a rush to bring that back to wherever?"

Hellboy thought he caught something in her inflection, and the glint of her gaze—a pleasant curiosity that he might have thought flirtatious if she'd been talking to anyone else. Anyone not huge and hooved and red. Anyone not Hellboy.

"I appreciate the help," he said.

Disappointment flickered in her eyes. "Ah. You've got to be off, then?"

He frowned. "I don't think Martin wants me hanging around."

"Bugger Martin," she said, and the bartender gave a good-natured shout of protest. "Fancy a pint? On me. For now, at least. I'll give the check to Dr. Campbell. Come, sit and talk. All the ruins you've visited, the ancient tombs you've unearthed. I want to hear about every one. The archaeologist in me is fascinated."

The words were all business. Natural inquisitiveness. But the way she said it, the flash in her eyes, if he didn't know better . . .

"You've done the job. Now you get the reward," she said.

Under her expectant gaze, Hellboy found it impossible to refuse.

"My kind of philosophy."

"Ah, no, sorry. No philosophy allowed in the pub until you're too drunk to walk. Only then can true wisdom be found."

Hellboy set the vacuum cleaner with the blue goblin smoke inside on the bar and glanced at Martin. "Keep that back there for me, will you? Don't want it getting into the wrong hands. And don't use it."

Martin started to protest, but Anastasia was walking back to her table, where her mates waited in amazement, and Hellboy didn't hear a word the bartender said.

He followed her.

For the better part of two years.

Chapter 3

The village of Nakchu lay five miles northwest of Lake Tashi, still in the foothills of the snow-capped Nyenchen Tanghla mountain range, but at a slightly higher elevation. They were already at fifteen thousand feet on the plateau where Lake Tashi pooled among the mountains. They had prepared for the breathlessness caused by the elevation and the hard work, but when Anastasia led a small party on a hike to Nakchu, they were out of breath fairly quickly.

She had left Mark Conrad in charge of the dig, and Eleanor Morris to keep an eye on Conrad. Danovich had to oversee the safety of the whole circus, so he had to be left behind as well. There were seven people in the detachment she led to the village that morning—herself; Professor Kyichu; a communications man named Horace Trotter; their local guide, Tenzin; a representative from the government in Beijing named Mr. Lao; and two diggers she had chosen for sheer muscle.

Anastasia carried a gun. She didn't let anyone else have one except for Tenzin, who carried a rifle slung over his back every waking moment. In fact, she thought that the slim, powerful guide with the intense eyes might have been born with a tiny rifle across his back.

Far too many times, they were forced to pause to rest. Tenzin became restless as a hunting dog with a snoutful of his prey's scent, but the rest of them weren't entirely used to the elevation. Tenzin understood this—his English was perfect; it was why they'd chosen him—but it didn't make him any less impatient. If she'd had to guess, Anastasia would have expected Han Kyichu to hold them up the most. He was the eldest among them by at least a decade. But it was the man from Beijing with his black eyes and black hair and new boots who slowed them down. His feet hurt.

Anastasia didn't much care.

Diplomacy was a part of her job. It came with the territory. But if the representative of the government that held Tibet against the will of its people had blisters on his toes, she figured that was a small price for him to pay.

Tenzin led them to a narrow stream that flowed down from the foothills of the mountains and from there they turned northwest, following the water. A flock of black-necked cranes rested beside the stream but took flight at their approach. Anastasia paused and watched in wonder as they skirted low to the land. It seemed impossible to her that they could thrive at such elevations, but she did not question it. Many things she had seen in her life were impossible, and they had already seen ducks by the lake.

As they went up, the terrain became rough, with patches of rocky soil interrupting the sprawl of brownish yellow scrub that was the yak herds' main source of sustenance. A fox raced from a hole and away across the hill, a red streak against the brown land. They followed the stream for several miles, and it seemed to Anastasia they were getting nowhere. Looking back the way they'd come, she could still see Lake Tashi. But ahead were only the mountains, and the higher they climbed, the colder it became.

Then, just as she was about to question Tenzin's sense of direction, they topped a rise to see a flat stretch of grassland below them, covered in grazing yaks. Opposite the rise, in the shadow of the mountain, was a village.

Anastasia smiled at what passed for a modern village in the mountains of Tibet, so far from the nearest city. There were perhaps sixty or seventy dwellings clustered around the base of the mountain, half on either side of the stream—which seemed almost wide enough to be a river here. A wooden footbridge spanned the water. The homes were small, but elegant in design, and smoke rose from several chimneys, reminding her how much chillier it seemed than at the dig site. Farmers' fields spread out for many hundreds of yards in either direction, though the yak herd lazed in the middle, kept away from the crops—or what remained of them.

Perhaps there were generators in the village for electricity, and maybe even a two-way radio. She'd stopped in similar places, where some of the village elders had radios with tall antennas that pulled in a rough static with the occasional melody.

"I simply don't understand it," Horace Trotter said, coming up beside her.

"What don't you understand?" Anastasia glanced at Horace, then surveyed the rest of the group. Mr. Lao, the man from Beijing, only smiled thinly to show his relief that they'd rested and that their uphill climb was finished. The diggers stood near Professor Kyichu, watching him warily, though because of his age or his grief, she did not know.

"Why do they live so far away from the lake? Surely crops would grow better there. It's not quite so cold. There are several caves they could have used to store goods. Where we're conducting our dig, there isn't much land to graze their herds, but the area where this stream runs into the lake is broad enough."

Anastasia had her theories about why no one had settled on the rim of the lake, but only Professor Kyichu knew about those theories, and she wasn't going to start talking about the Dragon King Pool now. Trotter ought to have known enough to realize that ancient superstitions lingered for millennia in such remote places.

"Tenzin?" she asked, turning to their guide.

The Tibetan turned his impassive features toward her and looked at Horace Trotter. "The mountains are sacred."

Trotter scoffed. "I thought the old temple city we're unearthing was sacred. Come to think of it, I thought the lake was sacred."

"Sacred too," Tenzin agreed. "Just different. The mountains are holy. Pure. The lake is not a place for people."

"But we're there," the communications man pointed out.

Tenzin fixed him with a meaningful look. "Perhaps you should not be."

That shut Trotter up. Tenzin descended the other side of the rise and started toward the village, yaks ambling lazily out of the way. The rest of them followed. Anastasia hurried to catch up to their guide.

"That wasn't very helpful," she said in a low voice as she came up beside Tenzin.

He smiled sidelong at her. "Helpful to me. No more stupid questions."

"Are they stupid questions?"

Tenzin gave a small shrug of his shoulders. "Any question is stupid when the man asking is not smart enough to understand the answers."

They trekked into the village. Even before they

reached it, people started to come out to watch their approach. Little girls and women with mesmerizing eyes stood together, many of them wearing thick, soft head scarves. A pair of small boys in dark caps marched out as if to meet them, but then only stood aside to watch them pass. The man from Beijing glared at them, and they glared back. But when Anastasia smiled at them, they giggled and ran away.

Staying by the river, they entered the village unhindered and passed among the houses. It was still only late morning, but Anastasia smelled something delicious cooking in one of the houses. The wind stole the scent a moment later, but her stomach rumbled with the memory of it. Clothes hung out to dry on lines. Dogs raced around, barking at the newcomers and each other, then tearing off across the village on some other mad errand.

The gun felt heavy against the small of her back, beneath her jacket.

Half a dozen men stood on their side of the wooden bridge, waiting for them. Others stood in front of homes but did not come any closer. The men wore drab grays and browns, or white. Though several were ancient—including one whose face was so wrinkled his eyes were almost hidden in the folds, and one whose long, thin, white beard was tied with a cord a few inches below his chin—most of them were of indeterminable age. They might have been thirty or fifty. Some had their heads shaved bald, while others had black or black-and-silver hair.

All were as expressionless as Tenzin, save for the man with the white beard that hung like a braid. He smiled and, as Anastasia gestured for her party to halt, he nodded to her.

Anastasia had found that the Tibetan language often sounded sharp and abrupt to her. But when this man spoke, there was a softness to his words that made the language sound beautiful. He looked at her as he spoke—she presumed because he had seen the others defer to her—but when he was through, she glanced at Tenzin.

"He welcomes us to Nakchu village with all appropriate prayers and hospitality," Tenzin said.

She nodded. The six men had been joined by three elderly women, and their expressions were not as muted as those of the men. They glared at her with open suspicion and hostility. One of them muttered to the man next to her and touched her hair, glowering at Anastasia. Something about her red hair being sinister, she was sure. Tenzin didn't need to translate that one.

"Thank him. Say whatever you have to say to not offend these people. All the customary niceties, please. And then tell them of our missing girl and ask if any of their herders or anyone else might have seen her."

A chill went through her, and she glanced back to see the man from Beijing watching her with grim disapproval.

"What?" Trotter said. "Why don't we just look for her ourselves? If they snatched the poor thing, they're not likely just to hand her over."

Professor Kyichu whipped his head around and froze Trotter with a glance. "Don't be a jackass, Horace. You don't honestly think this entire village kidnapped my daughter? If anyone did, it would be one, among them. One twisted spirit. When they hear what's happened, we need to know if they suspect one of their own could do such a thing."

"And how will we know?" Trotter replied testily.

"We'll know," Anastasia said. She glanced at Tenzin. "Speak. We're going to offend them, making them just stand here."

Tenzin nodded and began to rattle off a stream of Tibetan. He gave a respectful bow of his head and gestured to Anastasia, then to the group in general. She recognized only a handful of words, including her own name. At one point, when Tenzin paused, the old man replied.

"They're aware that you're digging at the lake. He worries that you will disturb spirits of their ancestors."

Anastasia bowed her head just as Tenzin had. "Tell him we will preserve anything we find, that we're there to study, only, and that our respect for what we discover knows no boundaries. Tell him that nothing will be removed from the site without the proper authorization."

Tenzin shot a glance back at the man from Beijing,

then looked at her. "They'll want to know what you consider the proper authorization."

She flushed. "Right. Leave off that bit."

The guide started speaking again. The villagers did not seem at all comforted by her reassurances, but Tenzin forged ahead. When he gestured toward Professor Kyichu and said Kora's name, the professor closed his eyes in momentary anguish before opening them and fixing his desperate gaze upon the white-bearded man.

The village elder's eyes filled with sorrow, and when Tenzin stopped speaking, he nodded toward Professor Kyichu and spoke words no one needed to translate. Then he looked at Tenzin again and made a suggestion in that mellifluous voice. Several other villagers nodded and murmured their assent.

The response made Anastasia look around. She scanned the faces of several who stood nearby, then the people beyond them. A figure caught her eye, a young man washed in sunlight, standing between two small dwellings. While the other villagers focused on Tenzin or Professor Kyichu, this young man stared directly at Anastasia.

A bright red stain blossomed on the right shoulder of his pristine white shirt.

Her eyes went wide.

"No, it was not, damn it!" Professor Kyichu shouted.

Anastasia turned to stare at him and Tenzin in

alarm. The village elder still wore his implacable, soothing smile, but several of the other men had adopted stern expressions.

"Han," she said, pinning the professor with a look.

But Professor Kyichu ignored her. He met the elder's gaze with a dark look, and when he spoke, it was to instruct Tenzin.

"My daughter was not taken by a bear," the old archaeologist said. "We've a hunter and tracker along on the project, and there's been no sign of any bear. Black bears may make their home here, but we haven't seen one, nor has one come anywhere near our camp or the dig. Have you seen any sign of a bear, Tenzin? Or any sign that Kora might have been taken by one?"

The guide shook his head. "No, Professor. I haven't."

Tenzin began to rattle off words to the elder, who only nodded solemnly. The two diggers had begun to look a bit puffed up, as though they might be expecting a fight. Missing the pubs back home, she had no doubt. Anastasia caught the eye of the older of the two and shook her head. He took a deep breath and nodded.

The man from Beijing looked on in apparent disgust, but she was not sure who or what precisely disgusted him. The answer was probably everyone and everything.

Horace Trotter looked queasy and frightened.

As if it had suddenly been deposited there, she felt the weight of the pistol against the small of her back again.

Anastasia glanced back between the two dwellings where she had seen the young man with the crimson spot on his shirt, but he was gone. Again she scanned what she could see of the village, but though she saw several men with similar white shirts, she did not see the one she sought. Her pulse raced as she told herself that it might not have been blood, that it could have been some kind of adornment on the shirt. But she didn't believe that. She told herself that the saboteur—the intruder who had been in their camp—had not been human. He'd had eyes on fire and jagged fangs and twisted features.

But how could she know what that young man might look like after dark?

Tenzin, the village elder, and Professor Kyichu continued to talk a few moments longer, but then the guide turned to her.

"He promises to send someone to our camp if they see any sign of Kora. That's his polite way of telling us it's time to go."

Her skin flushed with alarm. "They're not going to invite us for tea?"

Tenzin smiled. "That doesn't seem likely."

Her whole party nodded respectfully and began to withdraw, turning to leave the village. Trotter smiled at a group of children that had inched toward them during their long exchange, as though they might be dangerous. When he grinned their way, they scattered, laughing. That was about Trotter's speed—

amusing children. Anastasia knew the thought was uncharitable, but she didn't like thinking she couldn't rely on him, and that was certainly the impression she'd gotten.

Professor Kyichu had kept his shoulders squared and his chin high with determined hope for most of the time since Kora had vanished. Now, the light in his eyes had gone. An air of defeat hung about him.

Anastasia wanted to scream. She turned to stare at the man with the long, tied-off white beard. He gave her a curious look.

She wanted to shout at him, to demand that they be allowed to search the village. If that had been blood on the shirt of the man she'd seen, he might very well be their saboteur. Human or not. Sometimes, there was a fine line, and there were creatures that existed right on that line. The blood would be from the bullet wound she'd put in his shoulder last night.

It made sense that Nakchu village had a saboteur in its midst. The elder himself had cautioned them against disturbing the spirits. Maybe the villagers all wanted to drive the archaeology expedition away.

And yet, what were her options? She could draw her gun and forcibly search the entire village. Tenzin had his rifle. But chances were good that some of these farmers and yak-herders had rifles, too, and if not, they'd have knives. Anastasia had no doubt the villagers would defend themselves as necessary.

If Kora was still alive, the clock was ticking. She hated

to leave the village, just on the chance that the girl might be there, but there was only one alternative to drawing her gun. She calculated how long it would have taken word to get back to the States, to the Bureau for Paranormal Research and Defense, how long to prepare a team, how long to travel to Lhasa, and then up into the mountains.

Hellboy would come. She couldn't let herself think otherwise.

If there were answers to be found in this village, he would find them, and damn the consequences. That had been one of the reasons she had fallen in love with him, so long ago.

"We'll be coming back," she told the elder, who only smiled and nodded, not understanding a word.

She turned and stormed after her companions. When she came abreast of Tenzin, she fell into step with him, her eyes on Professor Kyichu.

"We're coming back," she told the guide.

Tenzin nodded. "I did not doubt."

Hellboy watched the land whip by beneath the helicopter and felt boredom scraping against the base of his skull like grinding teeth. The prickle of surreal excitement brought about by the idea of seeing Anastasia was still there, but numbed now with the lull of constant travel. He'd journeyed home from Chile, been back in Connecticut for only a handful of hours, then gotten on a plane headed for Tibet. It felt like he'd been in constant motion for a week.

The constant travel was only part of the problem, though. The real boredom, now, came from the sameness of the terrain. There were only so many herds of sheep and yak and deer that he could see before they stopped being a pleasant distraction and just became a part of the monotony of green and brown grass, mountains, and valleys. It was beautiful, certainly. Breathtaking. But now he just wanted to stop. Stop moving. Stop flying. Stop thinking.

They were at the top of the world. The air was so thin that at times it took an exceptionally skilled pilot to keep the helicopter aloft, but he had faith in Redfield. Hellboy sat in front, next to the pilot. Sarah, Meaney, and Neil were in the middle of the big chopper, and Professor Bruttenholm and Abe were in the far back, wrapped in blankets and sleeping like babies.

Hellboy couldn't sleep. He stared out at the night and the dark hills and tried to keep from screaming in frustration at being cooped up for so long. And just when he thought he couldn't take it another second, Redfield reached up to scratch his beard and cleared his throat.

"There's the lake," the chopper pilot said.

Redfield took the helicopter across the water low enough that the force of the air rushing down from the rotors churned the surface. Hellboy scanned the shore ahead of them, where gentle hills rose up into slopes that might have been confused for mountains if not for the snowcapped peaks in the distance.

Five years since he had seen Anastasia. He tried to figure how old she'd be now, but time didn't mean as much to him as it did to other people, and it took him a moment to work it out. Forty-one, he figured. Maybe forty-two.

The tents of the expedition's camp were ghosts on the shore of the lake. Lights burned against the moonlit stone face of the hillside, marking out the boundaries of the archaeological dig. Gray figures milled about the camp, drawn out by the sound of the helicopter. Hellboy wasn't sure of the local time, but he figured it had to be going on 11:00 P.M. A lot of people weren't sleeping. Not that he blamed them. If there were monsters lurking around their camp, sleep wouldn't come easy.

As Redfield circled in search of a likely landing spot, Hellboy couldn't help searching the upturned faces in the moonlight below. He caught a glimpse of a figure that might have been Anastasia, hair pulled back into a ponytail, then the copter swung around, and he couldn't see the expedition members anymore. The pilot set the craft down a hundred yards or so from the camp on a broad, flat stretch of lakeshore, and only when Redfield killed the engines and the noise of the rotors chopping air began to subside did Hellbody realize how grateful he'd be for the quiet. The hum and whine of aircraft engines had been his near-constant companion for three days.

In the back, Neil and Sarah were up immediately, sliding a door open. Neil jumped down and stretched, muscles popping. Tough as nails, but he looked like death warmed over with his twenty-four-o'clock shadow and dark circles under his eyes. Hellboy wondered how Stasia would look after five years.

He blinked. "Oh, crap," he whispered. Maybe she'd be wondering how he looked, and if he looked anything like Neil after this trip, the answer wasn't a happy one.

With a sigh, he ran his left hand over his stubbly chin, then the leathery pate of his head. The stumps of his horns probably could use filing—he hadn't done it in forever—but he wasn't some giggling schoolgirl preening before a date. Still, he ran his tongue over his teeth and cupped his hand in front of his mouth, trying to smell his own breath. He reached back and tightened the knot of hair at the base of his skull.

"Moron," he whispered to himself.

Beside him, Redfield had just removed his comm. unit.

"What's that?"

Hellboy shook his head. "Not you, pal."

He popped his door and climbed down from the helicopter. The brick wall, Meaney, was still up in the chopper, handing gear and travel bags out to Sarah and Neil, who piled them on the ground a few feet away.

"There he is," Neil said by way of greeting, as though Hellboy'd just shown up for a meeting. "What's the plan, boss? Where do you want us to set up camp?"

A group of perhaps a dozen people from the archaeologists' camp were making their way along the shore toward the helicopter. Hellboy felt his attention pulled toward those gray figures, but he turned to Neil.

"The professor's got command of this op. You know that."

Neil smiled, his face almost indigo in the darkness of night. "'Course. But Professor Bruttenholm's still kippin' in the back."

Lithe, tiny Sarah did not smile, just stared at him expectantly, even as she caught a duffel that Meaney chucked to her from within the helicopter. Hellboy looked at her, then back at Neil.

"You want me to give orders? Fine. Wake Professor Bruttenholm. That's an order. After that, it's up to him. I'm a grunt on this op, no different from you."

"Whatever you say, mate."

Hellboy left them to it. The archaeologists arrived, along with a little weasel of a guy in a dark suit who could only be some kind of government representative. In Tibet, that meant Chinese government. No way was Beijing going to allow representatives of the government of the United Kingdom to spend any time in Tibet, digging up ancient civilizations, without some kind of monitoring. They wouldn't want anyone stealing or destroying historical artifacts, of course, but that was just part of it. What they would really want to avoid would be any official interaction between British and local government.

To his credit, though, the Chinese government monitor hung back, acknowledging that this was Stasia's expedition, her team.

"Hellboy," she said as she walked up, the others making way for her. Several people went to help the BPRD operatives unload, and a couple were helping Redfield tie the chopper down in case of wind. Hellboy barely noticed them, now.

"Stasia. It's great to see you."

"And you. Thank you for coming."

He raised his hands. "How could I stay away? You always bring me to the most interesting places."

"By interesting you mean 'remote.'"

"That too."

Introductions were made. A couple of the names stood out to Hellboy from the report he'd read on the dig, the temple of the Dragon King, the supposedly inhuman saboteurs, and the missing girl. The first was Frank Danovich, an American site engineer from Seattle, Washington. His job was to make sure that none of the dig construction or excavation came down on their heads. He was also one of the first to see the creature plaguing the expedition. The other names he recognized from the report were Dr. Mark Conrad and Professor Han Kyichu.

Nobody offered to shake hands. With the size and weight of his right fist, he could not blame them. When people did summon up the courage to offer their hand to him, he was never quite sure what to do, so he was glad to be spared that moment.

He nodded solemnly to Professor Kyichu before explaining to all of them—and the government man in particular, though without speaking directly to him—that Professor Bruttenholm was leading the investigation. After several more welcomes and grateful appreciations, they began to drift away, most back to their tasks but others to wait as a sleepy Professor Bruttenholm climbed out of the helicopter, wrapped up in conversation with Abe. The two of them kept gesturing toward the lake, and Hellboy had a feeling Abe would be going for a swim very soon.

"I worried you wouldn't arrive tonight," Anastasia said.

Hellboy frowned. "We came as fast as we could. Left six hours after the briefing."

"That's not what I meant," she said, a bit worriedly. "You got here quickly. I just . . . I'm glad we don't have to spend another night with this mysterious, troublesome business without you here. The BPRD, I mean."

"The BPRD, right."

"So, thank you."

"You keep saying that."

"Can't seem to stop."

"You look . . ." he glanced away, then down at the ground. "You know."

He lifted his gaze to find her wearing that lopsided, sweetly amused grin that had done him in from the moment they'd first met.

"It's been too long, love. But it's so strange. Every time I see you, it feels as though it's only been hours since the last time. Why is that?"

Hellboy had several ideas on that score, but none of them were things he would ever have spoken aloud, even back in those times when he and Stasia had talked about things like love and fate as though they had some secret knowledge that others didn't share. Couples were like that. They had the key to the universe, or so they thought. He'd never felt that way before or since, and looking back, he remembered it with awkward distance, like something slightly embarrassing that he'd overheard people talking about at the next table in a restaurant.

"Don't know. But, yeah. Weird, huh?"

Anastasia laughed. "Ever the soul of eloquence."

"You know me."

With anyone else, he might have muttered something sarcastic. But it was Stasia. She was allowed to bust his chops the way no one else in the world could. Well, no one but Abe and Liz, and sometimes, not even them.

The thought of Abe made him blink and glance around, but the amphibious man was talking quietly with Professor Bruttenholm, while Redfield and the three BPRD field operatives got situated with the gear and started to put up their tents. Hellboy saw his father look up from the conversation with Abe, and the old man narrowed his eyes. Hellboy caught the subtle concern and disapproval on the old man's face though no one else would have noticed any change.

Hellboy returned his gaze to Anastasia.

"You do look amazing," he said. "Haven't aged a day. Almost didn't recognize you without the damn Yankees hat, though."

"Back in my tent, actually," she said. "Well, not the same one. Dropped it into a volcano a couple of years back and had to replace it."

"You did not."

Stasia gave him a tiny shrug. "Really did."

They stood for a moment, just looking at each other. The last time they'd crossed paths, it hadn't been like this at all. Hellboy had harbored some resentment toward her—and toward himself—that they hadn't been able to make things work. The attention of the media and all the church groups and others who were so vocal about their disapproval of the relationship had been too much stress. Hellboy didn't like the constant reminders that to much of the world, he would always be a monster, no matter how many lives he saved. The United Nations had declared him an "honorary human" decades ago, but even that label made his skin crawl. What the heck was it supposed to mean, anyway?

He'd lied to her. She looked damned good, but she had gotten older. Even in the dark, he could see that her hair still had the luster it had always maintained, no matter the climate or how long she'd been toiling in ditches and tombs. Her eyes were still as bright, and she was fit as ever. But the crow's-feet had deepened around her eyes, and small lines had formed at the corners of her mouth. How to explain that these things made her more beautiful, that the life in her—the living—made her sexy as hell?

Not the things you said to your ex.

"You haven't changed at all, either," Anastasia said. "You look—"

"Like a donkey's ass? Cuz that's how I feel."

A kind of sadness touched her features. "No. You look well. Healthy. Strong."

The strength in her faltered, and she stepped nearer, took his hands in hers, not differentiating between his ordinary, flesh-and-blood hand and the massive, destructive fist of his right.

"Thank you for coming. You have no idea how relieved I am that you're here."

Hellboy's voice dropped nearly to a whisper. "No sign of the girl?"

"Nothing. But there have been developments. Last night, our saboteur returned. I shot him, but he fell in the lake. I'm certain he swam off, despite the bullet wound."

"You got a good look at him?"

She nodded. "It's just as was in the report. Subhuman. I've reason to believe he might be a shapeshifter. And I may know where he is. If he is the one who took Kora—"

Hellboy had been unable to focus on anything but her hands in his. He broke that contact and took a step back, feeling the anxious attention of his father's eyes on his back without even turning around.

"Whatever's going on here, we'll work it out as fast as we can. Professor Bruttenholm is leading our investigation, but I'm sure the first thing he'll want is a meeting where you can lay out the background of the dig and what you've uncovered thus far. If your saboteur fell in the lake, then he may have come from there in the first place. Abe will probably recon the lake bottom tonight. And we'll take it from there."

He looked around to make sure none of the other archaeologists were close enough to hear him. The last thing he wanted was for Professor Kyichu to eavesdrop on this conversation.

"If this girl is still alive, we'll get her back, Stasia."

Ever since they'd landed, he'd had an ominous feeling, like something wasn't right. He wasn't the type to put much stock in precognition—not in people like himself who'd never shown any aptitude for it—but there was a kind of menace on the shore of the lake. When Anastasia smiled again, so full of her fondness for him, he wondered if the danger he sensed had anything to do with monsters, or if it was all about the ghosts of the past.

Abe Sapien slipped beneath the surface of Lake Tashi with a shudder of pleasure. The water caressed him, invigorated him. Though he had slept a great deal during their long journey from the United States, a shroud of sluggishness had blanketed him since he had stepped off the helicopter. When Professor Bruttenholm had asked him to recon the lake while the others prepared a debriefing with the archaeological team, he'd felt absurdly grateful.

Not that he expected to find much. The lake was vast, and the moonlight did little more than give a glow to the first few feet of its depths. His eyes were keen, at night or underwater, but when he was dealing with both darkness and depth, even his vision had limits. The only way he was going to find the remains of a little girl in the lake was by accidentally swimming into her floating corpse.

Another shudder went through him. *What's wrong with you?* Abe thought to himself. He wasn't normally so callous.

And yet, it was the truth. If the girl had drowned or been murdered in the lake, there was little chance he would find her body at night. Even in the daytime, it would be a huge job for him to search the entirety of Lake Tashi. Likewise, he calculated slim odds of finding any trace of the saboteur that Dr. Bransfield—Anastasia—had mentioned.

Professor Bruttenholm knew that. Abe knew that he'd been asked to do the recon for other reasons—first, to make sure the people they'd been sent to help felt that help had arrived, and that the BPRD was not going to waste any time getting started, and second, because they had no idea what was truly going on here. Hellboy was the closest friend Abe had ever had, but that didn't make him the best field leader. If they knew what they were up against, or knew where to look for the threat, no one could close a case faster than Hellboy. March in, get his butt kicked, then dish it out.

But this was going to be a real investigation. There was reason to believe something supernatural was going on here, but beyond that, they had to start from scratch. While Abe swam the lake, Hellboy and Bruttenholm would be touring the dig site and the expedition camp.

Abe knew the purpose of this swim.

It could wait.

He kicked and thrust his arms forward, pulling himself deeper into the darkness of the lake. Total immersion meant utter bliss. He swam for a few minutes, simply allowing the pleasure of the water to seep into him, acclimating himself to the temperature, the saline level, and the fish that darted up to him to gaze curiously for a moment before streaking away.

His mind drifted, and he found himself thinking about Hellboy and Anastasia. Professor Bruttenholm's concern for his foster son was badly concealed. Abe had met Anastasia several times—at the beginning or end of some expedition on which Hellboy was accompanying her—and he'd always found her to be intelligent and charming. But once their relationship had ended, he had also been there to see the way it had ravaged Hellboy's spirit. The breakup had been more his idea than Anastasia's, but the separation from her had taken a terrible toll. Never had he spoken a word against her, but Abe had seen between his words. Hellboy had brought up the troubles they faced, the pressure of their public image, and Anastasia had agreed that it was best to end things. It was clear he had wanted her to argue, to fight for what they had, but she had not.

Hellboy had done his best to put it all behind him, no matter how much he missed her. Then, five years ago, he'd seen her again, and the numb distance between them had been erased. When he'd come back from Egypt after that case, he'd been unusually quiet, even for Hellboy.

Having Anastasia as a friend ought to have been a pleasure, at least as far as Abe was concerned. They had loved one another—maybe still did—but decided they were better off apart than together. Yet the bond between them and their abiding fondness for one another remained. It would, of course, be bittersweet, but he had read a thousand novels in which similar relationships existed.

Now, though, he had seen them together. Professor Bruttenholm had watched them warily as they greeted one another, and Abe had watched as well—had found it impossible not to watch. It was all still there, between them. Hellboy pretended he didn't still feel what he once felt, and Anastasia pretended not to notice. Abe had spent months floating in a tank studying the people around him—even as they were studying him—and the dynamics between Hellboy and Anastasia were impossible to miss.

If Professor Bruttenholm disliked Dr. Bransfield, he could hardly be blamed. She would likely be a source of both happiness and sorrow to Hellboy as long as he lived; after her death, his memory of her would linger. It was natural for a father to wish his son's sadness away.

What the professor did not see was that Anastasia carried a similar melancholy with her in Hellboy's presence. She was as helpless as Hellboy to prevent it. Circumstances had brought them together again. Professor Bruttenholm might blame Anastasia for requesting the BPRD's involvement in the first place—she would know that Hellboy would come, no questions asked—but what else could she have done, given the situation?

Abe swam. The lake surrounded him with solace and pleasure. Yet he could not swim far enough to escape the inevitable sadness of this venture. Hellboy, Anastasia, and Professor Bruttenholm would all come away from this case with heavy hearts. There was no avoiding that.

In the meantime, all they could do was their best. The missing girl, Kora Kyichu, would be their focus, as it should be. And the desperation of searching for her, wondering if she was alive, would protect them all for a while.

Reluctantly, Abe focused on the task at hand. He'd have a better look in the morning, but for now he swam along the lake bottom, searching for some kind of ancient ruin or even a lair where a mystical creature might be hiding. Nothing was beyond imagining. They knew so little about what was going on here that he had to consider every possibility.

From what he could see in the dark, however, there was nothing unusual at the bottom of the lake. The only oddity he discovered was a strange featurelessness. There was little vegetation down here, and no rough terrain at all. The bottom consisted of soil so loose that when he paused a moment in his swimming and tried to put his feet down, he sank halfway to his knees.

The soil was warm. He shook himself loose, worried that it might be like underwater quicksand, and he'd find it difficult to free himself. But he slid out as easily as he'd sunk in, and began to swim for the surface. In the morning, he would return to the lake bottom, but he already knew he would find nothing but sand. If there was anything to find, it would have buried itself in that shifting silt by now.

Only when he had nearly reached the surface, not far from shore, did it occur to him that the soil had been too warm. He paused, floating for a moment. It wasn't just the soil. Given the time of year and the chilly air up in these mountains, the lake ought to have been fairly cold. Near the surface, it was, but it should have gotten colder the deeper he swam.

Instead, the depths of the lake were warm.

CHAPTER 4

Hellboy took an instant dislike to Mark Conrad. When Anastasia had met him, getting off the helicopter, he'd been too distracted by her to pay much attention to the people with her. Now, though, Conrad had an arrogant-rich-boy thing going on that made Hellboy want to hammer him into the ground with his fist. Dr. Conrad had a three-day stubble of beard that seemed by choice of style, and wavy blond hair that hung to his shoulders. He was fit, but the red in his eyes said he normally drank too much. And he occupied the space within Anastasia's tent as though they were serfs and he their feudal master.

Rich, uptight, English prig. It didn't help that he was handsome, and aware of it, and that he had a kind of proprietary air about him when standing beside Anastasia. From the way Conrad kept looking back and forth between Hellboy and Anastasia, it was obvious he was aware of their past relationship. It was also pretty clear how he felt about it. His nostrils flared with barely disguised disgust whenever he had to address Hellboy directly.

Which meant Hellboy tried to force Conrad to address him directly as often as possible, just to bother the asshat, and to amplify his own desire to pummel him.

They had all gathered in Anastasia's tent for the debriefing—Hellboy, Professor Bruttenholm, Dr. Conrad, Anastasia herself, and the man from Beijing, whose name was Lao. No first or last. Just Lao, like Madonna or Cher. As annoying as his superior smugness was, it didn't make Hellboy want to break him in two the way Conrad's attitude did. Maybe that was because Lao hadn't so much as flinched upon meeting him, had barely spoken to him or looked at him. Lao wasn't fazed by the presence of an enormous guy with sawed-off horns, bloodred skin, and a tail.

Hellboy liked that. Flunky for insidious secret government masters he might be, but Lao didn't look down his nose at the red guy.

The tent was huge. Given that it doubled as the command center for the dig, it had to be. Still, Hellboy had to crouch a little to stand inside, and he didn't like that. It made him feel foolish, so he tried not to meet Anastasia's gaze when he could avoid it.

Professor Kyichu hadn't been brought into the briefing, and that was good. Hellboy had felt the urge to say something to the man, to offer him some comfort or reassurance, but he'd been unable to come up with anything that didn't sound hollow or insincere. Better to have the man elsewhere, at least for the moment.

Conrad had finished giving them all a rundown of the discovery of the dig site and their operations up until now. Anastasia had asked him to do so, ceding the floor to him, and he took it as though he was entitled. Now that he was done, though, he looked up at Professor Bruttenholm, as if they were equals, and nobody else was in the tent.

"It's late, Professor. What can we tell you that isn't in the documents you received?" Conrad asked.

Professor Bruttenholm nodded, clearing his throat. "Thank you, Dr. Conrad. Perhaps you and Dr. Bransfield would be so kind as to—"

"Shouldn't we wait for Abe?" Hellboy interrupted.

His father raised a bushy white eyebrow. "Abe will be along shortly. Dr. Conrad is correct. It's quite late. Still, we ought to learn what we can."

Conrad started to speak again, but Anastasia cut him off, both talking over him and stepping closer to the center of the tent.

"What can we tell you, Professor? Where should we start?"

Professor Bruttenholm cleared his throat. "Perhaps you could begin by telling me what you expected to find when you began the excavation."

Conrad smiled thinly. "Surely, that's in the file, sir. Our mandate was to locate and restore the fortress city of an ancient warlord known in those times as the

Dragon King, due to his symbolic use of the Asian dragon motif in his city and the temple he built to the gods. Dozens of references in scrolls from those times refer to the deadly power of the Dragon King, raining fire and destruction down upon his enemies and all of the villages in the area, whom he forced to worship him."

Hellboy threw up his hands. "Yeah, yeah, pal, we read all that. But that's just a version of the story. You found this Dragon King Temple, and there's something about local legends of real dragons and the lake. Now you've got monsters rousting your camp, causing trouble, maybe taking this little girl away, trying to stop you. Gotta tell you, everyone's worried about the girl, Kora, but the way the report read, nobody seemed all that stunned about subhuman creatures sabotaging your dig."

Professor Bruttenholm nodded and gestured his agreement with a flourish of his right hand. "Precisely. Which prompts the question, why is no one surprised by this? What were you really looking for?"

Conrad sneered. "You people are off your nut. Our intent here isn't at issue. Can you help us, or not?"

But Professor Bruttenholm wasn't looking at him anymore. He was staring at Anastasia, who glanced reluctantly at Conrad before nodding. "You're right, of course, Professor."

Hellboy loved the look of confusion and consternation on Conrad's face. He wasn't used to being out of the loop, obviously. Cut off his self-image at the knees.

"Talk, Stasia. Let's not waste any more time," Hellboy said.

She nodded, and when she spoke, her gaze shifted between him and Professor Bruttenholm, ignoring Dr. Conrad and Lao entirely. Hellboy thought it was interesting that Lao seemed to be able to disappear in a room so that nobody noticed him at all.

"If Dr. Conrad's interpretation of those ancient texts had been accurate," Anastasia began, "this would still have been a wonderful bit of archaeology, and an important opportunity to study ancient Tibet. But Mark, along with my employers at the British Museum and the Chinese government, arrived at their interpretations by first discounting the folklore involved."

Conrad laughed and shook his head. "Stacie, what are you talking about? Are you trying to imply the Dragon King—"

Hellboy held his breath when Anastasia looked at him.

"Was a dragon," she said, casting a quick glance at Conrad. "Yes. That's precisely what I'm saying." Her gaze returned to Hellboy and Professor Bruttenholm. "Oh, call it whatever you like—whatever fits your narrow imagination. Monster. Giant Gila monster. Miraculous survivor of Paleolithic times. All of that would be utter shite, of course, but if it makes it easier for you to accept . . ."

Professor Bruttenholm stroked his goatee, studying

her. "Obviously, Hellboy and I have no difficulty—"

"Dragons!" Dr. Conrad said, too loudly. When he realized the volume of his voice, he hushed himself and looked around incredulously. At last he set his sights on the man from Beijing, thinking perhaps that Lao was the sole voice of reason remaining in the room. "Are you truly listening to this? This isn't science, it's childish nonsense. Dragons and princesses. Next she's going to tell me she believes in vampires."

Lao smoothed the lapels of his black jacket and fixed Dr. Conrad with a dark stare. "Of course she does, doctor," the man from Beijing said, in perfect, crisp English. "And with good reason."

Conrad spun, nose wrinkled in revulsion, and turned to Professor Bruttenholm. "This is absurd!"

"Not at all, Dr. Conrad. Vampires are, I assure you, quite real. Seventy-seven different breeds have been cataloged by the BPRD, and I can only presume there are others. Fortunately, they do not seem to be the problem here. Now, if you'll be so kind as to allow Dr. Bransfield to speak, perhaps we can return to my original question."

The man fumed, but he crossed his arms and said nothing further. Hellboy almost wished he would. At some point, his father would have told him to remove Conrad from the tent if he continued to impede their investigation. Would've been fun.

"Go on, Dr. Bransfield," Professor Bruttenholm said.

Hellboy couldn't have missed the cold professionalism in his father's tone, the distance there. The way Anastasia blinked, it was clear that she heard it as well. But she was used to being clinical and meticulous.

"Thank you, Professor," she replied, glancing from Bruttenholm to Hellboy and back. "Han Kyichu is the only member of my team who was aware of my beliefs regarding our discovery. He concurred with them. The legends about the Dragon Pool and the temple of the Dragon King are fairly straightforward. In fact, just before Kora was reported missing, he'd found writing within one of the excavated structures that indicated it was the actual temple of the Dragon King."

Conrad waved a dismissive hand. "Which it wasn't."

Anastasia nodded. "On that, I'm afraid Mark is correct. What we'd thought was the temple turned out to be something else entirely."

Hellboy ran a hand over his stubbly pate. "You've lost me, Stasia. There's some stuff about the legend in the case file. But gimme the short version. What are we dealing with here, and when do I get to hit it?"

She smiled wanly and went across the tent to a table upon which lay stacks of journals and thick sheaves of bound documents. Anastasia pushed a couple of them out of the way, picked up a phone-book-sized report, and flipped it open. She made as if to bring it to Hellboy, then raised an eyebrow at her folly and handed it to Professor Bruttenholm instead. She knew Hellboy wasn't good with the homework.

"In the morning, you can see the room itself. The

preparatory chamber, according to Dr. Conrad, and I concur."

Hellboy threw up his hands. "Preparing for what? And whose chamber was it? Lay it out for us."

"The Dragon King Pool is an ancient legend that describes a large, turbulent lake, beneath which resided an evil dragon who caused devastation, fire, and floods, and brought misery to all those who would not serve him . . . and often those he had already conquered and forced into his service."

"Swell guy," Hellboy muttered.

"He was a king," Anastasia said, as if that explained it all. And, in a way, it did. "The Dragon King's subjects were forced to build a temple to worship him. He considered himself a god. Not exactly unusual back then. Every silly bugger with a bit of power fancied himself a deity. Same thing happens nowadays, they just don't let on that they've promoted themselves to godhood. Anyway, point is, the Dragon King was supposed to be huge. Many other, lesser dragons served him. And then there were the conquered people, the slaves.

"His subjects built a temple, and some kind of city around it, where they lived. We are one hundred percent certain that what we've found is the city of the Dragon King, and that Lake Tashi is the legendary Dragon Pool. But the temple is still a mystery to us. The geography doesn't suggest any buildings of the size that would be required for such a temple."

Professor Bruttenholm looked troubled. He also looked tired. Hellboy wished Anastasia would offer him a chair. Not that his father would take it.

"And this preparatory chamber?" the professor said.

"The legend states that the only way for the locals, even those who were his subjects, to placate the Dragon King was to offer him a child in sacrifice. Once a year, a child was chosen and thrown into the lake, which would churn and steam with the fire of the Dragon King. The child would never be seen again. The figures and characters on the door to the preparatory chamber referred to the sacrifice and to the temple, which made Professor Kyichu think that it was the temple itself. The saboteur caved in the entrance to the chamber, focused there, as though it was of far more importance than anything else we're excavating. And I suppose it is. Once we dug it out, Dr. Conrad discerned the true nature of the place."

Hellboy took a few steps toward his father, but Professor Bruttenholm waved him off, a stern expression on his face. He didn't like to be fussed over. *Stubborn old goat,* Hellboy thought.

He looked at Anastasia, Lao, and Conrad, each in turn. Nothing that had been said seemed to have fazed Lao, but Conrad kept rolling his eyes and sighing in obvious dismay that they were all speaking with such credulity about dragons and their human worshippers.

"Let's talk about this saboteur," Hellboy said. "Mr. Lao?"

The man from Beijing regarded him coolly, without speaking.

Professor Bruttenholm cleared his throat again, a reminder that he was leading the investigation. "Mr. Lao, does the Bureau have your assurance that your government is in no way involved in the sabotage of this expedition?"

Lao revealed no emotion at all. "You insult us, Professor."

"And you have my apologies. That wasn't my intention. But the question had to be asked, and answered. I take it your official answer is 'no.'"

The man from Beijing flinched, almost imperceptibly. He did not like to be pushed. "That is correct."

"Thank you," Professor Bruttenholm said.

"Okay," Hellboy began, turning the focus back to Anastasia. "What, then? You shot the guy, you said. He dived into the lake—"

"Several miles to the northwest there is a village. Nakchu. I took a small party to the village this morning to ask about Kora. I was as diplomatic as possible. Only the elder spoke, and he didn't offer his name. No one in Nakchu had seen Kora, or so he told our guide, Tenzin. But when I was there, I saw a fellow with a bright red spot on his shirt, right where I'd shot the . . . intruder, the night before."

"Blood."

"Probably."

"So you think he was your guy? That he took a bullet, dived into the lake, and hiked back to his village before daybreak?"

Anastasia nodded. "Yes. I do."

"Bollocks!" Dr. Conrad said. "And I suppose he was wearing some sort of monster mask every time he came into camp? The man you and Danovich and the others spotted was disfigured, Stacie, you said so yourself."

"Hideous," she replied, and Hellboy was troubled by the disquiet in her voice. "He had fire burning in his eyes."

"You mean they glowed?" Professor Bruttenholm asked.

"No," Anastasia said, shaking her head. "I mean they were on fire. Flames flickered from his eyes like . . . have you ever seen a building on fire, the way the blaze shoots up from the burned out windows? Like that."

Hellboy stared at her. "So, when you said you had reason to believe he was a shape-shifter?"

"What I saw wasn't a mask. Danovich will tell you the same. This thing wasn't human. But the young man I saw—handsome lad. Nothing out of the ordinary at all, except that bloodstain on his shirt."

"He could have gotten that a thousand ways. You don't even know it was blood!" Conrad protested.

"It was blood," Lao said, and from the way Anastasia

and Conrad glanced at him, Hellboy had the impression the man from Beijing was being downright verbose with them tonight in comparison to his usual MO.

Professor Bruttenholm crossed his arms. This time when Hellboy went to him, he allowed himself to be escorted to a chair and slid down into it gratefully, deep in thought.

"Tell me, Dr. Bransfield," the professor said, stiffly formal. "How does this legend end? Such bits of folklore always have a colorful ending."

"This one is no different. An order of monks refused to serve the Dragon King. He burned many of them and threatened to destroy them all if they would not worship him. But among them was a monk who was a warrior and sorcerer, though small in stature. A dwarf."

"A dwarf," Hellboy repeated.

"Yes," Anastasia said, glaring admonishment at him.

Hellboy shrugged. "Just saying."

"His name was Dwenjue. He posed as a child and was thrown into the lake by the subjects of the Dragon King. Dwenjue battled the dragon for seven days and seven nights, and slew the dragon . . . or at least wounded it mortally and trapped it forevermore. From that day on, the area became prosperous, and the people were happy. At least . . . that's the legend."

Professor Bruttenholm mumbled something that might have been "interesting." Mr. Lao only watched the interplay with cool, distant eyes. Dr. Conrad shook his head in disbelief. Hellboy and Anastasia found they could not hold one another's gaze for very long without looking away.

"Okay, let's see what we've got," Hellboy said at last, just to be saying something. "Sabotage guy, who might be a shape-shifter, fire coming out of his eyes kinda suggesting dragon-boy. Village protecting him, or maybe actually clueless. Either way, that's a problem. Missing girl, in a place where they used to drown kids sacrificially to appease the local bully."

Alarm flared in Anastasia's eyes. "Please don't say that out loud again. Professor Kyichu is holding out every hope. I'm sure he's thought of it himself, but until we know for sure—"

Hellboy held up his left hand. He almost told her not to get her knickers in a twist. Any other Englishwoman, he might have. But this was Anastasia.

"Relax. Not another word. Besides, I've got a feeling the kid's still alive."

Anastasia frowned. "I hope you're right, but what makes you say that?"

"Hey, nobody's used that preparatory chamber in how many centuries? Could be why they've been trying so hard to keep you from opening it up. Maybe that's all part of the deal."

Professor Bruttenholm twisted around in his seat and stared at Hellboy. Anastasia covered her mouth in horror.

"What'd I say?" Hellboy asked.

"Something logical."

He shrugged. "Give enough monkeys enough typewriters, you get Shakespeare, or something like that. I'm just saying if somebody wants to worship the Dragon King the old way, they'd have to use that chamber, right?"

"It does make sense," Dr. Conrad said, though it was obvious the words pained him.

"So if no one's been in there with the kid yet, then she's probably still breathin'."

Anastasia started to swear under her breath, then shot him a hard look. "Are you suggesting that the saboteur was trying to stop us so that . . . you're saying by opening the chamber, we may have somehow set those old rituals in motion again, that we've woken something—"

She was interrupted by a flap of canvas, then Abe Sapien walked into the tent, dripping with water from the lake.

"Abe," Professor Bruttenholm said, staring at the amphibious man intently. "Did you discover anything?"

All eyes were on him, and Abe looked at Conrad and Lao warily. Hellboy gestured for him to speak.

"Nothing. It's very dark, Professor, but I don't think the morning will show me anything either. No sign of ruins. No creatures other than fish. No bodies. Nothing but loose soil and a few plants. I've never seen a lake bottom so bare."

"Another puzzle," Professor Bruttenholm said.

"There is one odd thing," Abe added.

Hellboy didn't like the way he said it.

"What're you talking about, Abe?" he asked.

"The lake . . . it's cold at first, what you would expect. But as I went deeper, the water felt warm. There's heat coming from somewhere down there, as though there might be a volcanic fissure beneath the lake. I saw no sign of—"

"No," Anastasia said. "There's no volcanic activity on this plateau."

Hellboy saw the idea illuminate her features. Even Lao reacted, eyes narrowing with dark worry. Conrad only looked confused.

"Well," Professor Bruttenholm said, "obviously, something must be providing that heat."

Hellboy stared at Anastasia.

"I think we need a plan."

The Island of Crete, 6 April, 1980

"Nice place. Kind of a change of pace."

Anastasia turned and smiled at him from the balcony. Hellboy stood in the airy living room of the villa that the British Museum had provided for them on the outskirts of Anoyeia. White curtains billowed in the breeze like some kind of princess's dream or a bad coffee commercial. Any minute, Hellboy expected to see unicorns—or a Colombian guy in a bad hat with a burro.

"It's beautiful," Anastasia agreed. "Come out here."

Hellboy hesitated only a moment before stepping out to join her, careful not to break the tiles with his hooves. The view was spectacular. In one direction they could see St. John's Church, and in the other, the peak of Mount Ida.

"Quite romantic, don't you think?"

Hellboy cocked his head, knitting his brow. "Not much of a romantic. Not really built for it, you know? They don't paint guys like me on the covers of those novels."

Anastasia slid her arm around him, forcing him to do the same. She nuzzled against his chest, and something inside him hesitated. Her touch was so soft. Holding her was like holding a bird in his hands. He liked to feel her heart beat against his chest when she lay next to him in bed, and the way she looked at him . . . these were all new experiences for him. Hellboy had always thought he was prepared for anything, would walk blindly into any trap, stand toe to toe with any danger. But he hadn't been prepared for this.

"You don't fool me," she whispered, reaching up to undo the knot of hair at the base of his skull, teasing it with her fingers. "Don't ever think you can."

"I'll keep it in mind," he said, looking down at her, smiling what he knew was a brutal, almost indecipherable smile. "How do we warrant this VIP treatment, anyway?"

Anastasia shrugged. "The museum likes the work I've been doing. They like having you associated with them, even unofficially. Since this dig is Dr. Campbell's baby, and we're only here to assist until they get the funding up for my Iceland dig, they don't need us on the site."

"I could get used to it. Iceland, on the other hand—"

She bumped him with her hip and gazed up at him. "It's beautiful there. You're going to love it."

Hellboy laughed softly. "Is that an order?"

"It is."

"Yes, mistress."

"Bloody well right."

Delicious aromas of Greek cooking wafted up from the village. The spring air felt a bit cool, but Hellboy relished it. Anastasia had taken him to some remote areas of the world in the time they'd been together—which was nearly every day since they'd met in that pub in London—but there seemed to be beauty everywhere. Maybe just having something to do besides hunt monsters and ghosts and debunk legends made him see the world differently. Oh, there'd been a fair share of supernatural encounters since they'd gotten together—that crap seemed to follow him around, and the BPRD still tried to keep him busy when they could, sending him on jobs in the areas where Anastasia was already working—but places like Mount Ida made it all worthwhile.

"We need spinach pie," he announced.

Anastasia slipped out from under his arm. "Spinach pie it is. Just as soon as we're unpacked."

"Is that my stomach growling or impending volcanic eruption?"

"All right," she said, rolling her eyes. "Spinach pie first."

He didn't smile. Squeezing his eyes closed, he brought his left hand up to his face and felt himself sway.

"Hey. You okay?"

Anastasia's voice seemed distant and muffled. He frowned as he looked at her.

"Yeah. I think so. Head feels a little oogy all of a sudden, like I had too much ouzo last night."

"You did have too much ouzo last night."

Hellboy nodded, trying not to ruin the lighthearted moment they'd been sharing. "Yeah. But I didn't have it for breakfast. Anyway, it'll pass."

Concern lined her face. "You want to lie down a while?"

"No, no. I'm good. Just give me a minute."

Hellboy turned away from Anastasia, not liking her troubled expression . . . not wanting her to see the expression he knew must be on his own face. They'd been together almost a year, so maybe she didn't notice, but he didn't get sick. No flu. No colds. No fevers. The only thing that ever affected him was sorcery. And sorcerers pissed him off.

His tail dragged across the terra-cotta tiles as he

walked across the living room and into the bathroom, trying to figure out if he was swaying, or his equilibrium just felt off. He hoped Anastasia hadn't noticed.

In the bathroom he turned on the tap and let cold water run into the sink. When he bent to splash water onto his face, the whole world tilted around him. Hellboy fell. He reached out to steady himself, enormous right hand closing on the edge of the sink, which shattered. As he collapsed, he pulled the sink with him, breaking it off the wall. The mirror above it exploded in a shower of reflective shards. Water spurted from the pipes behind the sink, quickly pooling on the floor.

The dizziness pulled him down into darkness.

Cold water sprinkled his face. He blinked and opened his eyes, and the world was gray around him. The smell of the water and his own musky odor filled his nostrils. Hellboy shook his head and pulled his legs beneath him, standing unsteadily.

He breathed deeply, straightening up, and kept one hand on the wall as he left the bathroom, mirror fragments crunching under his hooves. In the living room, he paused a moment and glanced around. The world hadn't turned gray . . . the day had turned to evening. Dusk had arrived.

"Stasia?" he whispered, glancing around. The suitcases lay on the huge king-size bed, just as he'd left them, open but still packed.

A frisson of fear went through him, not for himself,

but for her. For them. He spun and looked out through the curtains at the balcony. The dusk had a rosy glow—not long at all since the sun had gone down. Moments, really. In that glow, he saw the silhouette standing out on the balcony, and relief flooded through him.

"Damn, you gave me a scare," he said. He strode toward the balcony doors.

The silhouette shifted and became clear.

It was not Anastasia.

Fists clenching, Hellboy froze just inside the doors and stared at the man on the balcony. The first thing he noticed was the glowing orange tip of the cigarette the man held down at his side, nearly cupped in his palm. A trail of smoke curled upward, though Hellboy felt sure the cigarette had not been there a moment before.

He had olive skin and raven black hair, but his features might have been Middle Eastern or Egyptian or Greek. His large pupils glowed with the same heat as the tip of his cigarette. He dressed with casual elegance, in a beige linen suit and a cotton shirt, open at the neck.

Hellboy spent his days and nights trying to ignore the reaction most people had to his presence. There were positives and negatives to his infamy, but perhaps the best thing about being a public figure was that, more often than not, people knew whom they were seeing when they encountered him for the first time. The ones who'd never heard of him—they were the ones that troubled him the most.

They reminded him, every day. He didn't have to look in a mirror to see that he wasn't like most people, that he could be terrifying to behold. All he needed was the looks on the faces of the people he encountered. And when they realized he and Anastasia were together—together—it was that much worse.

Not this guy. He smiled and nodded a silent greeting. He stood in front of the seven-foot, four-hundred-pound, red-skinned guy with the sawed-off horns and the hooves and tail—and the ugly disposition—and he was *cool*. Not just acting cool. Hellboy could see it in his body language, in the bright intelligence of his eyes.

He had never wanted to kill anyone so badly.

"Where is she?"

The man leaned against the balcony railing with the island sunset behind him and Mount Ida on the horizon, and he lifted his cigarette and took a drag.

"The Obsidian Danse has decided that you have ruined enough of our plans," the visitor began.

Hellboy narrowed his eyes. "The what? Obsidian what?"

The man's composure slipped. A tic of anger twitched at one corner of his left eye.

"Honestly, with your lady friend vanishing, I wouldn't have expected such obstinacy."

Hellboy's right hand was not made of stone, but that ancient substance had the texture and weight of stone, and it often felt heavy to him. Just then it had no weight at all. It seemed to float upward. All Hellboy had to do was give himself over to the urge, and he'd be snapping the guy's bones in a heartbeat.

But not until he knew where Anastasia was and that she was safe.

"You've plagued us these past few years, Hellboy," the elegant man with the ember eyes said. "The Obsidian Danse has lost talented operatives, dozens of invaluable artifacts, alliances with gods and monsters, and several opportunities for apocalypse because of you."

"Good for me," Hellboy muttered. He wanted to add, *still never heard of you,* but thought of Anastasia and kept silent.

"Now you're here. We're on the verge of returning to this world three of the most powerful supernatural creatures ever to walk the earth, and here you are to thwart us again. You and your lady friend and her sniveling little friends from that damnable museum. If not them, your precious Bureau. You vex us, sir. With the Daktyloi as our slaves, we will have all the power we have ever dreamed. Apocalypse will be ours. The Forge, the Hammer, and the Anvil *will* rise. The weapons they forge will make the Obsidian Danse the masters of the world."

He took another drag on his cigarette, the tip flaring along with his eyes. "And you might have stopped us. My brothers and sisters in the Danse were filled with such consternation when we learned of your arrival, your participation in the excavation—the foolish diggers trying to reach the Daktyloi before us. They feared you because you are like a bull. You would keep charging until we killed you, or you destroyed us, just as you have before. Even in the face of the fury of the Daktyloi, you would not stop."

The man flicked his cigarette over the balcony. His pupils changed color, taking on a shade of violet, like storm clouds at dusk.

"I told them this was not true. I told them you could not stop us, that you would not try, as long as we had your Dr. Bransfield."

Hellboy ground his teeth together so hard that his jaw ached. At length, he opened his mouth, unclenching his fists.

"I'll ask you one more time. Where is she?"

Genuine amusement blossomed on the man's face. "I have delivered a message, nothing more. You will not trouble us any further."

"Man," Hellboy said, shaking his head, "you're making a huge mistake."

"And you watch too many of your American films."

Hellboy stood taller, moved a few inches nearer. "Says the guy who talks like a Bond villain. Thing is, Hocus Pocus, I never heard of you idiots until today. If I wrecked some of your operations, it's sheer coincidence. I mean, I was doing my job, sure, but nobody in the BPRD ever said a word to me about any connection between any of that. I doubt they even knew you existed. Course, you just screwed the pooch on that one."

At last, the moron's arrogance crumbled.

"That's not possible. It couldn't all be coincidence."

"I told you, pally. It's my job. Now, I know you and maybe your other dance partners, or whatever you call them, are into magic. Someone—I'm betting on you—screwed me up bad, dropped me in the bathroom back there. But I've fought sorcerers before. Legends. And I broke them into little pieces. You can slow me down, but you can't keep me from doing the same to you.

"Bring Anastasia here. Now. The same way you poofed her gone. And I'll pretend we never had this conversation. I'd make a whole bunch of threats about what I'll do to you otherwise, but there's no point. I guess you've seen my work."

Dark and elegant, the man regained his composure. Though he'd tossed his cigarette over the balcony, another had appeared in his hand without Hellboy noticing. He took another drag. Hellboy thought about mocking him for the parlor trick, asking if he could pull a coin out of his ear—or some other orifice—but he didn't feel like talking anymore. Again, he slid nearer.

"Perhaps we did make a mistake. But now, the error is yours. Do you want her to die?"

Big as he was, Hellboy was fast. The bad guys always seemed to underestimate him on that score.

"Son of a—" he growled as he lunged, reaching out with both his ordinary hand and the massive, crushing grip of his right.

The sorcerer didn't have time to wave his hands or utter a single word before Hellboy was on him. His left hand grabbed the guy's right wrist and twisted. Bones snapped, and the cigarette dropped from his fingers. His huge right hand closed around the guy's head.

Hellboy opened his mouth to issue the threat, to tell the man with his polished English and his perfect hair that he was going to crush his head like a grape if he didn't bring Anastasia back in five seconds.

Before he could speak, the man's flesh changed. His linen suit felt even softer, and it moved, tickling Hellboy's palm. His hair came alive, undulating beneath that carved, stone hand.

His entire body trembled, then tore apart, separating into a flock of birds. Sparrows. Dozens, perhaps hundreds of tiny sparrows. They fluttered their wings, then flew off above the village and into the sprawling evening.

Hellboy stood on the balcony alone, watching the birds fly as though Anastasia might be among them.

He couldn't stop the self-mockery that came to his lips. "Oh, that went well." But panic seethed inside him.

Whoever they were, the Obsidian Danse were no poseurs. They had Stasia. The question was how long they would keep her alive.

CHAPTER 5

"Caves," Hellboy said.

The helicopter rotors chopped the air, and he had to raise his voice to be heard. He glanced at Abe and Anastasia. Abe stood and peered out the window without leaving his seat. Stasia leaned over Hellboy to get a look at the valley below them. Her hair smelled like mangoes.

"I didn't see them when we were up here," she said.

"You weren't in a helicopter."

Anastasia nodded, knitting her brows. Hellboy knew what she was looking at. They were above Nakchu village, and from above they could see the cave mouths that dotted the face of the mountain just to the north of that settlement. From the ground, and at a distance, they would have looked like outcroppings of rock, or just shadows.

The guide, Tenzin, sat quietly in the back of the chopper. He seemed anxious, and Hellboy figured maybe this was his first time flying. His eyes were wide, and he clutched his rifle tightly.

Abe settled back into his seat, his heavy leather jacket creaking. It was cold up in the chopper. Though his amphibious body could endure great variations of temperature in the water, he preferred to be warm.

Hellboy wore his long coat and the heavy belt he always used on missions. The belt had a dozen or so pouches filled with various things he might need, from occult artifacts to silver bullets.

Anastasia put up the hood on her parka.

Out the window, they could see people coming out of their dwellings—they were too nice for him to think of them as huts or shacks—and staring up at the helicopter.

"Redfield, bring her down to the north!" he called. "Between the village and those caves."

The pilot raised two fingers in a kind of salute and guided the helicopter around and set it down. Brown grass bent with the air pressure from the chopper's approach; then the rotors began to slow, and go quiet.

"Keep her primed," Hellboy said. "You know SOP."

Redfield pulled off his headphones, smiling through his bristly beard. "Course I do. I just don't know why we didn't bring the whole team."

Hellboy frowned. This was what he got when Professor Bruttenholm was leading the investigation instead of him—Redfield questioning the plan. The guy was the ultimate professional and one hell of a pilot.

Hellboy knew he was just cautious. But the only person giving orders on this op was Professor Bruttenholm.

"We don't know what's going on at the lake, or if the people at the dig are still in danger. We don't know a damn thing, yet. Someone's gotta look out for Anastasia's crew and do a new search of the dig area for the missing girl. Everyone's got their job, pal."

Hellboy didn't have to add any emphasis to his last statement. Redfield got it. His job was to fly the chopper.

"SOP," the pilot said, nodding.

Anastasia slid back the door with a rattle and clank, then she and Abe dropped to the ground. Hellboy climbed out after them, Tenzin behind him, rifle slung over his shoulder, and the four of them started toward the village.

"We're coming at this from the opposite side from my last visit. They weren't too thrilled before. They're not going to like this," Stasia said.

"All that concerns us is Kora Kyichu," Abe replied.

The morning sun shone on his blue-green flesh, making him glisten. Hellboy had seen him take a swim in the lake just after sunrise, which was good. Abe always seemed more focused after immersion.

"Agreed," Hellboy replied.

Stasia nodded.

A group of villagers in wool and linen clothes emerged from among the dwellings, not far from the place where the narrow river entered Nakchu. They seemed to be waiting for something. Then a slender old man with white hair and a long white beard, tied a few inches below his chin, strode toward them.

"That him?" Hellboy asked.

"Yes," Stasia said.

"He moves well for an old man," Abe noted.

Hellboy had noticed the same thing. Despite his age, the man moved with assurance and strength. The others fell in behind him, as though his appearance had flicked some sort of switch to start them walking. Perhaps two dozen villagers—mostly men and mostly young, but not entirely either—crossed the space that separated them.

"Hunh," Anastasia grunted.

"What?" Hellboy glanced at her.

"No kids this time. They've left the children in the village."

Hellboy didn't like the sound of that. Maybe Redfield was right. They should've taken the investigation more slowly, started by searching the dig site and left only one guard on the excavation of the preparatory chamber. But it was too late to change the plan, now. And he knew his father had not wanted to waste another moment—not with the girl missing.

Tenzin had the rifle. Stasia had her pistol holstered at the small of her back. Hellboy carried his big hand cannon. Abe, though—Abe didn't screw around. Under his leather jacket he had an Uzi hanging from a strap. Meaney and Sarah had sneaked it in on the

BPRD transport, along with several other things. They were going into an unknown situation. Best to be prepared.

As the villagers approached them, then surrounded them, Hellboy watched their eyes. Though they studied him and Abe closely and curiously, none of them looked frightened by the appearance of the newcomers.

"They've seen monsters before," he said softly.

"What?" Abe asked.

Hellboy shook his head. "Never mind."

The village elder came and stood right in front of Anastasia, glaring at her, barely acknowledging the others. He snapped something off in his own language, and Anastasia glanced at Tenzin.

"He wants to know what you want," the guide translated.

Hellboy took a step closer, narrowing his gaze as he studied the old man. "They call me Hellboy. You've met Dr. Bransfield. This is Abe Sapien." He thought about explaining that they were from the BPRD, but that would mean nothing to the old man. "What's your name?"

Tenzin rattled off the translation.

The old man stared up at Hellboy defiantly as he replied. "Jangbu."

Stasia nudged him. "My guy's here."

Hellboy looked around at the faces of the villagers. "The one you shot?"

"Think so."

"Tell him we're here to find the girl. We think they've got her, or someone in the village does. If we're wrong, we apologize in advance, but we're going to search the village now. Every structure."

Tenzin nodded, trouble in his eyes. Hellboy understood. Trouble was likely. But they had to find the girl and the shape-shifting saboteur, and he thought it was likely the two would be in the same place. Right here.

The guide translated.

A flash of anger crossed Jangbu's face. His spindly fingers tugged his beard. A number of other villagers began to protest, several of them coming forward.

Jangbu held up a hand and barked a command at them, then paused. With a slow, deliberate nod, he stepped to one side and bowed deeply. He spoke without rising.

"He says you are welcome to search if it means you will leave Nakchu alone after," Tenzin said.

Anastasia let out a breath of relief. She started forward, and Abe joined her.

"Wait," Hellboy said. He studied the faces of the villagers around him, wondering which was the saboteur Anastasia had shot.

Abe frowned, large eyes blinking. The ridges on his neck rose slightly, as they often did when he was alarmed. "What is it?"

Hellboy ignored him, staring at Jangbu, who rose to his full height again, regarding them all with a troubled expression.

"Sir?" Tenzin asked.

"If he's so willing to have us search the village, I'm gonna guess the girl isn't there." Hellboy glanced at Abe and Stasia. "So let's check the caves instead."

They started to back away. Jangbu barked a question, suspicion and anger on his face. Tenzin replied in rapid-fire gibberish, and Jangbu shouted something, pointing at Hellboy, then at the helicopter.

Anastasia moved over beside the guide. "What's he saying, Tenzin?"

"We're forbidden from entering the caves. No outsider is allowed there."

"Yeah," Hellboy muttered. "Just little girls they snatch to sacrifice to their fiery dragon god."

Abe unzipped his jacket to free the Uzi as they backed up farther. The villagers had surrounded them, and Hellboy wondered if they were going to charge.

They did. But not in the direction he'd figured.

Half a dozen of them ran, shouting, toward the helicopter. A couple of them had long sticks. Hellboy touched the grip of the big pistol that had been custom-made for him, about to draw it. He figured he could fire it into the air, scare them off, before any real shooting started.

"Hellboy!" Abe snapped.

Hellboy twisted around, even as he drew the pistol, to see the face of Jangbu changing, flesh changing texture, jaw protruding. His eyes began to burn, fire licking up from the edges.

"Him? This old guy was your guy?" he shouted to Anastasia.

"No. It wasn't him," she said, her voice curiously lifeless.

Which was when Hellboy noticed that it wasn't just Jangbu. They were all changing, skin turning to rough, scaly hide, fangs protruding, eyes on fire. Jangbu hissed and started toward them.

They were all shape-shifters. Or, at least, all subhuman. From the look of them, they were part human, and part dragon.

Abe squeezed the trigger on the Uzi. Bullets dug up earth just a few feet in front of the dragon-men. They paused. But the others, the ones who were changing even as they lunged at the helicopter, didn't slow down.

The chopper blades whirred, and Redfield took her up. The helicopter rose quickly, one of the Nakchu dragon-men hanging from the left skid. He let go and fell thirty feet to the ground, landing on his feet without any injury at all.

"Stupid git, where's he going?" Anastasia snapped, drawing her pistol and waving it around to help keep the villagers back.

"Standard operating procedure," Hellboy said. "We don't have another chopper. If there's trouble, orders are to dust off, get help."

Abe swung the barrel of the Uzi around. "Help isn't coming before we run out of bullets."

"Guess not," Hellboy replied, turning quickly, long coat whipping around his tail behind him. "So we do what we came here for. We find the girl."

"The caves?" Tenzin asked, a grim determination in his eyes. Hellboy decided he liked the guy.

"Yeah. The caves. Abe?"

Abe fired another few rounds into the dirt, scattering the dragon-men. Hellboy took one look at Jangbu—even as half dragon, the little white beard hung from his chin—and saluted as they started to run toward the caves.

The dragon-men opened their jaws and let out a horrid screech, some kind of battle cry, and started after them.

Tenzin paused, squeezed off a shot from his rifle, and one of the creatures fell dead. Hellboy hammered another to the ground with the punishing weight of his right hand, then they were running full steam toward the caves.

What they'd do once they found Kora, he didn't know.

Professor Bruttenholm left Dr. Conrad, Ellie Morris, and young Rafe Mattei in the preparatory chamber and emerged into the sunlight. He raised a hand to shield his eyes from the midmorning glare off the lake.

"Any luck, Professor?" asked Sarah Rhys-Howard, who stood on the edge of the excavated entrance with a very unpleasant-looking black submachine gun in her hands. A pistol jutted from its holster on her hip.

Timothy Meaney stood on the opposite side of the excavation, similarly armed. He didn't even look down. His eyes were busy scanning the lakeshore and the ridge of rocky hillside above them.

"Nothing that would indicate the presence of magic or provide a clue as to the identity or location of the saboteur," Bruttenholm replied.

Conrad and his team were still working on deciphering the pictograms and characters in the preparatory chamber. The professor might have been of some use to them, but his focus was elsewhere. If Hellboy and his team did not return with Kora Kyichu, they would have to start a more widespread search. Meanwhile, Bruttenholm was searching for any clue that might lead them to Kora or the saboteur.

"Has Neil not returned?"

"Not yet, professor," Sarah said.

Bruttenholm looked at her. The woman gave him an enigmatic smile. She was a field operative for the BPRD, which meant she had seen things both terrible and terrifying. He'd read her file, and in truth she had also done terrible things. That was why he had chosen her—and Tim Meaney and Neil Pinborough as well. They were total professionals, not afraid of the ugly, dirty work that sometimes came with the job, or of the ancient darkness the BPRD often faced.

This beautiful woman would not kill unless she

had to, but in dire circumstances, she would not hesitate to pull the trigger. Bruttenholm hated to need such people, but it came with the territory.

"Walk with me, Sarah. Mr. Meaney, when Neil returns, ask him to report to me, please. I shall be preparing a report upon our activities thus far."

"Yes, sir," Meaney said, gaze still roving, watching. The man was a born sentinel.

Professor Bruttenholm started carefully across the rough terrain of the dig, where dozens of members of Dr. Bransfield's team were hard at work unearthing a variety of structures whose features were only slowly becoming visible. It was important work. Bruttenholm wondered if any of them truly understood, though, how dangerous it was. Oftentimes things were buried for a reason, ancient things put to sleep. Waking them could be fatal.

Sarah might have been tempted to offer him aid as they made their way down the rocky slope toward the lake, but she was better trained than that. She kept her hands on her weapon.

Every member of this operation had surveyed the ground that the saboteur had covered in his escape two nights past and come up with nothing useful. Nevertheless, Professor Bruttenholm studied the ground as they descended, leading Sarah toward the edge of the lake.

"Sir?" Sarah said.

Bruttenholm looked up to find that they were perhaps fifty yards from the water. Professor Kyichu stood on the shore in the very spot where Anastasia had shot the saboteur.

Dr. Bransfield, he mentally corrected himself. *Don't think of her as Anastasia. Don't make it easier for her to hurt him.*

He understood that those who loved were helpless against the power and confusion of that emotion. There was no malice in Dr. Bransfield. But that did not mean he could ignore what havoc her mere presence played with Hellboy's heart.

Professor Kyichu turned, hearing their approach. The sorrow in his eyes seared Bruttenholm, and thoughts of melancholy lovers left his mind. What did that compare with the grief of a father who has lost a daughter?

"Good morning, Professor," Kyichu said with a nod.

"Good morning, sir. But, please, call me Trevor. You're nowhere near my age, but still, let's leave the formalities for the youngsters."

Again, Kyichu nodded. "As you say, Trevor. And I am Han."

For a moment, they stood in silence. Sarah stood a few yards away, scanning the lake and the north ridge just as Meaney had. Then Bruttenholm broke the quiet.

"I know promises would sound hollow, my friend. But if it provides any comfort, I truly believe that

Kora is still with us. And my team will not rest until—"

His words were drowned out by a sudden barrage of sound. The helicopter. Redfield had brought them back safely. A sense of relief swept through him, along with hope. Professor Bruttenholm turned—and as he did, he saw the look of unease upon the face of Sarah Rhys-Howard.

The chopper roared over the top of the north ridge, whipping up clouds of dust in the archaeological dig. Redfield was not a fool. Such a close approach would infuriate Dr. Bransfield's team, disturbing their work, perhaps damaging delicate artifacts. Protocol would have been to approach along the lakeshore, as they'd done last night.

But protocol was out the window.

Red emergency lights blinked urgently on the undercarriage of the chopper. They meant crisis. They meant disaster.

"Sarah," Professor Bruttenholm said calmly, "fetch Meaney and Neil, and rendezvous with me at the chopper with all speed."

The dragon-men were fast. One of them caught up to Tenzin when they were still eighty or ninety yards from the nearest cave entrance. Hellboy cursed as he heard the guide cry out in pain. Jangbu started shouting, but he couldn't figure out if the village elder wanted the other one to gut Tenzin or leave him alone. His hands—long, yellow talons, really—were gesturing wildly.

"Stasia! Abe! Get in there and find the girl!" he shouted as he skidded to a halt in the brittle grass and switched directions.

"Try not to kill them," Abe called back.

"Doing my best!"

Hellboy understood. Despite the Uzi, Abe tried his best to be a pacifist. Hellboy didn't mind beating the crap out of dragon-men if they were attacking him, but he'd also like to avoid killing any more of them if it could be avoided. Whatever was in their genetic makeup, these people had children, right in that village.

Tenzin slammed the butt of his rifle into the skull of the creature on top of him. The dragon-man rolled into the grass, and Tenzin was up. He was a smart guy. He didn't even think about trying to use his rifle. There were too many of them, at least fifteen, and more coming from the village.

Hellboy reached his side just as several of the dragon-men leaped for Tenzin. They fought side by side, the guide grunting with frustration, anger, and effort as he clubbed them with his rifle. Hellboy back-handed one of them with his stone fist, slapped another away with the gun in his left, and grabbed a third with his tail, slamming the creature to the ground hard enough to break bone.

Jangbu kept shouting. Lucky for the old one that he was slower than the others, but still he was coming.

Hellboy grabbed Tenzin's arm and pulled him toward the caves; then they were running again. "What's he saying?"

"Until now, he was telling them not to take our lives."

"And now?"

"Stop us entering the caves, no matter the cost."

"Wonderful."

Hellboy barreled onto the rough, rocky soil that marked the base of the mountain. The cave entrance lay just ahead. The dragon-men were swift. He was just glad they didn't have wings. That would have been very bad. It also made him wonder what they were, really. It was easy to think of them as dragon-men, given the local legends, but he had no proof of that.

Jangbu started shouting the same thing over and over.

"Stop them," Tenzin said quietly.

A strange feeling passed through Hellboy as they ran up to the mouth of the cave where Abe and Stasia had gone into the mountain. Something in the desperation of Jangbu's shouts did not seem savage to him, only sorrowful.

Then they were inside the cave. The morning light did not reach very far into the dark depths.

A snarl came from behind them. Hellboy spun. One of the dragon-men tackled him, and he fell, one sheared horn scraping the stone wall of the cave. The thing grabbed him by the head and started slamming his skull against the floor of the cave over and over. The pistol flew from Hellboy's grasp. Fire flickered in its eyes like a reptilian jack-o'-lantern.

Hellboy caught the motion of Tenzin raising his rifle from the corner of his eye.

"No!" he shouted. He bucked against the dragon-man and threw it off. The creature tried to lunge for him again, and Hellboy grabbed hold of it in midleap, redirected its momentum, and slammed it against the wall. The dragon-man's skull made a dull, unpleasant thunk against the rock, and when he slid down to the ground, he left a streak of blood behind.

"Crap," Hellboy muttered.

He had dropped his gun. Now he snatched it up and turned toward the cave entrance. Backlit by the morning sun, he saw several more of the villagers rushing in after them.

Hellboy pulled the trigger. A spray of rock chips erupted from the wall just inside the cave, but it gave the men of Nakchu village pause.

"Go," he snapped.

Tenzin ran. Hellboy followed, still aiming at the cave entrance, until they were around the corner and out of sight. The caves were riddled with small shafts that let light in at intervals, and they hurried through patches of light and darkness.

"Abe! Stasia!"

The tunnel became narrower, and lower. Hellboy

bent and kept going. Tenzin was ahead of him, which was good. Hellboy was pretty durable. The guide somewhat less so.

"Stasia!" he shouted.

The whispering and clicking sounds of pursuit came up the tunnel behind them.

"Here!" came the call from ahead.

Her voice.

Hellboy followed Tenzin into a vast cavern. Far above their heads, small windows in the rock allowed light in. He spotted Stasia first, almost in the center of the room. She had her gun in her hand, but her features were twisted in anguish.

"What is it?" he asked. "The girl? Did you find her?"

With the look on Anastasia's face, he didn't know if he wanted an answer. But then she shook her head. Hellboy didn't understand. He glanced around, looking for Abe. He spotted his friend in a darker corner of the cavern. Abe emerged into a shaft of morning sun. He had the Uzi in both hands, but it was almost as though he'd forgotten he was holding it.

"Abe, what—"

But then Tenzin started to whisper a prayer, and Hellboy looked past Abe, focusing on the walls of the cavern for the first time. Boxlike shelves had been hewn in the wall, and upon each of them lay a corpse in death's repose. Some of the remains looked almost human. Others were twice ordinary size and had skulls with jaws like a crocodile's. He spun around. Every wall was the same.

Then Hellboy saw the strange crenellated shapes in the floor where Stasia stood, and he knew that the pale things jutting from the ground were the bones of a true dragon.

"This is why they didn't want us to come in," Abe said.

Stasia gazed at Hellboy. "It's their crypt."

The sounds of pursuit grew suddenly much louder. All four of them turned at once, leveling their weapons at the same entrance Hellboy and Tenzin had used, though there were at least two other tunnels leading away from the burial chamber—probably to other crypts.

Two dragon-men burst into the chamber. Upon seeing the intruders, they stopped, threw back their heads, and howled in grief. Then, with a hiss, they started across the crypt, flames licking from their eyes.

A voice barked behind them.

The two dragon-men stopped and turned to stare at Jangbu, his white, knotted beard making him unmistakable.

Then another villager slipped past Jangbu and into the chamber. He raised his hands as though in surrender. Smoothly, his features changed again, and in the space of a few heartbeats, he appeared human again.

"What's this?" Abe asked.

"I don't know," Hellboy replied.

"It's him," Anastasia said. "The one I shot."

She and Tenzin moved toward one another, closing ranks. The guide spoke, addressing Jangbu, but the old man only shook his head sadly. It was the younger one who replied.

"What's he saying?" Hellboy asked.

Tenzin held up a hand, wanting him to be patient as he listened to the creature, the saboteur.

"He's the one who kept trashing the camp," Hellboy said. "He collapsed the excavation of the preparatory chamber."

The guide shot him a quieting look. Hellboy gestured for him to speed it up. Abe kept his Uzi leveled at the dragon-men.

At length, Tenzin nodded respectfully to the villager, then turned to Hellboy and the others.

"His name is Koh. Jangbu is his father. Yes, Koh is one of the men who have been sabotaging the dig. The villagers have been trying to prevent you from opening the preparatory chamber. They believe that now that it is opened, the Dragon King will rise to terrorize the plateau and mountains once more, unless a sacrifice is made."

"Oh my God," Anastasia breathed.

Hellboy still held his gun, but lowered the barrel. "Then they did take the girl? Is she alive?"

The question felt like poison on his tongue.

Tenzin turned to Koh and shot off the question. The answer came slowly, and when Hellboy saw the regret and humanity in Koh's eyes, he felt sick to his stomach, thinking the worst.

"The girl was taken by several of the men of Nakchu. They believed that since they were not the ones who disturbed the preparatory chamber, they should not have to sacrifice one of their own. They are the tribe of legend, who provided that sacrifice for centuries, once every year. Their ancestors bred with the dragons who served the Dragon King."

"It appears we were correct," Abe said.

"Yeah. Great," Hellboy replied.

"The girl is alive," Tenzin said.

Anastasia cocked her pistol and pointed it at Koh, obviously more than willing to shoot him again. "Where is she?"

"Not here."

Abe took a step nearer, staring into Koh's eyes as though trying to understand him on some level the others could not. "They only tried to stop us to keep us from defiling their burial chambers."

Tenzin spoke to Koh.

Jangbu shouted angrily, emotion seared into his dragon features. The fire that fell from his eyes seemed like flaming tears.

Hellboy wasn't buying it.

"What about the ones who tried to stop Redfield from taking off? He wasn't going to fly the chopper in here, so what's that about?" he demanded.

When Tenzin translated the question, Koh and

Jangbu began to argue. Father and son shouted at one another. Hellboy holstered his gun, trying to understand their language. He thought if he could just listen a while longer, he might be able to get it. Languages made sense to him.

Anastasia took a step nearer to Koh, pistol still raised.

It was Abe who reached out and took her wrist, pushing the gun's barrel toward the ground. With a sigh, Stasia seemed to deflate, and she held the gun at her side.

"What are they arguing about?" Abe asked.

Tenzin looked stricken. In the pale daylight of that chamber, he appeared as though he might throw up.

"The village is torn. Some want the girl to be sacrificed. Some cannot condone it. Those who want to see Kora given to the Dragon King tried to stop the helicopter from taking off so that he could not warn them."

"Warn them of what?"

"That the girl's abductors are bringing her, even now, into the camp. They mean to prepare her for sacrifice. They will kill her today."

Hellboy felt rage ignite within him. He glared at Jangbu, then at Koh. But when he spoke, it was to his companions.

"You guys get what that means?"

Anastasia went to him, staring into his face. She'd see the fury there, he knew, and unlike so many other times, she would not be able to defuse it. Hellboy wasn't even sure she would want to.

"What are you talking about?" she asked.

Abe swore under his breath. "SOP. Redfield will bring back the rest of the team to try to retrieve us."

"No," Anastasia said. "Professor Bruttenholm wouldn't send all three of them. Surely he'd have someone guarding the preparatory chamber, for this purpose alone."

"Maybe," Hellboy said. "Or maybe he'd be more worried about us than something that right now is only a theory to him."

"We've got to get back," Abe said.

Hellboy unholstered his gun again. He lifted it and pointed it at Jangbu's head.

"Tenzin, tell them we're leaving. We're sorry about coming in here, into the crypt. But we're going back to the dig and stopping their buddies from murdering that little girl. Tell them there won't be any sacrifice. Not ever. The Dragon King's dead. And if they don't get out of the way, they'll join him."

As the guide translated, Abe and Anastasia raised their weapons again. Hellboy might have questioned Abe's willingness to shoot the dragon-men before, but if they tried to stop them from getting back to save that little girl, he'd pull the trigger.

So would Hellboy.

Jangbu clearly did not doubt it. And now that they'd already been inside the crypt, the villagers had little reason to fight them. At least two or three of their number were dead, but they'd been killed in self defense. Jangbu did not want any more of his people to die. Maybe he didn't want the little girl to be murdered, either; maybe he didn't want her blood on his hands. He and his people had set all of this in motion.

Now Jangbu stepped aside. He ordered the others to do the same. Some of them withdrew down the tunnel. Others came into the cavern and stood out of the way.

Hellboy started toward the tunnel through which they'd entered. Tenzin, Anastasia, and Abe followed warily.

Koh said something, reaching out for Hellboy, who glanced at Tenzin.

"He wants to come with us. He wants to help save the girl."

For a long moment, Hellboy glared at the dragonman. Then he nodded.

"Come on, then. Maybe your idiot friends will listen to you."

CHAPTER 6

No wind came off the lake. No dust rose from the digging of the team of archaeologists, and though they must have been speaking to one another, Professor Bruttenholm heard no voices. Other than the sifting noise of shovels striking dirt and the occasional chip of tools on stone, there was little sound at all on the plateau of Lake Tashi. The whole mountain range appeared to be holding its breath.

In his hand he held a bit of potsherd that had been given to him earlier in the day by Dorian Trent, one of the junior members of the British Museum archaeological team. Although in his midthirties, Trent lacked the dynamic ambition of people like Bransfield and Conrad, and as such held a position on the expedition that ranked only a little higher than the students who'd come along. In fact, as far as Bruttenholm could see, the thoughtful, intelligent Trent might well be here primarily to babysit the young men and women who were here to learn. But a single conversation had revealed Trent to be at least as knowledgeable as his more accomplished associates. Bruttenholm had been considering recruiting him for the BPRD's research division.

That had been hours ago.

Now, Dorian Trent had been nearly forgotten. Bruttenholm idly ran his thumb over the smoothness of the potsherd, careful not to cut himself on its sharper edges. The design of the piece was typical of the region, according to Trent, save for the repetition of an image along the bottom of a single, strangely hypnotic eye, drawn inside concentric circles. The eye of the Dragon King, Bruttenholm presumed, though he would let the experts make that determination for certain.

The shush of shovels in dirt became the regular rhythm of his heart as he stood there on the ridge above the slope that led down to the lake. Normally, he found such work fascinating, the unearthing of the history of a people and their customs and beliefs.

Today, he could only stand, numbly clutching that bit of potsherd, and stare at the sky above the hills into which the archaeologists were digging. He waited for the sound of rotors chopping air or the sight of that helicopter, dark against the sky. Redfield hadn't had time to say more than that the team was under attack, and terrible images wormed their way into Bruttenholm's mind. He feared for his son, and he feared for the others as well. Life had been a chain of such moments ever since he had helped to found the BPRD. Sometimes he wondered why he had not gotten used to it, but he knew the reason.

Hellboy.

Having to look out for the lad had kept Trevor Bruttenholm from losing his perspective. Hellboy had kept him human.

He reached into his pocket. In his kit, he carried a rosary blessed by Pope Joan. In times when he could only wait, and worry, it helped him to hold that talisman. He drew it out of his pocket and wrapped it around his fingers. For a moment he closed his eyes and just breathed in the thin, cool mountain air. Already he had tried to radio Redfield in the chopper but had been unable to get anything but static.

Professor Bruttenholm had not been put on this earth to wait while others acted. Age had made it difficult for him, and more often than not he remained at BPRD headquarters while field agents performed the tasks he wished he could still manage. But today, he discovered that being in the field, this close to the action, and being unable to help, was far worse.

"Come back," he whispered.

With Pope Joan's rosary still twined in his fingers, he turned and glanced east along the ridge, to the place where the preparatory chamber had been unearthed. He'd sent the rest of his team off with the chopper to retrieve Hellboy, Abe, and the others. Young Rafe, one of Dr. Bransfield's prize students, had been set as a guard at the door, along with one of the diggers, a Russian-born Londoner called Sima.

The Russian was armed with a pistol. No one

would give Rafe a gun, though he'd wanted one. Bruttenholm and Dr. Conrad had both forbidden it.

The professor started toward the excavation of the preparatory chamber. Some of its exterior wall had been revealed, now, and its design and adornment seemed to have once been similar to the interior. There had been no question about the purpose of this structure in those ancient days.

A sudden clamor arose ahead of him. Shouts and cursing and cries of alarm. A chill went through Bruttenholm. If the trouble was at Nakchu village, what was going on here?

Quick as he was able, he jogged along the ridge, never more conscious of his age. Half a dozen men and women had gathered at the rim of the hole that led down to the excavated entrance into the preparatory chamber. He saw Han Kyichu and Dorian Trent, an engineer named Priya Arora, and several others.

As Bruttenholm hurried to join them, Frank Danovich fell in beside him.

"What the hell's this?"

"Not a blessed clue, I'm afraid."

When they'd come within twenty feet of the hole, Professor Bruttenholm saw someone pulling the corpse of Anastasia's prize student from the excavation. Rafe Mattei had been broken so badly that his limbs flailed like a rag doll's as he was lifted from the hole.

"Goddamn it," Danovich breathed.

Bruttenholm did not argue.

Others moved aside to make room as they reached the edge of the hole that had been dug to expose the entrance to the preparatory chamber. The Russian, Sima, also lay in the hole. Bruttenholm recognized him by his belt buckle—an American cowboy buckle—and the still-holstered pistol on his hip. Sima had not had time to draw the weapon before whatever had attacked the men decapitated him.

His head was nowhere to be seen.

Dorian started for the open door, which yawned wide with shadows.

"Not another step, Mr. Trent," Bruttenholm said.

As one, all of those gathered turned to look at him, some of them with obvious surprise. Until now, though he was the field leader of this BPRD investigation, they'd all seen him as an eccentric old man. Now their eyes said something different.

"Anyone have a clue who is working in the chamber at present?"

Professor Kyichu looked at him. "Ellie Morris is there, with Dr. Conrad. I was about to join them."

"Good that you had not," Professor Bruttenholm said.

"Who would do this?" Danovich asked.

Bruttenholm preferred not to reply, but his gaze shifted for just a moment to Kyichu, who understood immediately.

"They mean to use the chamber," the man said, realization thinning his voice. "My daughter's in there?"

"Dorian, Miss Arora, be so kind as to fetch as many of your colleagues as you can, and as many weapons, and return here as quickly as possible, please."

Trent and Arora hurried away, calling for aid.

"You think my daughter's in there?" Professor Kyichu shouted, a frantic, mad light in his eyes.

The white-haired man did not wait for a reply. He jumped down into the hole and started for the entrance to the chamber. A young student and one of the diggers tried to grab him, but Kyichu slapped their hands away. Fools that they were, they allowed him to do so.

"Danovich, stop him, please," Bruttenholm said.

As the engineer jumped into the hole and lunged for Han Kyichu, Professor Bruttenholm climbed carefully down after them. He bent over the corpse of the headless Russian and slid the pistol from his holster with the same hand that still clutched Pope Joan's rosary. When he held the gun tightly, the beads of the rosary dug into his fingers and the flesh of his palm.

Kyichu screamed and railed against Danovich, but the engineer easily overpowered him.

Professor Bruttenholm walked over to him. "Your daughter is still alive, Han. If we are very fortunate, so are Doctors Morris and Conrad. If you go in there, that might change. Kora, they will not harm unless they can reach the lake, where they intend to sacrifice her. We will not allow them to leave the chamber with your daughter in their hands."

Even as he spoke, sounds of shouting and running feet filled the air. Diggers came with shovels held like baseball bats. Pistols and rifles and a shotgun or two were leveled at the entrance to the chamber. This was not a military operation, but security dictated the presence of guns, and Bruttenholm felt sure he was now seeing every weapon in the camp.

The brave members of the expedition surrounded the hole that led to the door into the preparatory chamber. Professor Kyichu stared at them, chest heaving in grief and fear for his daughter, but slowly he relaxed in Danovich's grip.

Bruttenholm gestured with his free hand for them to leave the excavation, and they began to climb out, leaving Sima's corpse where it lay.

"How did they get through the camp without anyone seeing them?" Danovich asked quietly as he reached down a hand to help Bruttenholm out of the pit.

The professor glanced upward at the sheer, treacherous ridge above the excavation. "They didn't come through the camp. They came down."

"Climbed down that?" Dorian Trent said, coming up beside him. "What are these people?"

Bruttenholm held the pistol in front of him, barrel pointed toward the chamber entrance, the rosary of Pope Joan digging into his palm. A silent circle followed suit, waiting breathlessly to see what would happen next.

"I'm not certain they're people at all," Professor Bruttenholm said.

In the quiet that followed, he thought he heard a sound from within the chamber, the sobbing of a little girl. Professor Kyichu covered his ears and shot a hateful glance at him. Bruttenholm understood. Better to be with his child and die than endure this.

Still, they waited.

Kora thought Dr. Conrad might be dead.

She wept, her eyes tightly closed, and tried to be quiet. Not being quiet, that's what made them kill Dr. Conrad. He'd shouted at them, asked them what they were going to do to her. He'd even tried to grab one of them, but that wasn't why they killed him. Kora was certain of it. When the dragon-man had rushed at Dr. Conrad, grabbed him by the face and smashed his head against the rock wall, it had been only to shut him up.

Ellie Morris wasn't saying a word. She was a doctor, too, but the medical kind. Still, she was so kind that Kora couldn't think of her as anything but *Ellie.* She'd whispered to Kora a couple of times when the three dragon-men had first carried her into the chamber. But once they killed Dr. Conrad for not being quiet, Ellie stopped talking. Every time Kora opened her eyes, Ellie looked at her with wide, hopeful eyes, maybe trying to tell her everything was going to be okay, or just hoping that Kora would keep quiet.

If Kora hadn't been afraid to talk, she would have told Ellie it wasn't going to be okay at all. She didn't understand a word the dragon-men said, but she knew that much. They were monsters, with their long claws and their snouts and their scaly flesh, and fire burned in their eyes. When one of them carried her, Kora could feel the heat from inside it, from those eyes.

Sima and Rafe were dead, too. She'd seen them murdered.

One of the dragon-men hissed at her. Kora just kept her eyes closed. She could feel them pulling at her, tearing at her clothes. They poured warm water over her, and she smelled something awful, some weird, earthy stink like rotting plants, before one of them started to smear some gristly goop on her forehead and cheeks, on her throat and arms and legs.

Kora cried harder, thinking that rough hand, that stinking smear, would be used to cover her body. They all hissed at her, and she knew they wanted her to be quiet—knew if she didn't, she might end up like Dr. Conrad—but she could not help it. The tears came. The sobs came up out of her, and she couldn't stop them.

But then the hands went away, and she let out a breath of relief. She tried to get hold of herself, to slow her tears. Her chest rose and fell in even breaths.

The dragon-men began to chant in a language that was not what she had heard them speaking before.

Language was her specialty. Her father loved language—old, dead languages especially. Kora was only eleven, but she found the different tongues people spoke around the world fascinating, and spoke half a dozen languages passably well. But she only liked the languages people still used.

This wasn't what they were speaking before. This tongue was harder, uglier, with little howls and yelps that made it seem as though it wasn't a human language at all.

A little sob escaped her. Of course it wasn't a human language.

Her eyes opened. The three dragon-men stood around her, one at either shoulder and the third at her feet. She lay atop some kind of altar. Dr. Conrad's corpse was sprawled on the ground beneath the streak of his blood on the wall. Only a few feet from him, in the light from the lamps that had been rigged in the chamber, Ellie stared at Kora, still trying to communicate some hopeful message without speaking.

The dragon-men weren't even looking at her. They had their heads thrown back, weird, crocodile jaws moving with that chant, and the flames danced up from their eyes.

Tears still spilled down Kora's face, but she was catching her breath at last. She glanced quickly around the chamber. In the light she could make out some of the images on the walls that illustrated the ancient purpose of that room . . . she saw the lake, and a group of people carrying a child toward the water, hung upside down. The child had designs on her skin and a red cloth tied around her waist.

A red cloth, just like the one she'd seen around the neck of one of the dragon-men.

Kora stared at the ancient, faded images on the wall, studying them.

A child, painted with designs and tied with that red cloth, plunging into the lake . . . and up from beneath her, jaws opening wide, and fire raging upward, scorching the drowning girl.

Kora's tears stopped, and she began to scream.

Outside the preparatory chamber, Professor Bruttenholm heard the terrible sound emerging from the doorway—the terrified cry of that girl—and for a moment he couldn't breathe. That scream would drive Kora's father into a frenzy, would surely make some of the others want to rush into the chamber. These people had no history with crisis situations. They would not be thinking rationally.

He glanced down at the gun in his hand. *What precisely do you know about rational thinking, Trevor?*

The girl's screams were drowned out by a sudden roar from above. Professor Bruttenholm threw back his head and watched as the helicopter came slowly over the ridge. Redfield was jockeying it into a holding pattern just above their position.

Two hundred feet above their heads, the side door

rattled open. When Hellboy thrust his head out and looked down, Professor Bruttenholm laughed out loud in joyful relief.

"That's my boy," he whispered.

Hellboy turned to shout something back to the others inside the chopper. He braced himself a moment, then leaped out of the helicopter. The chopper swayed badly from the sudden release of ballast, but Redfield knew what he was doing. The pilot got the helicopter under control even as Hellboy careened through the air and struck the face of the ridge above them. He hit the sheer, rocky surface with hands and hooves thrust forward, but the impact slammed him hard. His heavy, arcane hand caught a grip, the fingers plunged into rock and earth, and he dangled there a moment.

Then he started to try to climb down, and the ridge gave way.

"Move!" Professor Bruttenholm shouted.

Guns and shovels clattering, the archaeologists and diggers scrambled to get out of the way as Hellboy slid down the ridge amid a small avalanche of stone and dirt. He hit the lip of the ridge above them and plummeted to the ground, landing right in the hole that had been excavated to enter the preparatory chamber.

"Ah, crap!" he barked, as bits of stone and dirt hailed down upon him.

Professor Bruttenholm was only glad that he seemed unharmed and hadn't completely caved in the entrance.

The helicopter roared toward the lakeshore, hovering a moment before beginning to set down.

"Hello, sir," Hellboy said.

"You're all right?" the professor asked.

Hellboy stood and brushed off his long jacket, then twisted his head to stretch the muscles in his neck.

"Ambush. Sort of. We're fine. We were on the way back when Redfield picked us up." He looked around at the guns and other brandished weapons, then at the corpses of Sima and Rafe Mattei. "Guess it's not news that the dragon guys are bringing the girl here."

Professor Bruttenholm stared at him. "Dragon guys?"

Hellboy drew his gun and turned toward the entrance to the preparatory chamber. He walked two steps toward it before glancing back.

"Yeah. Nakchu village. Dragon-human half-breeds. All of 'em. They think opening this chamber's gonna make the Dragon King rise, and he's gonna want breakfast. Some of them figure since it was this crew that woke him up, it should be one of theirs that gets sacrificed. Others disagree."

He gestured toward the chamber with the barrel of the gun. "Is anyone else in there?"

"Eleanor Morris and Mark Conrad, we believe," Professor Bruttenholm replied.

"All right. When Abe and Stasia and the others get up here, you hold them back. Nobody comes into that room but Tenzin and Koh."

Professor Bruttenholm held the pistol down at his

side, his fingers still wreathed with the rosary of Pope Joan. He had been studying the supernatural for most of his life, had been in dire circumstances more times than he could recall, and now he wracked his brain for some solution that would not require Hellboy to enter that chamber.

He had none.

"You do realize I'm field leader on this investigation?" he said.

Hellboy gave him a look of exhaustion only sons could ever give their fathers. "Do you *not* want me to go in and save the cute little human sacrifice?"

Bruttenholm fixed him with a withering stare. "We have the only exit surrounded."

"If we wait until they come out, there's going to be shooting. Guaranteed. We have a better chance if someone tries to talk to them."

"And you think you're best suited for that? That you won't startle them? You've already drawn your gun, and you can't even speak their language."

Hellboy shook his head in frustration and set the gun down on the edge of the pit. "Did you notice me jumping out of the friggin' helicopter? We're kind of in a hurry, here. I don't need to speak the language. That's what Tenzin and Koh are for."

"Who is this Koh?" Bruttenholm snapped.

"Dragon guy. He's on our side."

"What?" the professor began, but Hellboy was already disappearing into the chamber, tail bobbing behind him.

Conversation started all around the excavation, mutterings about the girl, about Professor Kyichu, who stood next to Frank Danovich with his arms crossed, rocking a bit, lips moving wordlessly, perhaps in prayer. Professor Bruttenholm turned to watch Abe and Dr. Bransfield hurry up the slope toward the dig with the three other field agents he'd brought along, for all the good they'd done so far. He supposed that was the intention of backup—they were there in case the lead agents failed. The guide and translator, Tenzin, ran alongside, accompanied by a man dressed in the mountain garb particular to the region.

Bruttenholm raised an eyebrow. If this was Koh, he didn't look much like a dragon.

Hellboy made his way through the corridor that led into the preparatory chamber, ducking his head to avoid the lights the archaeologists had hung. They were bright enough to piss him off. The place was lit up like a night game at Fenway.

He tried his best to tread lightly, but his hooves crunched on the stone floor, and his jacket made a kind of shushing noise when he walked, like the nylons of the old German lady who ran the library at BPRD headquarters and was so ancient and militant she'd probably been Hitler's nanny.

The corridor took a little jog to the right ahead and opened into the chamber. A low chant whispered around him, echoing off the walls. Some kind of prayer to the Dragon King, he figured. Hellboy tried to count the voices, but all the echoing made it impossible. Not too many of them, though. Two or three, maybe four. Above the sound of the chanting, he could hear the little girl whimpering, and it set his teeth on edge and his fingers to flexing. The flexing wasn't good. It usually led to him breaking things—likes bones. So he put his hands up in a gesture of surrender and stepped around the corner into the chamber.

He saw Kora first. Her shirtsleeves and the legs of her jeans were torn open, and weird sigils had been painted on the skin there, and on her face. Her eyes were squeezed shut and three of the dragon-men surrounded her, one at each shoulder and one by her feet. Beyond them, he saw Ellie Morris, kneeling beside the corpse of Mark Conrad. Hellboy figured he was dead because of the bloody streak on the wall and the way his head didn't look quite round anymore.

Keeping his hands up in that peaceful gesture was just about the hardest thing he had ever done.

"You boys should just go home, now," he said, in as reasonable a tone as possible.

The chanting stopped. All three of the dragon-men twisted toward him, crocodile jaws opening in a hissing chorus. The fire that flickered up from their eyes didn't seem very bright amid the spotlights set up in that chamber, but that didn't make it any less freaky.

He raised his hands a few more inches, and their wary eyes followed the motion. The chamber was fifteen or sixteen feet high, but he couldn't put his hands up any farther. Hellboy wanted to make sure they didn't see him as threatening.

It didn't seem to be working. The two at the girl's shoulders gathered closer to her, putting protective hands on her. The third, at her feet and nearest to Hellboy, took a slithering kind of step toward him.

"Don't do it, Puff. I left my gun outside and everything. This doesn't need to get messy."

Which was when Kora spoke. Her eyes were still squeezed tightly closed.

"Who's there?" the little girl asked, her voice breaking with hope and despair in equal parts.

"A friend," he said. "Don't be afraid, Kora."

"I don't know how to not be afraid," she said.

"Hellboy—" Ellie Morris said.

A bad idea. One of the dragon-men twisted around, reached out, and grabbed Ellie by the hair, and hauled her, screaming, toward the altar where they'd been preparing Kora for sacrifice. Ellie screamed as her scalp tore, her shriek ragged in her throat.

"Son of a—" Hellboy began.

Kora opened her eyes. Maybe she'd been expecting the Dragon King to come and claim her, to eat her, to kill her . . . when she saw Hellboy, her eyes filled with such terror that she began to shake all over, her arms and legs trembling so hard on the altar that she seemed almost to be having some kind of fit.

Ellie was talking, maybe begging the dragon-man to let her go, or telling Kora that Hellboy really was a friend, even though maybe he didn't look like one. Either way, Hellboy didn't hear more than a muttering jumble of words, because he was otherwise occupied.

The dragon-man who'd slunk closer to him lunged, hissing.

Hellboy hissed back. It sounded and felt foolish, but he'd lost patience. The dragon-man reached hooked talons out to grab him, wide jaws opening. Hellboy didn't even try to avoid the thing's hands. The talons gripped him with enough strength to make small punctures in his thick hide. He didn't even feel it. In the same moment, he grabbed the dragon-man by the throat, raised his right fist, and hit him as hard as he could.

Bones broke in the dragon-man's face. His eyes rolled in his head, he let go of Hellboy and staggered backward, then fell down, either unconscious or dead.

The other two stayed on their side of the chamber. Hellboy figured they were having second thoughts about how to proceed. Ellie was kneeling beside the altar, bent over and whispering to Kora. A trickle of blood ran down the woman's face from where her scalp had torn. The dragon-man who'd grabbed her, a big, ugly bastard with yellow-and-red flesh and very little fire in his tiny, black eyes, held one of her shoulders. The second stood on Kora's other side, one hand closed over the girl's biceps.

He started talking to Hellboy.

"Sorry," Hellboy said, spreading his arms. *"No comprendo."* He pointed to the girl. "But I know you *comprendo* this. They're coming with me."

He tapped his chest, pointed at Kora and Ellie again, then repeated the gestures several times.

The dragon-man who'd tried to speak with him hissed.

Which was when Tenzin and Koh stepped into the chamber behind him. He could tell by their footsteps, but also by the spark of hope that flared in the eyes of the two dragon-men who weren't lying on the ground with a broken face. The guy on the floor twitched a little, so maybe he was also feeling hopeful, though Hellboy didn't think so.

The one holding Ellie's shoulder starting shouting at Koh, who immediately starting shouting back even louder. Koh was the son of the village elder, so Hellboy hoped he had some kind of authority over these guys. From his tone and the commanding hand gestures he made, Hellboy figured Koh at least thought he did, which was a start.

"How's he doing?" Hellboy asked, taking a quick sidelong glance at Tenzin.

The guide stepped up beside Hellboy, face grim. "Not well. They keep insisting that the sacrifice must be made or the Dragon King will rise."

"Has Koh mentioned all the people with guns waiting to kill them if they try leaving this room with the girl?"

Tenzin shrugged. "No one will shoot if they have the girl."

Hellboy frowned. "Whose side are you on? There are too many guns for them just to walk out there. Someone will get a bead on the backs of their skulls. They'll never make it down to the water alive. Tell them."

His voice shook when he translated what Hellboy had said. Then the dragon-men started screaming at Tenzin, too.

"I'm going to be very disappointed in you if you get me killed," the guide said.

"Me too. What are they saying now?"

Hellboy watched Ellie and Kora, ignoring the dragon-men now. He tried to nod to the girl, give her some kind of reassurance, but she only whimpered and twisted on the altar to bury her face against Ellie.

"I'm quite the charmer," Hellboy muttered.

"Still no good. Koh's arguing with them, but they just keep saying the sacrifice has to be made, and they'll die to save their village if they have to."

Hellboy sighed. Zealots were the worst.

"Look, Koh," he said.

All of them fell silent at his use of the name. Koh turned to look at him.

"Tell them that they're right," Hellboy said, and Tenzin translated. "If us opening up this chamber brings the Dragon King back, it's our fault. Tell them I'll take the blame. I'll make sure the village is safe."

As the guide translated his words, the two dragon-men holding Ellie and Kora started to laugh.

Hellboy lowered his head, staring up at them with the light on his filed-down horns and dark shadows under his eyes. He let anger fill him. If not for the innocent people in that chamber, he'd already have brought the roof down on these guys.

"Tell them I don't need to sleep, but that I bet they do. I'm between them and the only way out, and if they try to get past me with Kora, I'll break them into pieces. And if they fall asleep, I'll break them into pieces. And if we're still talking about this thirty seconds from now, I'll break them into pieces."

Tenzin translated quickly, shooting worried glances at Hellboy. Ellie looked pretty concerned as well. Kora, though, seemed at last to be listening to precisely what he was saying, and a kind of peace had come over her.

"They won't kill the girl," Tenzin whispered—as though they might be able to understand English, "but they could still kill the woman."

Ellie's mouth gaped. She had good hearing.

"They won't," Hellboy said. "Appearances aside, they didn't come here to kill, or to die. Even Kora, they weren't thinking about killing. They were gonna throw her in the lake and wait for the Dragon King to come up and claim her. They killed to get the job done."

Hellboy didn't bother to add that he'd just made it

clear to them that there was no way to get the job done. No exit.

Koh let out a breath and moved to the end of the altar, putting his hands on the stone. He turned and asked Hellboy something, and though his flesh had not changed, there was fire in his eyes.

"What's that?"

"They're afraid you'll kill them anyway if they let the girl and the woman go," Tenzin said.

Hellboy shook his head. He thought about the BPRD trying to hold a couple of shape-shifting dragon-men in their custody for the duration of the case, then trying to get them extradited to face charges in the U.K. or the U.S. Even if that were possible—which he wasn't sure about—trying to keep them prisoner here at the camp would be dangerous and difficult, and probably foolhardy. The rest of the village would probably come down and try to break them out, and the bloodshed then would be far worse than what had already happened.

"I don't work that way," he said. "But when this is all done, they're going to face charges for what they've done, either under whatever the local laws are or under international law."

He hoped Stasia and his father understood.

When Tenzin translated, Koh twisted toward Hellboy in a fury, hissing, and the dragon came out in him. His jaws extended, his flesh became yellow-red and rough as scales, and he sneered something.

"Oh, my Lord," Ellie gasped, when she realized Koh was one of them.

Kora cursed in words eleven-year-old girls wouldn't want their fathers to know they knew.

"He says you killed several people in his village this morning. This only makes you even," Tenzin said warily, taking a step back and reaching for a long knife that hung from his belt.

Hellboy raised a hand to calm him and stared hard at Koh.

"We were under attack. That was a misunderstanding. We didn't know we were going into their burial ground. We were looking for the girl, and they tried to kill us. What happened here, what they did to the two outside and to Dr. Conrad over there . . . that's murder."

Tenzin translated.

The fire burned higher from Koh's eyes as he stared at Hellboy a moment longer. Then he turned and snapped at the others. Reluctantly, the two dragonmen nodded.

All three of them shifted back, their flesh almost liquid, and in a moment they appeared to be human again. Koh stepped forward and said something.

"They give their word they will await any punishment in Nakchu and not make any further attempt to take the girl, or any other action, so long as you vow that you will keep the village safe from the Dragon King. But if you break your vow, theirs is also broken."

Hellboy stared at them each in turn, then nodded slowly.

"As long as we're clear that there isn't going to be any sacrifice. Not Kora or anyone else."

Tenzin translated. One of the villagers shook his head sadly and shot Hellboy a meaningful glance as he replied, and then they all stood aside.

"Take her out of here, Ellie," Hellboy said.

Kora slid from the altar, wide-eyed, and kept glancing around at them all. As she passed Hellboy, she gave him a shy smile, and he resisted the urge to smile back for fear he'd scare her again. Then she and Ellie Morris were gone.

"What'd he say to me?"

Tenzin shifted his gaze, like he didn't want to reply.

"What?" Hellboy prodded.

"He said you'd find out soon yourself. That when the Dragon King came, you'd feed the little girl to him yourself if it meant sending him back under the lake."

A chill went through Hellboy. His nostrils flared, but he said nothing as he turned his back on them.

"I'm gonna go out and nicely ask a bunch of frightened, pissed-off people not to shoot them full of holes when they walk out. You might want to tell them to go slow, with their hands in the air, then get their butts back to their village and stay there until someone shows up to put them in prison. And tell Koh no more midnight raids. The dig goes on. No more trouble from them, there'll be no more trouble from me."

"It's not you they're worried about," Tenzin replied.

Stooped in the corridor, Hellboy turned to glare at him. "Are you the translator or their mommy?"

He followed Ellie and the little girl out into the sunlight, looked up at the blue sky and all the curious faces waiting for him, and wondered why he felt so sure that he hadn't really brought an end to the situation, just a pause.

CHAPTER 7

Anastasia stood on the ridge, leaning on a shovel, and used a handkerchief to wipe sweat from her brow. A chill ran up her back. Evening was not far off, and she had been digging for hours. There were dozens of other things she ought to have been doing, but she had needed simple, mindless, backbreaking work to cleanse some of the horror and sadness from her soul. The beauty of the mountain range and the lake ought to have helped, but instead, the entire landscape haunted her.

How had it come to this? They'd never meant to disturb anything sacred, certainly never thought to find anyone still living, who would hold such ancient sites sacred.

Mr. Lao had returned to Lhasa to make a full report about the murders at the dig site and the status of Nakchu village. Redfield, the BPRD pilot, had flown him there. She wondered if Lao's superiors would stop the dig, but presumed they would not. The Chinese government did not care if Tibetan sites were being unearthed, only that they reaped any benefits that might accrue. In fact, she suspected that if it bothered the local Tibetan peoples, the man from Beijing's bosses would be even happier.

Though they probably hadn't expected the local Tibetan people to be descended from dragon-human interbreeding.

Anastasia had reports to write as well. Professor Bruttenholm was already down in his tent, hard at work on his own. There would be an inquest, and further investigation, and her leadership and reputation would be called into question.

She felt it ought to be.

Kora Kyichu was back with her father, and she would not trade that for anything. The relief on Han's face and the joyful tears the little girl had cried convinced her that she would have done it all over again, even with the same results.

But three men were dead, and she found the burden difficult to bear. Conrad had been a pompous ass, but his arrogance was well-founded. He had been brilliant. She had not known Sima, the Russian digger, other than to say hello, but he had been a hard worker, and she had learned he had a family—a wife and two sons. Then there was Rafe—sweet, young Rafe, who had been her most promising student in years and had been willing to flirt with her a little, just to make her feel good about herself. He'd been little more than a child himself.

All three of them lay dead, wrapped in cloth in the preparatory chamber to keep the bodies cool while a message was sent to London and Beijing to get a team up to Lake Tashi to retrieve their bodies. The irony of their remains lying in the sacrificial chamber was not lost on her. It made her feel sick.

"Stop it," she whispered to herself.

Anastasia took a deep breath and lifted her shovel, driving it into the earth. The preparatory chamber was off-limits for now, but all of the other excavations continued. She bent to the work, letting the ache in her bones wash away all thoughts of death and blame for a time.

Until she looked up to see Professor Bruttenholm standing nearby, watching her as he stroked his white goatee.

Anastasia stood up, stretching her back, and regarded him curiously. The cool breeze dried the beads of sweat on her skin.

"Is something the matter, Professor?"

Bruttenholm produced a pocket watch and clicked it open, glancing at it a moment before snapping it shut. He looked around, scanning the area, though what his gaze sought, she had no idea.

"Professor?"

"Yes, sorry," Bruttenholm said, clearing his throat. When he spoke, it was with a low, sonorous voice, grimly sincere. "I'd hoped you might spare me a moment, Dr. Bransfield."

"Anastasia, please. Or Stacie."

The old man flinched, as though the informality pained him.

"What can I do for you, sir?"

"I fancy myself a practical man, Dr. Bransfield. I know that the idea of a father wishing to shield his son from the complexities of human emotion beyond childhood is awkward and even somewhat ridiculous. But he is no ordinary son."

Anastasia stared at him. "I'm not sure what sort of point you're trying to make—"

"One would think I would be ecstatic to have him endure such trials, that I would be overjoyed by the real humanity in his heart. To the latter, I say that I am. But as to the former . . . I am only human myself, and a father, and no amount of practicality can cure me of the wish not to see my son endure disappointment and heartbreak."

That was enough. She let her shovel fall aside and crawled out of the hole she'd been digging. Professor Bruttenholm was a diminutive man, an inch or so shorter than Anastasia, but he did not back up an inch as she bent toward him, finger wagging. She knew she must look a fright, dirt and sweat streaking her forehead and cheeks, her ponytail and Yankees cap the only thing keeping her hair from falling wild as a mane around her face. Bruttenholm did not blink.

"You see here, old man!" she snapped, all sense of propriety lost, her face flushed will ill temper. "I've said and done precisely nothing to indicate to Hellboy that I hoped to rekindle old flames. Dear God, you think, what, that all of this is some kind of enormous ruse for me to play some kind of romantic charade? People are dead, Professor! Friends of mine are dead, up in that damned chamber!"

Anastasia fumed, wanting desperately for Bruttenholm to shout back at her so there could be a proper screaming match. She needed that. The old fool didn't know what he was in for, making such accusations.

He did not rile so easily.

"Forgive me, Doctor, if I've been unclear. Age causes one to ramble. I know the cost of this journey has been high, and I meant to imply no such thing. The truth is, I know that calling upon the BPRD and upon my son was the only sensible, rational thing for you to do when you were faced with the unfortunate circumstances that arose here. Though I'd be lying if I said I didn't wish you had thought of some other course of action. My point in speaking to you on this matter was only to make an observation."

Anastasia wiped dirt from her cheeks and bent down to pick up the shovel. The dusk was coming on, night beginning to spread across the plateau. She was tempted to jump back down into the hole, but they both knew the digging was done for the day.

"Say what you've got to say," Anastasia muttered.

"He still loves you, but you know that. And now I see that he is not the only one who still lingers in the past. With all that is happening here, it would be quite easy for old habits to reemerge, for old feelings to come alive."

"It was ten years ago!"

"Sometimes embers take only an errant breeze to ignite again."

Her face flushed, and she was glad of the dark, hoping he didn't see how much the words affected her. Bruttenholm spoke the truth. He knew it, but Anastasia didn't want him to see that she knew it as well.

"Maybe you've forgotten," she said, half-turning away from him. "Hellboy is the one that ended the relationship."

Bruttenholm nodded slowly. "And perhaps you have forgotten, Anastasia, why he felt compelled to do such a thing and why he has maintained a solitary life in the years since."

She shivered, and it wasn't from the cold.

"He said it wasn't fair to me, all the attention we drew, all the things that were said in the media—"

"That was part of it, I'm sure," Professor Bruttenholm said, smoothing his lapels, dignified as always. "But you know there is more to it."

"You said all the things he's felt have made him more human," she protested, hearing the sorrow in her voice, the heartbreak, and cursing herself for showing such weakness in front of this stern old man.

"They have," Bruttenholm replied. "But every time the media mentioned you and him together, every time he saw the expressions on the face of those you met in your travels . . . every time he held your hand, Dr. Bransfield, it reminded him that he is only human in his heart."

With that, the old man turned and strode away.

Anastasia could only watch him go, feeling bitterness welling up within her. Hellboy could not help what he felt, and nor could she. If he had never been the same after the time they had shared together, she could not regret that. She had never been the same, either.

Some things weren't meant to be forgotten.

The Island of Crete, 14 April, 1980

Hellboy was dead.

Anastasia staggered along the slope of Mount Ida, hands manacled behind her back, a thick gag in her mouth. The men behind her did not touch her, and the two in front—the sorcerers—did not so much as glance back. It sickened her to know how little they considered her. She represented no threat, so she registered only for what use they could make of her. She was only bait, the worm at the end of the hook.

But she had been bait for a week, perhaps more. Locked in the wine cellar of some villa, gagged and blindfolded, she had wept, and she had cried out in pain. They had burned her for their pleasure with the tips of cigarettes. Some of them had pawed at her in the way that men did. They had taunted her in a dozen languages and spit upon her. But no worse.

No worse.

Anastasia had found that strange. For days she had pondered her good fortune. They hadn't raped her, or tortured her in earnest, or slit her throat. When they'd taken her out of the wine cellar, away from the rich, earthy aroma of that room, and paraded her outside, still blindfolded and gagged, she had not understood. At first she'd thought they were taking her elsewhere to kill her, but after an hour or so of this, they'd returned her to the wine cellar.

They'd fed her and given her water. Kept her alive. And the next day, they'd paraded her again, as though showing her off to some unseen watcher.

And then she'd understood that she was bait. They wanted Hellboy to come after them. They'd prepared for him, and for whoever else he might bring along. Twice, when her blindfold had been removed while she was allowed to use a filthy child's potty as a toilet, she saw the sorcerers at work, men and women who slipped in and out of shadows with a flourish, as though they were dancing in darkness.

Sorcerers.

Whenever they were there, she caught a scent that reminded her of burning plastic. Now she knew the odor of dark magic. Snatches of conversation she'd overheard spoke of the hammer and the anvil and the forge, none of which made any sense to her.

A week. More. Behind her blindfold, sleeping only in fits and starts, afraid at every moment that her usefulness was at an end, the days blurred into one another. Days and days, and at first she had been filled with righteous anger along with her fear. Hellboy would come, and he would make them pay. They would hurt. God, would they regret having taken her, touched her, burned her.

But Hellboy never came.

In her heart—where she cherished her love for him and all the little moments they'd shared, despite the world's ignorance—she knew that he must be dead. He would have come for her, otherwise. It was the only possibility. And if Hellboy was dead, then she truly had outlived her usefulness.

Now, tonight, the proof had come.

Two of the sorcerers had come. Four others—three men and a woman—had taken her at gunpoint out of the villa and loaded her into the back of a truck. They hadn't bothered with her blindfold, and then, of course, she had known. She'd tried not to think about it, looking down at the beauty of Crete in the moonlight, sprawled around them. The sorcerers had not vanished into darkness this time. They had sat with her in the back of the truck with two of the gunmen.

The truck had rattled all the way along the rutted road that led up the side of Mount Ida, then off the road, at an angle that made her fear they would tumble over, the vehicle rolling all the way down the side of the mountain. They'd stopped and dragged her out, and for the first time in days, Anastasia had screamed against the inside of her gag.

She felt too numb to cry as they marched her toward a scarred and pitted area of the mountain, where tall caves stood open. Scaffolding had been erected all over the entrances to the caves, and in the pits in the mountainside, tiny flags dotted the soil, strung with twine, bits of the archaeological dig partitioned off so that it could be searched more methodically.

Paul Campbell's dig, she thought. Yet the only people in sight were the two sorcerers who strode ahead of her and the woman and three men who followed her, prodding her now and again with the barrels of their guns. She staggered and went down on one knee.

One of the sorcerers, whose dark, Mediterranean features would have made him exotically handsome if not for the cruel flint of his eyes, turned and hissed at the lackeys who escorted her.

"Careful, idiots," he commanded them in archaic Greek. "We haven't time to find another sacrifice now."

Sacrifice.

Anastasia searched her head trying to find another translation from the Greek for the word, but came up with nothing. Her bones were cold, despite the heat of the night. The smell of wildflowers carried to her on the mountain breeze. She found pleasure in them, though inside she felt empty.

Hellboy would have come for her. He had to be

dead. They'd wanted to use her as bait, but now that that didn't work, they'd found another use for her. Whatever they were up to—whatever the reason they'd arranged somehow to get Campbell's entire archaeological expedition away from the dig tonight—it required blood sacrifice.

"Move," said a gunman behind her, prodding her with his weapon.

Anastasia planted her left foot, spun, pushed off with her right, and drove her head into the man's ugly face. His nose shattered. She felt his blood spray across her cheeks. One of the others shouted. With her hands cuffed behind her, there was no hope of her getting the fallen man's gun, so she simply ran.

Half a dozen steps, and she tripped, tumbling, then rolling down the side of the mountain. Stones cut and scraped her as she fell end over end. A thick bush tore at her right arm as she plunged past. Anastasia held her breath because trying to breathe through her nose with the gag over her mouth would only have panicked her. She whipped her legs around, trying to slow herself down, and her right ankle struck a rocky outcropping with a crack that sent spikes of alarm through her heart.

The slope leveled out for a few feet before dropping off again. Anastasia managed to stop. Bruised and bleeding, trying to breathe through her nose, trying to shake the gag out of her mouth; she put her legs under her and tried to stand.

The pain in her ankle put stars in her head.

At last, fresh tears came.

And then a voice.

"No need to cry, little one," said the sorcerer as he stepped out of a cloak of night, and her nostrils filled with the stink of burning plastic. The handsome magician in his stylish clothes—one of the two who had stolen her away from the balcony that night—gestured with one hand and the darkness enfolded her, picked her up.

He moved toward her. Anastasia tried to pull away, but the night held her fast. The sorcerer gathered her up in the darkness and reached out a hand. She spun toward him as though they were locked in some marionettes' tango, and then she felt it happen. Just as it had the night she'd been taken by the Obsidian Danse, the world rushed into darkness around her. Anastasia felt plucked from the ground, thrust into the air, then released.

When she came down on her shattered ankle, the pain drove a scream up out of her throat.

The darkness cleared, leaving her in the midst of Paul Campbell's excavation. Lights had been strung through the cavern on the face of Mount Ida. Perhaps twenty of the men and women who served the Obsidian Danse were spread about the place, guns at the ready, watching every corner for some surprise attack. Others covered the entrance.

There were eight sorcerers all told. Five men and

three women. Anastasia found that she hated the women more. She knew her own sex could be just as vicious as men, perhaps even more savage at times, yet still she felt a strange betrayal at their presence.

They were elegant people, these sorcerers, sophisticated and well-dressed. Perhaps they hoped to persuade those around them that they had some gift of enlightenment, but their eyes were full of the same dull motivations she'd seen in far less powerful creatures—greed, zealotry, lust for power. Why was it that such characters were always so full of ignorant and destructive notions? She wished she knew.

Of course, it would do her little good. Their notions were about to spill her blood in sacrifice to some ancient deity.

Anastasia felt tired. She wondered if she would see Hellboy again, afterward, if there was some place their spirits might be able to encounter one another. She didn't expect eternity with him. What a naïve hope that would be. All she wanted was an opportunity to tell him good-bye, and that she'd loved him.

"Bring her," one of the female sorcerers shouted in French. She had long, red hair that fell in curls around her shoulders, as though she'd just come from the salon. Likely she had.

The three thugs who'd escorted her before surrounded her.

"Where's your friend?" she asked. "Migraine?"

Anger flickered across the faces of the two men,

but the woman was stoic. She merely gestured with her gun toward the rear of the cavern. The sorcerers were gathering there, and the shadows slithered along the floor. The bright lights set up by the archaeologists could not penetrate them.

Then, for the first time, Anastasia looked carefully at the strange columns that lined that wall. A wave of understanding crashed upon her, and she stared, shaking her head. For those four columns were not stone at all. They were something else—something no human could have identified, though it must have been some kind of flesh. They were the fingertips of something unimaginably large.

And the huge rectangle that jutted up like a table from the floor of the cavern—thirty feet across—that was not stone, either.

The hammer. The anvil. The forge.

Vague recollections of conversations she'd had with Paul Campbell came back to her, now. He'd talked to her of local folklore before he'd departed for Crete. Paul knew she fancied such tales. The Daktyloi. Demons or gods or simply monsters, beings who should not exist in this world; they were the Forge, and the Hammer, and the Anvil. She did not remember their names of legend, but what did that matter, when she could see the anvil on the floor, see the four fingers of some antediluvian deity jutting from the stone?

The Obsidian Danse meant to use her blood to bring them to life.

Why? she wondered, before realizing that *why* mattered not at all.

Tendrils of shadow pulled at her, wrapping around her arms and legs and sliding her through the air, placing her gently upon the anvil.

Close your eyes, she told herself.

But Anastasia could not look away. They were going to kill her, but she wondered if she would live long enough—her blood seeping away—to see that hand come to life, and what might come up out of the mountain behind it.

The red-haired sorceress stood above her, a silver knife appearing in her palm as though it had been forged in darkness and produced through some sleight of hand. Only then did the weight of reality descend upon Anastasia. Death had come for her.

She trembled in dreadful anticipation and wondered how much pain there would be.

An explosion rocked the cavern, and part of the roof caved in.

Rock rained down only a few yards from her. She rolled herself off the anvil. The sorceress cursed in some ancient tongue and grabbed a fistful of her hair, silver dagger raised high.

And then the woman's gaze shifted toward the sounds coming from the pile of rubble from the collapse of the roof. The movements, there.

Hellboy stood, and the shattered rock fell down around him, so that for a moment he looked quite like a statue himself, save for the leather satchel that hung from one shoulder. He glanced once in obvious curiosity at the giant hand thrust out of the stone behind him, then ignored it. Anastasia's breath caught in her throat, and she quivered with relief to see that he was alive and had come for her. Even if neither of them got out of there alive . . . he had come for her.

"Fool," said that elegant, exotic sorcerer who had picked her up off of the mountainside.

"Yeah. Hey. How's it going?" Hellboy asked.

The idiot lackeys with their guns started to gather around, but the sorcerers waved them away. Those arrogant magicians circled him like lions on the veldt, all save the redhead who still twisted her hand painfully in Anastasia's hair.

"You've given us precisely what we wanted," the sorcerer continued. "I thought you had abandoned the woman. Instead, you deliver yourself to us. It's a gift, Hellboy. You will make a far more substantial sacrifice than Dr. Bransfield . . . and then you will plague us no longer. What is it they say? Two birds with one stone."

Hellboy narrowed his eyes, and the anger there was more powerful than any sorcery. "See, there you go again. I told you, dumb-ass, I never heard of you losers before. Just so we're clear that you brought this on yourselves."

The redhead was the first to laugh. Then the other two sorceresses joined in. The men shook their heads in amusement. One or two of them seemed actually nervous, but they were confident in their greater power. There were eight of them, after all, and twenty fools with guns.

"We shall try to remember that when the world is ravaged by fire and despair."

Hellboy sighed, reaching into the leather satchel he carried. "You guys ever heard of Aksobhya the Immovable? He was one of the Five Jinas, the guys with the Mandala, all that? Point is, he didn't like magic, wouldn't have it in his presence."

The sorcerers moved nearer as he spoke.

"What are you prattling about?" one of them snapped.

But the most vocal, the one Anastasia thought of as the leader, scowled. "Don't listen. The fool is going to try some enchantment. Just kill him."

Whorls of darkness filled the air, rushing toward Hellboy across the cavern. In the same moment, Hellboy pulled his hand from the satchel.

He held a yellowed, human skull.

The shadows dissipated, the lights flickering once, then the sorcerers stood there, gaping dumbly at Hellboy and at one another. Their hands danced in the air uselessly, and they twisted their bodies in spastic motion, but to no effect.

"Meet Aksobhya," Hellboy said. "Toldja he didn't like magic."

The grip in Anastasia's hair tightened. The sorceress

holding her screamed in fury, and she felt her head jerked back. She saw the silver dagger flash down out of the corner of her eye, then it wavered. The knife slipped away, and Anastasia found herself free. Behind her, she heard the sorceress crumple to the ground, and she turned to see the woman lying there, her beauty gone, her flesh withered, now that the magic that had preserved her had been dispersed.

A blowgun dart jutted from her throat.

Anastasia spun to see Hellboy just tossing the small blowgun aside.

The thugs in the employ of the Obsidian Danse started shouting. Sorcerers called out orders. Some of their lackeys fled. One of them shot a sorceress through the head in what Anastasia could only imagine was revenge for some slight—or a thousand. The rest of them started to move toward Hellboy, weapons at the ready.

Shouts came from the entrance. Many of the thugs turned to watch as dozens of soldiers and BPRD agents swept into the cavern.

Hellboy didn't even pay any attention as the Obsidian Danse began to surrender. His eyes were on Anastasia. He carried the skull under one arm like a football and ran to her, leaping up on top of the anvil.

"Hey," he said, reaching down for her with his free hand.

"Hey." Careful with her broken ankle, she let him help her up onto the stone platform. Shouts and activity were all around them, but neither of them were paying any attention. "Took you bloody long enough. Got it in my head you might be dead."

He cocked his head, a mischievous light in his eyes, and held up the skull of Aksobhya. "Nah. Just knew it wasn't going to be a matter of busting in and beating these guys into submission. For morons, they had some serious mojo. I needed to do a little research first."

Warmth spread across her chest, and she reached up to trace the contours of his face. "You hate research. You did your homework for me?"

Sheepish, he shrugged. "Yeah. Of course."

"God, that's romantic."

CHAPTER 8

Abe Sapien emerged from the water of Lake Tashi and stood on the shore, surveying the tent village that the archaeologists had created with their camp, and the BPRD tents erected nearby. Ever since they'd arrived, Abe had felt the terrible weight of some imminent terror. At first, when they had discovered the true nature of Nakchu village and its inhabitants, and when it seemed the missing girl, Kora, might be murdered as a sacrifice, Abe had presumed those things had caused his unease.

Now the dragon-human half-breeds had returned to their village, and the little girl was safe. Though three men were dead, the crisis appeared to be at an end.

Yet Abe felt more unsettled than ever. He'd never been a precognitive—this was more primal than some kind of clairvoyance. The fish in the lake had been darting back and forth erratically. He could not ignore his own nature. Abe Sapien might not know his origins, but he existed as both a humanoid and an aquatic being. And something primeval in his makeup was reacting to a disturbance in the natural order of things.

Hellboy would tease him mercilessly if he brought it up. Just as Abe would have done the same had it been his friend who broached the subject. But they would both take the ominous feelings seriously, regardless of how odd things might seem.

Abe had other reasons to seek Hellboy out. In fact, he thought it was time to have a conversation with Professor Bruttenholm as well. The behavior of the fish in Lake Tashi wasn't the only unusual thing he'd encountered in the water. The weather had not changed substantially since they had arrived here. The sun was warm, the wind off the mountains quite cool, and at night it grew cold.

But in the depths of the lake, the water had gotten warmer. Down near the shifting, formless bottom, the temperature had risen enough that he would almost say it was hot.

Under the circumstances, this seemed like spectacularly bad news.

Long arms swinging at his sides, Abe walked toward the cluster of tents at the edge of the camp. His gaze scanned the ridgeline above. Though evening had arrived, lights burned around the main excavations, and a number of people were still at work up there. The dark shape of Hellboy was unmistakable. He stood on an outcropping of rock with a silhouette that had to be Anastasia. This time of day, when the darkness had not fully gathered, his eyesight was not what it became in the fullness of night.

Abe did not attempt to get Hellboy's attention, reluctant to interrupt. Instead, he continued toward the tents that had been set up for the BPRD operatives at the edge of the archaeologists' camp. Voices carried, some of them hushed with worry and grief, but others filled with the enthusiasm an endeavor such as this always created.

He passed between two tents and emerged at the center of the camp, where the entrances to most of the tents opened. In front of the nearest of the BPRD tents, Neil Pinborough smoked a filterless cigarette, gaze roving as always, gun slung across his shoulder. His dark skin seemed almost blue in the early evening gloom.

"Hello, Abe," the man said, amiably enough. They'd worked together only once before, and didn't know each other well, but it seemed as though everyone felt comfortable calling Abe by his first name.

He'd never been sure how he felt about such intimacy from acquaintances.

"Agent Pinborough," Abe replied. "Evening. Has Professor Bruttenholm heard anything further from Dr. Manning, do you know?"

Pinborough nodded, drawing another lungful of smoke. When he spoke, it ghosted from his mouth like hot breath on a winter morning. "He did, yeah.

It's all sorted. Manning's sending a cadre of our people and the U.N. have struck a deal with Beijing. Joint mission between U.N. and Chinese military. Couple of hundred, if I heard it right. They'll deal with Nakchu. Part of the reason Redfield's flown Lao down to Lhasa."

Abe sighed. "I almost feel bad for them."

"Yeah?" Pinborough said, glancing around again, his eyes always in motion, watching for more incursions from the dragon-men. He plucked his cigarette from his mouth, wet his thumb and forefinger on his lips, then snuffed the burning tip with a pinch before slipping it into the breast pocket of his military jacket.

That was the kind of operative Neil Pinborough was—he wouldn't leave a trace of his presence behind if he could help it. When dealing with such men and women, Abe often wondered why the Bureau put up with its more unique agents. He and Hellboy and Liz had been trained, of course. But none of them had ever been very skilled at the espionage sort of tactics that were standard fare for other BPRD field agents.

Then again, Pinborough and the others couldn't light fires with their mind, breathe under water, or pummel a Hydra into submission with their bare hands, so maybe there had to be a give-and-take.

"Did Professor Bruttenholm say how long before they would arrive?" Abe asked.

Pinborough spoke as though to himself, all of his attention focused on the nighttime landscape around them. "Two or three days. After that, the rest of us go home and leave the grunt work to the grunts."

"A lot of things can happen in three days," Abe replied.

A troubled expression crossed Pinborough's face. He turned to Abe as though he were about to ask a question. The moment was interrupted by Professor Bruttenholm, who appeared from within the largest of their tents.

"Ah, good evening, Abe," the old man said.

Abe nodded. "Professor. I have troubling news."

Bruttenholm smiled. "Of course. Nothing is simple here. Do come in." He stood back and held the flap of the tent aside.

As Abe started toward him, he heard a low sound like distant thunder and felt the ground tremble, just slightly, beneath his feet.

His stomach lurched. He stared down at the ground, then quickly looked up at the professor. "Did you feel that?"

Bruttenholm frowned. "Feel what?"

It happened again, the slightest tremor.

Abe glanced back and forth between Agent Pinborough and Professor Bruttenholm. "We don't have three days."

Inches. Maybe a foot. Hellboy had never been so aware of distance as he was of the small space separating him from Stasia as they started down the hillside toward the shore of Lake Tashi. That gap between them seemed somehow charged to him, like the air heavy with moisture and electricity right before a storm. Anastasia had seemed awkward when he'd run into her, just a few minutes before, and she'd been acting skittish ever since. Her gaze shifted away from him, and she seemed constantly on the verge of putting into words whatever troubled her.

But Hellboy didn't push. He wasn't the type. And truth to tell, he had a feeling it might be dangerous for Anastasia to say out loud what troubled her.

"You're sure the museum's not going to pull you off the project?" he asked.

Anastasia had her hands thrust deeply into the pockets of a lamb's wool jacket. Her New York Yankees cap was nowhere to be seen. Her strawberry blond hair seemed golden orange in the moonlight. Hellboy took short strides as they went down the slope together, his long jacket flapping in the light wind. He kept his hands at his sides.

When Anastasia shrugged, she kept her hands in her pockets. He wondered if she sensed the charge of the space between them the way that he did, and guessed that she did.

"Once they've read the BPRD report and the statements of my staff, they won't pull me. They'll send an additional team including someone to replace Mark Conrad—probably Tott Peck, who's a decent bloke—and the newcomers'll have orders to keep an eye on me. Once all the excavation is done and it comes down to nothing but cataloging and photographing, they'll call me home. Which is fine, really. You know the initial discovery and interpretation is my real love. Then I like to move on."

Hellboy glanced at her in time to see her frown at her words and her eyes narrow with wrinkles of worry. She shot him a sidelong look, almost guilty, and he realized she was reconsidering her words, wondering if he would read any deeper implication into them.

"Tott Peck?"

She blinked, careful as she picked her way down a tumble of stones. "Hmm?"

"That's someone's name? Seriously? Tott Peck?"

Anastasia laughed a bit too much. "His name's Tottenham. Apparently where his parents conceived him. Some apartment on Tottenham Court Road. The sort of precious thing Americans do all the time, giving their children such names. Tott's parents are from Boston, but moved to London before he was born. If they've got to send someone to watchdog me, I hope it's him."

Off to the right, Hellboy saw Abe walking between two of the tents the BPRD had set up beside the archaeologists' camp. But here, in the shadow of the ridge where the city of the Dragon King was being excavated, no one was around. Everyone was either up at the dig or in camp. Hellboy and Anastasia walked together down to the shore of the lake, undisturbed.

At the water, they paused to stare out toward the far shore. Until now, they'd been talking about the horrid events of the morning and the deaths of Sima, Rafe, and Dr. Conrad. Professor Kyichu would be leaving the expedition, apparently. He wanted to take Kora home. Hellboy couldn't blame him. Anastasia was sad to see him go, but she understood.

Now, though, all discussion of work came to an end.

The space between them fairly crackled. The lake's surface rippled in the night breeze.

"How long before the BPRD sends someone to deal with Nakchu village?" she asked.

Hellboy glanced away from her, the moonlight on the lake suddenly fascinating beyond its beauty. "I don't know. Haven't spoken to the professor about it. A few days, I'd guess. Probably BPRD and United Nations."

"And then you'll be going?"

Her voice sounded small and faraway.

"Yeah. Our job's done."

Hellboy felt strangely warm. He glanced at Anastasia and saw that she seemed not to notice all the beauty around her, focusing on her feet.

"Your father would be pretty upset with me, but . . . are you sure you have to go?"

The moment seemed eternal, and eventually Hellboy became aware he had remained silent for far too long. His lack of answer would have stung her. He knew that, and couldn't do anything about it.

"I shouldn't have said anything—" Anastasia began.

"Why would he be upset?" he asked.

Anastasia laughed softly, hollowly. "Professor Bruttenholm basically warned me off an hour or so ago."

"He what?" He was often frustrated with his father, but he'd never felt anger like this at the old man before. The feeling didn't sit well with him. It seemed to sizzle inside him, like he'd been electrocuted.

"Stop. Wait," Stasia said, shaking her head. "He was fine. Respectful. He's just your father, and he worries for you."

"I'm not a child," Hellboy growled.

"We should all be so fortunate as to have someone who loves us as much as he loves you," she told him. It felt like an admonishment.

"What'd he say, exactly?"

Anastasia turned toward him. She didn't reach for his hands or slide into his arms or any of the things that would have felt so natural for them, so comfortable.

"It's absurd, you know. This is only the second time we've seen one another in ten years. I go all this time thinking I'm set. I miss you, right enough, but I don't remember why I miss you. Then here you are, and it all comes back, and ten years seems like ten days. So here I am, saying all these things I know I shouldn't say, because I'm a selfish bitch, I suppose. I'm not asking you to be in love with me, or to travel around the world with me, or to make things as they were, once upon a time. I would never presume. I know it can never be that way again.

"But I feel better with you here. Better about myself. Better about the world. And I'm just . . . I'm having trouble with the idea of you going home in a few days. It's too quick. So, I just wondered if you might be able to stay on for a little while. . . ."

A horrified expression crossed her face. "And now I've bollixed it up entirely, haven't I? Made a damn fool of myself."

Hellboy reached out his right hand, that huge destructive bit of him, and she lay her head against it, so gently. Anastasia was the only person in the world who'd never shied away from that hand.

"I'll always be here when you need me," he said. "I couldn't not come when you call. But you only think you want me to stay. Bad things happen when we're together."

A flicker of pain went through her eyes. "That's not . . . you're right, of course. You're right. I'm sorry. I know it isn't easy for you. I told you I was being a selfish bitch, and—"

"Yeah, no. Not what I meant," Hellboy interrupted. "I'm talking about the monsters, and the black magic, and the zombies and giant spiders and talking severed heads. Dragon-men are kind of a vacation compared to all that crap. But you know what my life is. You're sick with the horror of what happened this morning. You don't want that to be your daily routine."

Anastasia's gaze hardened. "That was never why it ended for us."

She didn't have to say any more. They both knew why it had really ended. Stasia had been courageous in the presence of darkness and evil, willing to stand with him no matter what kind of horror reared its head. It wasn't the monsters that had been the end of them, it had been the people—the looks and the whispers.

"So what happens if I stay, then?" Hellboy asked, surprised to hear his own voice. "How long are we talking about? A week? Two? 'Cause you know that's the problem, Stasia. I'm here now because you needed my help—the BPRD's help. The minute I'm sticking around just to be with you and not because there's something big and evil I need to hit, that changes things."

Seconds passed. The moonlight played across the night-cloaked lake. They stared at one another, standing on the shore, everyone else so far away.

"I didn't hear a 'no' in there," Anastasia said.

Hellboy hesitated. She was right. He hadn't actually said no. Was what she was asking so terrible? They were old friends who still cared deeply for one another. They were both adults, and they knew how things stood and what the parameters were between them.

He reached out his other hand, and she twined her fingers with his.

Beneath his hooves, the ground began to tremble. Hellboy frowned. He'd felt something before, when they were coming down the hill, but it had been so slight he had thought he'd imagined it or that it had just been loose earth shifting under him.

Stasia's eyes went wide. The shore of the lake shifted and bucked. She let out a scream, and had she not gripped his arm just then, she would have fallen. Hellboy pulled her into his arms and held her as the earth began to shake, and rocks tumbled down the hillside toward them. The surface of the lake churned like an ocean storm. Shouts of pain and terror rang out from the ridge as parts of the dig collapsed. The seconds passed like hours as the whole world tilted, and still Hellboy kept his footing, and held tight to Stasia.

As quickly as it had begun, it passed.

"Bloody hell," Stasia rasped, looking around frightfully. "Earthquakes—what next?"

Even as she spoke, Hellboy stepped away from her, turning to stare out at the lake. The quake had subsided, but the water still churned. And underneath the maelstrom, it glowed a bright orange.

"You had to ask."

The lake exploded in a gigantic fountain of water and fire, and the Dragon King hurtled skyward, erupting through a cloud of his own flames. The serpent had no wings, but still it flew. Its long body was covered with yellow scales, though its belly was a wide red stripe. Its snout opened wide, fire blossoming from its gullet as it twisted and squirmed across the sky above their heads. Upon its skull were the antlers of a stag, and its tiny limbs ended in talons like those of eagles.

"It doesn't make any sense," Anastasia whispered, so close to him.

Hellboy stared into the night sky as the worm wiggled through the air, fire streaming along its body, snorting from its nostrils. He figured it was over a hundred feet long, but told himself that he could kill it, if he could just get close to it. The inability to fly posed a problem.

"What doesn't?" he said, not tearing his eyes from the Dragon King as it twisted and coiled in upon itself, either exulting in its freedom or chasing its tail like a savage dog on a cocaine high. "This is exactly what the legend said would happen. We oughta believe legends more often."

"Legends are usually symbolic. They mean something beyond the words."

"Yeah, this one means we're screwed."

"You don't understand. It doesn't make sense that the Dragon King is here when we've found no trace of the temple."

Hellboy tore his gaze away from the worm snaking across the sky and stared at her. "I don't think not finding the temple is your team's biggest concern right now."

Anastasia's eyes were wide. Hellboy saw reflected in them the yellow-and-red dragon swimming in the sky above them, trailing fire. But then among the shouts and cries from the camp and from the dig up on the ridge, he heard a kind of low whistle. It came from the Dragon King. When Hellboy looked up again, he saw that the fire had ceased to trail from its snout.

Scales and antlers reflecting moonlight, the Dragon King slithered across the sky, then descended upon the archaeological dig.

"Son of a bitch," Hellboy muttered.

He pulled his gun, wondering what good it would do, and started up the rocky slope toward the dig as fast as he could. Someone screamed. The dragon landed on the ridge, talons gripping mounds of excavated earth and fish tail whipping around. Someone shrieked, and Hellboy saw a man clutched in the dragon's rear talon. The shriek cut off as the digger was crushed, bones snapping, limbs splayed from the dragon's grip.

The worm tossed its body around madly, tearing down scaffolding and collapsing the mounds that had been unearthed onto the parts of the city that had been revealed. Several people leaped off of the top of the ridge and struck hard, knees bending, tumbling end over end into a painful roll.

Hellboy was almost at the top. He paused and leveled his hand cannon.

The Dragon King slithered into the air, darting almost too fast for him to follow with the barrel of his gun. He squeezed off a round and it boomed across the sky, but the way the worm twisted, the bullet didn't even come close.

It seemed about to head north, toward distant mountain peaks, but then abruptly coiled in upon itself. A yellow-and-red blur, it snaked down from the sky toward the camp. Hellboy froze a single instant, then he ran, hooves pounding as he hurled himself down the slope, shouting warnings in words he didn't even hear coming out of his mouth. The gun dangled uselessly in his hand.

The dragon opened its maw, and the night lit up with fire once again. The tents set up by the archaeologists and by his fellow BPRD agents caught fire, and the blaze roared, licking at the night sky. Black smoke raced up from the camp. Holes circled in burning black widened as the fire consumed two out of every three tents.

Hellboy gritted his teeth and glared at the dragon as it slunk away across the sky. He did not call out his father's name, or Abe's, or anyone's. He simply ran toward the burning tents. As he reached the camp he saw a woman on fire staggering out of a tent. Hellboy pulled her to the ground and started to roll her roughly on the dirt, clawing up handfuls of soil to throw onto her. He doused the flames. She screamed in terror, though she was not badly injured. As he rose, he whipped aside the flap of the burning tent, checked to make sure no one else was inside, then he tore it down. *Safer if it burns on the ground.*

But he didn't slow down.

People shouted all around him. He saw a burning man run toward the lake, his hair ablaze.

Two of the BPRD tents were on fire.

Silhouetted against them, Hellboy saw Abe Sapien standing with his legs apart, holding the slender, white-haired figure of Professor Bruttenholm in his arms.

He heard Anastasia calling out to others somewhere nearby. She was seeing to her people, calming them down, getting them organized and seeing who was injured. Hellboy felt a vague, distant relief. With Anastasia there, he didn't need to worry about saving everyone. All he needed to worry about was his father.

"He'll be all right," Abe said.

Hellboy took the old man from Abe and carried him away from the burning tents, away from the camp, and set him down at the bottom of the slope that led up toward the dig. His father murmured something, and his eyelids fluttered. Parts of his white goatee had been singed. A portion of his jacket had been burned along one arm, but Hellboy put off trying to remove it. The flesh would be burned under there, and he didn't want to look just yet.

"What happened to him?"

"I went into the tent to get him. Pinborough kept the flap clear, but when we came out, the professor was on fire. He kept swiping at his eyes, the smoke stung him, I think. When he dropped to try to put the flames out, he simply passed out. He may have struck his head."

But Professor Bruttenholm was already coming around. He blinked several times, opening his eyes wide as though clearing his vision. For a moment he seemed disoriented, but then dark understanding etched a grim expression upon his face.

"What happened to you?" Hellboy asked.

"Too much smoke and excitement, I suppose," the professor replied, touching the side of his head. "Got a bit of a bump, that's all. I'll be fine. Look to the rest of them, now. There'll be a lot of wounded. And where's the damned dragon gotten off to?"

Hellboy stared at his father, then looked up into the sky.

The dragon had headed north, toward Nakchu village. It crossed his mind that he'd promised that he would keep the village safe after stopping them from sacrificing Kora. So much for that.

"North," was all he said.

"Damn it," Professor Bruttenholm whispered. He tried to rise, but swayed and lay back down. "Help the rest. I'll be all right here."

"You're sure?"

The old man fixed him with a determined stare.

Hellboy nodded and pulled Abe away from him. "Where's Pinborough, now? Where are the others?"

Abe gestured toward the burning tents. "Neil went to help them. Sarah and Meaney were up at the dig."

Hellboy felt a cold knot in his gut. "Take care of the professor. Work with Stasia and Pinborough to coordinate down here. I'm going up on the ridge. Anyone sees the dragon, they should start screaming."

A visible shudder went through Abe. "Somehow, I don't think that's going to be a problem."

Koh crouched just inside the mouth of the tunnel that led into the burial cavern of his people. Twenty feet away his father's body lay burning, flesh flaking like black parchment, charred bones still on fire. Koh wept tears of fire. Behind him, deeper inside the tunnel, dozens of men, women, and children of his village huddled together in grief and fear.

"Is it still out there?" asked a little girl, a daughter of his cousin.

He could only nod, staring at the figure slithering across the sky in flames. It seemed as though the heavens themselves were burning. Nakchu village crackled and raged with fire, all of the beautifully constructed wooden huts swallowed by orange flame and black smoke. The winding river disappeared into the rolling smoke. He could see only the arch of the bridge, on fire.

In the sky, the Dragon King seemed to grow bored

with them. It slid lower and glided, twisting, above the village in search of anything that might be moving—might still be alive. And then it whipped up toward the heavens again and turned southward, slithering away over the hills, toward the lake.

But Koh knew that the Dragon King would return. Its reign had begun anew.

Chapter 9

All of the archaeologists' work had been destroyed. Almost nothing remained undamaged. Areas that had been cordoned off and sectioned with rope and stakes had been churned up by a combination of the earth tremor and the Dragon King's arrival. Mounds of earth had been spread back across excavations as though no digging had ever occurred. The hole in front of the preparatory room had collapsed in upon itself or been torn asunder by one of the dragon's talons. The steep hillside above the entrance had caved in, sealing the chamber with the corpses of Sima, Rafe Mattei, and Dr. Conrad inside.

Two more people were dead—a digger named Kufs and one of Danovich's men—and the archaeologist that Professor Bruttenholm had befriended, Dorian Trent, was missing. It seemed obvious Trent had been buried in one of the cave-ins, but Hellboy couldn't be sure.

Hellboy had sent Sarah Rhys-Howard, the BPRD medic, down to help at the camp. She was rounding up supplies and helping Ellie Morris treat the burns of those at the camp. They were priority one right now. That, and getting Kora Kyichu away from this place, just in case there was some way for the Dragon King to sense her—to sense that she had been intended as a sacrifice to him.

Danovich stood beside Hellboy, his arm in a sling made of torn strips of his shirt. The engineer's arm was broken, but the man was tough as nails. He and Hellboy had been checking on everyone else for nearly half an hour. Hellboy was amazed that the death toll had not been worse. There were injuries, people with scrapes and bumps from tumbling rocks and earth, but mostly they were not serious.

"Time to leave all this," Hellboy said.

"What about Trent?" Danovich asked.

"Wherever he is, he's not going anywhere."

The engineer flinched. "That's cold."

Hellboy shrugged. "He may still be alive down there. But that dragon could come back anytime. We've got to get the injured treated and find some kind of shelter. Redfield and Meaney won't be back with the chopper—and our friendly Mr. Lao—until morning at least, and trying to evacuate people that way will take forever. We need to figure out how to fight this thing."

"Fight it? Fight the damn Dragon King?"

"You got a better idea?"

Danovich didn't.

They started down from the ridge. Some of the tent fires had been put out, salvaging part of the camp, but many of them had burned to the ground. In places, all that remained of tents were the bottom edges, strung from one stake to the next, still burning. In the moonlight, the flickering of those flames seemed unearthly. To Hellboy, it looked like a battlefield, and they were the army that had lost the war.

The Dragon King, he could handle. The trouble was going to be keeping the big worm from killing anyone else in the meantime.

The sky filled with a shushing noise. Hellboy and Danovich exchanged a glance. Then Hellboy left the engineer behind, running down the slope toward what remained of the camp.

"Cover!" he bellowed. "Everyone take cover! Don't let it see that the job isn't done!"

As they scattered, some into the tents that remained intact and others behind rocky outcroppings or beneath equipment, trunks, and blankets that had been salvaged, Hellboy stopped to stare upward. The red stripe of the dragon's belly coiled across the sky above him, silhouetted against the yellow flesh of its body. He thought of the dead and the injured and of the way his father had felt dead when Hellboy took the old man into his arms.

He drew his gun, raised it high, and pulled the trigger once, twice, a third time. Hellboy could have sworn at least two of the bullets punched into the

Dragon King's belly, but the worm was so swift that there was no time for a fourth shot. It swept across the sky above the ruined camp and hit the surface of the lake. The water roiled around it, and the Dragon King dived, vanishing beneath the surface. Small waves rolled out from the place it had gone under, but the dragon was gone.

Forty feet from where he stood, Abe Sapien knelt beside the expedition's M.D., Ellie Morris, while the two of them helped treat a burn victim who lay on a thick blanket.

"Abe!" Hellboy shouted, running toward him even as he holstered his gun.

The amphibious man stood and turned toward him.

"Go! Get in the water, now!" Hellboy barked at him. "You've gotta go after the dragon."

The fin ridges on Abe's neck rippled as though in a strong breeze, and he regarded Hellboy oddly. "Did you suffer some kind of head trauma?"

Hellboy skidded to a halt in front of him, staring down intently. "I'm not screwing around, Abe. Go after it. Now. I don't want you to fight it. Just track it. Figure out where its lair is down there. Without that, all we're doing is sitting here waiting for it to come back and kill us."

Abe cursed at the logic, turned, and ran swiftly but awkwardly toward the water.

The water did not soothe him. Abe Sapien knifed beneath the roiling surface of the lake, the water unnaturally hot. It slid across his flesh with the clinging film of mercury. Given a choice, he would have swum for shore, but he had a job to do.

He kicked and swam with all of his strength, propelling himself as swiftly as he could in pursuit of the great serpent. In the darkness of the deep lake bottom, he could barely make out the tail of the dragon whipping back and forth ahead of him. Its yellow scales gleamed only a little this far under water, at night. Instead, Abe relied upon the displacement of water, the disturbance of the Dragon King's passing, and the heat it generated to guide him.

The dragon sped up, swimming so powerfully that Abe felt himself caught and pulled along in its wake. He had to fight to keep from tumbling end over end in the water, and the Dragon King pulled ahead.

Alarm rippled through Abe. If he lost the thing's trail long enough for it to enter its lair unseen, his pursuit would be for nothing. Desperation raced in his blood, adrenaline surging. He gritted his teeth and swam harder, gills pulsing.

In his mind's eye he saw images of the Dragon King bursting from the lake in a spray of fire and water, saw the tents burning and the fear in Professor Bruttenholm's eyes as the old man had choked on the smoke and stared at the fire spreading along his arm.

A flash of yellow flickered through the water ahead—too close—and Abe drew back quickly. Somehow he'd caught up, and the terror of the Dragon

King's nearness struck him. Catching up to the dragon was the very last thing he wanted to do.

What are you thinking, coming down here after it?

But even as the thought struck him, he pushed it away—pushed away all fear and hesitation, and the knowledge that this flying, burning engine of destruction was way out of his league, and maybe out of Hellboy's as well. They needed way more firepower than they'd brought up here, to the top of the world.

And what about when they got that firepower? The only way to destroy the Dragon King or seal him under the lake again was to figure out where he'd been sleeping and how he got out.

He darted through the water again, redoubling his efforts. The heat and wake of the dragon's passing was simple enough to follow, but it would fade if he slowed down any further. Abe's heart thundered with the effort as he struggled to catch up with the Dragon King. Even as he did, he scanned the dark smoothness of the lake bottom, the soft, shifting, almost featureless terrain. There was so little plant life that the fish population of the lake was also quite small. But he had searched the lake twice already, by night, then by day, and he had seen nowhere that the dragon could have hibernated.

Yet he had come from the water, so there had to be an answer down here somewhere.

Long seconds of frantic swimming went by before Abe felt the real pull of the dragon's wake again, then he saw the flash of its yellow hide up ahead. This time Abe did not slow down. The dragon slithered upward and darted down again. Abe swam too close and nearly collided with the serpent as it twisted toward the lake bottom, eagle talons pulled up tight to its body.

Abe treaded water, eyes wide, peering into the gloom ahead. Where was the dragon going? It darted toward a place where the sandy bottom gave way to the rocky basin of the lake, sloping upward toward the surface. There was a cloudburst underwater, dirt swirling in the lake, and when it had sifted down enough Abe stared in astonishment.

The dragon was gone.

Heart racing, he swam toward the place where he had last seen the Dragon King. The water began to clear, the wake to diminish, and Abe saw that between the slope on the side of the lake and the sandy bottom, there was a dark crevice. An orange glow of fire flickered once in that darkness, then it was gone.

He felt positive the crevice had not been there before. He would have seen it. Somehow the rumbling underground had shifted the lake bottom, releasing the dragon. Or perhaps the dragon could have come out whenever it wanted, and it had made the exit itself. As Abe swam toward it, a chill went through him.

The loose soil of the bottom was sifting into the darkness of that crevice, spilling away into nothingness. Abe wanted to know what was down there, in the gloom, but trying to find out alone would be foolish. Hellboy had asked him to find out where the dragon went, and he'd done that.

If Abe went down there after the Dragon King, he wanted to make sure he knew how to kill it. In his time with the BPRD, he'd learned such things were never simple. Killing a legend was difficult business.

The breeze off the lake made Professor Bruttenholm shiver. To feel cold in the aftermath of the dragon's inferno cut him with the bitterest of irony. Even the burn on his left forearm no longer felt hot. It stung and pulsed, but the pain made him shiver, as though the flesh had been frozen instead of seared.

"You still with me, Professor?" Sarah Rhys-Howard asked.

Bruttenholm blinked and smiled up at her. "No more chest pains, my dear. And whatever knock I took to the head doesn't seem to have addled my brains any worse than they already were."

He hissed through his teeth as she moved his arm and tried not to wince. "That, however, is quite painful."

"I'd imagine," Sarah replied. Moonlight and the dim glow of the small fires that still burned limned her with an angelic light.

But she was an agent of the BPRD, not some angel of mercy. Sarah had cut away the sleeve of his jacket and shirt, and now she held his arm steady as she pulled bits of burned cloth away from the seared flesh. Bruttenholm hissed through his teeth. Sarah was not a doctor or nurse; she did not spare him so much as an apologetic glance. Though she had medical training, she was a field operative for the BPRD, and bedside manner was not her forte. She had retrieved her medical kit from the tent she'd been sharing with Agent Meaney, who was still off with Redfield, bringing help back from Lhasa, and now she squirted an antibiotic ointment onto the second-degree burn on his arm and began to bandage it.

"You were quite fortunate, really."

"I'm aware of that," he replied.

Sarah frowned and glanced at him, then surveyed their surroundings. Smoke still rose from the ruined camp, and tiny flames still lingered in places. Two people had been burned to death. Several others were badly injured, including one young man who might well wish he had died by the time real assistance arrived or he expired from complications due to the severity of his burns.

Anastasia's team had Ellie Morris. Every major archaeological expedition had a doctor on staff, but Ellie served double duty as both archaeologist and medic. Neil Pinborough had given them a report on the condition of the camp, the wounded and dead, and his admiration for the way the woman was dealing with the crisis had been evident. Then Bruttenholm had sent Neil off to lend a hand. There were lives to save.

The dig had come to a disastrous conclusion, and now their only concern was getting everyone away from Lake Tashi before the Dragon King resurfaced.

"There you are. That's you, done," Sarah said, standing up and brushing herself off.

Bruttenholm glanced at the bandaged arm. The burns sang with pain, but already it had begun to recede to a throbbing ache, thanks to the topical anesthetic she'd used with the antibiotic. There would be other painkillers to come, he was sure. But not yet. He needed his mind clear.

"Thank you, Sarah."

She nodded. "Not at all, Professor. "You've got a plan, I take it?"

"Not a good one," Bruttenholm replied. "Would be a damn sight better if we didn't still have a day or two yet before reinforcements arrive. For now, we'll simply—"

He caught sight of Hellboy, and all thoughts left his mind. Professor Bruttenholm had barely been aware of how worried he was until that very moment. Now, as Hellboy and Anastasia strode toward him across the remnants of the archaeologists' camp, a grim satisfaction filled him. When Hellboy had run off after the dragon as it made its return, firing his ridiculously enormous pistol, Bruttenholm had feared he would do something foolish—something that would cost his life. But, no, Hellboy was fine. Others had died, but not his son. It was dreadfully selfish, but he was only human.

Sarah turned toward the new arrivals.

"The dragon's back in the water?" Sarah asked.

Hellboy nodded toward his father in greeting, then turned to Agent Rhys-Howard. "Yeah. For now. I sent Abe down after it. If we're going to deal with this thing, we're gonna need to know where it's hiding out."

"You sent Abe?" Professor Bruttenholm asked, aware how cross he sounded. The searing pain in his arm grew worse.

"I know you're field leader, but you were off the board. Command decision."

"I see." Bruttenholm narrowed his eyes. "And has Abe returned yet?"

Hellboy met him with a slitted gaze that was almost a mirror of Bruttenholm's own. "Not yet. But he will. I see you're feeling better."

"Quite a bit, thanks to Sarah, here."

"How bad is the burn?" Hellboy asked her.

Sarah took a breath. "Could be worse. There'll be some scarring, but how noticeable it will be depends on how well it heals."

"What about the rest of the camp?" Bruttenholm asked.

Hellboy's expression darkened. "Redfield better get back from Lhasa quick, and with a full fuel tank. We need to get the injured out of here and get Kora as far away as possible."

As he spoke, Anastasia watched him. Her heart

must have been broken over the deaths of her team members and her friends, and the ruinous end to her expedition. But she gazed at him with such tenderness in her eyes that Professor Bruttenholm could not help being touched.

"The injured and the girl first," Sarah replied, "but we need to get *everyone* out of here."

"What we need is to kick the crap out of that dragon, put him back where he belongs," Hellboy said.

Bruttenholm grimaced. "It's never easy to put the genie back into the bottle. I suspect it won't be as simple as having superior firepower. Even if it were, I doubt the cavalry will arrive with rocket launchers and tanks. Assault weapons are not going to stop the Dragon King."

"It'd be a start," Hellboy said.

"Too right," Anastasia said bitterly. "But I agree with Sarah. The sooner we remove everyone from the area, the better."

"On that, my dear, we are all agreed," Professor Bruttenholm said.

Anastasia's expression remained grim, and she did not respond. After their last conversation, the professor could not blame her. Seeing her with Hellboy—witnessing for himself the way she obviously still felt about him—he felt regretful.

"Dr. Bransfield," he said.

Her brows knitted as she regarded him coolly. "Professor?"

"My behavior earlier was boorish and inexcusable. I'm an old man, and sometimes I come to believe my age allows me to speak with candor that I later regret."

She blinked, obviously startled, then tried to brush the words away. "It's fine. Really."

"No. It isn't at all fine. Regardless of my feelings, I have no right to meddle. I dislike viewing myself as a troublesome old crank. Please accept my apologies."

Anastasia smiled softly. "Of course, Professor. I do. Thank you."

He allowed himself a moment of contentment, nodding at the woman, then he glanced at Hellboy and Sarah.

"All right, then. All the injured will be prepared to travel to Lhasa. We'll give Mister Redfield a brief respite upon his return, then he'll have to fly again. Sarah, I'll want our entire team here on the ground, so Ellie Morris will have to travel with the wounded on the helicopter."

She nodded.

Bruttenholm went on. "Dr. Bransfield, you'll need to break camp. Anything that can be salvaged should be packed up and ready to move. In your survey of the area, did you locate any caves or other structures nearby to which we can retreat until help arrives?"

Anastasia glanced up at the ruin of the dig. "There are caves on the other side of the lake, but given what we've just seen, I think going inside of them would be a spectacularly bad idea. There is an abandoned monastery not far—"

"It'll have to do," the professor said. "Hellboy, talk to Anastasia, and to Professor Kyichu about what he read on the inside of the preparatory chamber. If there's a clue in the legend of the Dragon King about how to destroy it, or at least to defeat it, we need to know. And we must all gather whatever weapons we can find. Fighting the dragon may be useless, but we must make the attempt."

Bruttenholm had been sitting at the base of the slope that led up to the archaeological dig, in the same place Hellboy had left him after Abe had pulled him from the burning tent. Now, from the darkness of the slope above their heads, came a sibilant whisper.

Hellboy drew his pistol and aimed it at a scattering of large rocks on the slope. His tail swayed behind him, and his huge right hand clenched and unclenched.

"Who goes there?" he demanded.

Bruttenholm heard a hiss and narrowed his eyes until he could make out a figure among the rocks, perched at an angle, head downward. Twin candles of flame flickered to life, and as the figure moved, he saw that it was one of the dragon-men.

"Koh?" Anastasia asked.

Hellboy glanced at Anastasia and nodded. "Get Tenzin."

She turned and ran toward the makeshift camp,

calling Tenzin's name. The professor and Hellboy and the dragon-man, Koh, all stared at one another. Koh must have realized what they were all waiting for. Less than a minute after she'd departed, Anastasia appeared once more, walking toward them with the guide and translator, Tenzin, following behind.

Tenzin did not flinch at the sight of Koh, clinging to the ridge above their heads. He knew precisely why he had been summoned. Before anyone could ask it of him, he began speaking to the dragon-man. Agitated, Koh pointed to Hellboy and rattled off angry words.

"His village is destroyed," Tenzin translated. "His father is dead, burned before his eyes. At least half of the villagers are dead."

Tenzin's voice rasped as he repeated this horrid news. Though Koh spoke no English, the anguish in the dragon-man's voice was terrible to hear, in any language.

Hellboy slid his gun back into its holster. He shook his head slowly. "I couldn't stop it. I know I said I'd take responsibility, but I never thought—"

Tenzin began to translate.

Koh dropped to the ground, landing in a crouch among them. Sarah moved protectively to Bruttenholm's side. Anastasia took a step back. Tenzin glared at the dragon-man. But Koh paid no attention to any of them. His focus was entirely on Hellboy.

Koh spoke again, and Tenzin quickly translated.

"Those of us who survive will hold you to your

vow. To take responsibility, as you swore you would, there is only one thing you can do. You must destroy the Dragon King."

Professor Bruttenholm saw the tension in Hellboy deflate.

"Yeah. We're on the same page, there. We were just talking about that. I don't plan to leave without making sure the dragon isn't going to bother anyone else. The way it sounded in the legend, he'd just keep traveling farther and farther to get what he wanted—mainly, death and destruction and human flesh."

When Tenzin had translated, Koh shook his head, frowning.

"The Dragon King wants fear and worship," Anastasia said.

Sarah laughed softly, without amusement. "Well, he's got step one all sorted."

Hellboy stared at Koh. "If you have any ideas on how to take him down, chime in anytime."

Koh's fiery eyes widened as Tenzin repeated the words in his own language. He said something quick, his expression grave.

"What was that?" Sarah asked.

"The only one who was ever able to defeat the Dragon King was Dwenjue," Tenzin said.

Professor Bruttenholm frowned. "Even if we presume that because the Dragon King exists, the rest of the legend must be true, Dwenjue lived many centuries ago."

"According to the story, Dwenjue disguised himself as a child and had the villagers throw him into the lake," Anastasia said. "He fought the dragon for seven days and seven nights before slaying it . . . or, at least, mortally wounding it and trapping it beneath the lake."

"Yeah," Hellboy added, "that's not exactly helpful. Dead, dwarf, warrior monk isn't going to show up to save the day this time."

Koh crossed his arms defiantly.

"Are you quite sure of that?" Tenzin asked.

Bruttenholm stared at him. "Do you mean to say that Dwenjue is still alive?"

Tenzin asked Koh the question.

The man with dragon blood gestured toward the lake.

As he spoke, Tenzin gave voice to his words. "The Dragon King still lives," he said. "I do not know if Dwenjue is still alive, but the legend says that if the king rises, the monk will also return to battle him."

"So where is he?" Sarah asked, a bit snide.

Once more, Tenzin translated the question. Koh pointed to the east and replied.

"He says that he can guide us to the place where he is buried," Tenzin said.

"His corpse isn't going to do us much good," Hellboy replied.

But Anastasia's eyes were bright with hope. "We're living a legend, now. A myth has come to life around us. It seems only sensible to me that to destroy one bit of legend, we'll need another, even if it's Dwenjue's bones for daggers."

Professor Bruttenholm raised an eyebrow.

Hellboy reached out to take Anastasia's hand. "Anyone ever tell you, you've got a way with words?"

CHAPTER 10

Deep within the underwater crevice where the Dragon King had gone, an orange glow flickered like torchlight in a dark cave. Abe floated at the opening of that crevice and tried to make sense of it all. Did this lead to some kind of extension of the lake that stretched beneath the plateau around it, or were there pockets of open space beneath the bottom of the lake itself?

Abe swam away from the crevice—from that glow and the growing heat that emanated from it—and looked around in the darkness. His wide eyes went even wider as he turned the questions over and over in his mind. He flipped in the water and swam for the loose soil of the lake bottom. Rare vegetation wavered in the gentle eddying of the water. Abe wrapped a hand around the nearest stalk of that plant and pulled. It came away from the soil with only the lightest tug. Its roots had nothing in which to anchor.

The soil had been sliding into the open crevice where the dragon had hidden away. Now Abe touched the bottom of the lake, plunged his right hand in deeply. It felt like beach—like sand.

His fist broke through a kind of crust, and a hole appeared in the lake bottom. Sandy soil began to spill down into the hole, just as it had into the crevice entrance to the dragon's lair.

Abe pulled back, swimming in place, gills pulsing as he stared into the gloom, trying to make sense of the impossible geography of Lake Tashi. Beneath the bottom, there definitely existed some kind of underwater cavern, perhaps an entire warren of caverns. The Dragon King must have lingered in some kind of suspended animation there. A shiver went through Abe. He, himself, had been discovered in similar circumstances—though in a glass chamber in the basement of an old building rather than in some ancient, subterranean den.

As Abe hovered in the water, the hole he'd made quickly filled in, and in moments there was no trace of it. He glanced over at the crevice, and the glow from within seemed brighter to him now, the furnace in the heart of the lake burning stronger.

Only then did he feel the change in temperature.

The water had gotten hotter, just in the past few minutes. He wondered how hot it would get.

Troubled, Abe swam back the way he'd come. The dragon had inflicted horror upon the camp. His help would be needed. And he had to think about what he'd seen, and its implications. How many hollow caverns were down here? Lake Tashi was huge.

As he swam toward the far shore, where the ruined camp and the excavation of the city of the Dragon King lay, he slowly surfaced, waiting for the water to grow cool again. But though the temperature was not as hot as it had been near that crevice, the water did not feel cool anywhere. The temperature had risen all through the lake.

When he reached the shore, Abe climbed out of the water and stood for a moment, just taking in the awful scene. Perhaps half a dozen tents remained standing, but those were being taken down by members of Anastasia's team. Hellboy worked with them. Perhaps fifty yards from the camp, what appeared to be a makeshift field hospital had been set up. It consisted of blankets and cots dragged from tents. Those with burns lay on those cots or on the ground, being attended to by the uninjured.

All around this triage area, salvaged supplies had been haphazardly stacked and lined up, and even as Abe started up the shore toward the embers of the camp, the expedition team raced around, rescuing what other supplies they could and preparing to evac as soon as possible.

But Abe's flesh was still warm from the lake water, and he knew that it would only be getting hotter. If they were going to evacuate the area, it had better be soon.

Almost as if summoned by this thought, the distant sound of a helicopter reached him, and he turned to see the long black chopper they'd arrived in, flying low over the surface of the lake.

Redfield had returned. But he wasn't alone. Two more helicopters came over the horizon, falling into formation behind the first, and almost identical to it. The trio buzzed across Lake Tashi toward camp.

Apparently, Redfield had brought help. Or Mr. Lao had. It was too early for the BPRD reinforcements to have arrived, and that worried Abe more than a little. The Chinese government had welcomed the BPRD to Tibet—a land where their dominion was always in question—and given them carte blanche to conduct an investigation. But in crisis, Abe had a feeling that the balance of power was about to shift.

Redfield made a pass over the camp, staring down at the burned remains of the tents. There'd been a volleyball net set up in the midst of camp, and whatever plastic materials it was made of were still on fire, flames flickering along the net.

"Christ," the pilot muttered. "What the hell happened here?"

He could see injured people gathered in one place, others running around frantically, and he could feel their panic and urgency. Whatever had done this, the expedition team obviously was afraid that it was going to come back.

"Agent Meaney," Redfield said. "You seeing this?"

"Check," the burly orange-haired field operative

said from the rear of the chopper. Redfield glanced over his shoulder and saw that the man was staring out a side window.

"Looks like we've got our work cut out for us," Redfield said.

He glanced sidelong at the black-suited Mr. Lao, expecting at the very least some kind of surprise on the man's face. Instead, he only looked angry. Lao had been swift and decisive in Lhasa. When the BPRD team had arrived, Lao had been waiting on a helipad at the airport with this helicopter, courtesy of Beijing. They'd landed on the same helipad tonight and had been met within minutes by other men in dark suits. The helicopter had been refueled while Lao spoke to a pair of his colleagues, men who seemed simultaneously to speak with him and on their mobile phones.

Before that conversation was over—before the fueling was complete—nearly thirty men and women in black jumpsuits without insignia or identification marched onto the helipad and stood at attention, awaiting instructions. Redfield hadn't liked the way things were going, but he didn't have any kind of authority to argue about it.

He'd figured Lao's blacksuits would head up to Nakchu village and deal with the half-human, half-dragon people there. Redfield had done covert ops before he came to work for the BPRD, and he could imagine some pretty horrible outcomes for the half-breeds of Nakchu. The blacksuits might just take the guys who'd murdered Dr. Conrad and the others at the dig site, but Redfield had a feeling it would be more than that. Sure, some of the villagers would be kept for study, but the others would be eradicated. The whole place would likely be destroyed—erased from the face of the earth.

Governments did that sort of thing every day. And if his own government did it—he'd seen such atrocities with his own eyes—he couldn't expect the communist, oppressive government of China to behave any differently. There was a reason the jumpsuits on Lao's soldiers didn't have any insignia on them.

Now, as Redfield brought the helicopter down on a stretch of lakeshore a hundred yards from the ruined camp, he knew that everything had changed. The other two helicopters circled above them, awaiting orders. The plan had been for them to fly on to Nakchu village, but apparently the devastation at the expedition camp had given them pause.

Lao's smooth forehead creased as he reached out and grabbed the headset from Redfield and slipped it on. He started barking orders in Chinese. Immediately the two helicopters drew away from the lake, noses dipping as they ascended, buzzing northward.

"What are you doing?" Redfield snapped. "These people need help. Didn't you see the injured down there? We'll need more than one chopper to evac them to Lhasa."

Mr. Lao glanced at him without expression. The

rotors began to slow. The helicopter almost seemed to sigh as it settled down fully on the lakeshore. Lao popped open his door, dropped from the chopper, and started toward the remains of the camp.

"What's that creepy little shit up to?" Meaney muttered from the rear of the helicopter.

Redfield shook his head in disgust. "He ordered his spook troops to take the village, to continue with their mission. Son of a bitch just prioritized that over the lives of our wounded."

Meaney poked his head up from the back. "You speak Chinese?"

The pilot shrugged. "You pick things up over the years."

Anastasia stared at Han Kyichu. "You can't be serious."

The professor's white hair was wild, and he had scorch marks on his jacket where fire had singed the fabric. Dark soot streaked his face, probably where he'd touched his cheeks after handling some of the partially blackened equipment trunks or strips of tent that had to be stomped out. She thought she'd seen him helping to carry buckets of water up from the lake in an impromptu fire brigade that had included his daughter, Kora.

Now, though, the hard work was over. The only business left to attend to was getting the hell out of here. At least as far as Anastasia was concerned. Professor Kyichu had other ideas.

"Of course I am serious." He spread his hands to indicate the lake and the mountains around them. "I would ask you the same question, Anastasia. Are you serious about abandoning all of this? We have found the city of the Dragon King. The temple must be here somewhere as well. We have proven the existence of a myth! Dragons are quite real. Anthropologists must be brought to the dig as well. And biologists. Don't you think they will want to study the children of dragons and humanity?"

Anastasia whipped off her Yankees cap and shook her head. She stared at Professor Kyichu in horror. "I don't think they'll want to be burned to death, or eaten! People are dead, Han. The dragon is gone, but only for a moment. You cannot possibly think anyone will sanction the continued presence of an expedition or any excavation work on this plateau until the damned dragon is dealt with."

Pushing his hands through his white hair, the man glared at her. "Listen to yourself, Stacie. How can you suggest that we leave all of this unattended? We can take precautions, build shelters. Are you really going to surrender your claim on this discovery? The museum will certainly want you to follow through. Think of the paper we can present on this. It's a discovery unlike any other. It may be the single most important archaeological discovery of the twentieth century."

Ice gripped her heart and she gaped at him, sorrow embracing her. "My responsibility is to the members of this expedition, Professor. Yourself included. Perhaps you're in shock. Otherwise, I'd have to say that you're delusional. The museum would never condone my leaving any sort of team in place here as long as the threat to their lives was so significant. Too many have died already. They were my responsibility, don't you see?"

Professor Kyichu narrowed his eyes. "All I see is a woman without the courage to be great. No one would have believed this, but we believed, Stacie. We were right!"

"And I wish to God we hadn't been! What is wrong with you? Christ, Han, what about Kora? You're going to keep your daughter here, knowing that the Nakchu people will throw her in the lake if they've got a chance, never mind the danger she's in from the bloody Dragon King every moment she remains here?"

The older man flinched as though she'd struck him.

"I would never knowingly put my daughter in danger," Professor Kyichu said. "All of the injured are going to Lhasa. Ellie Morris is going to doctor them on the way. I've already asked her to look after Kora until I can join them there, or the trouble is finished here."

"Oh, you've asked her, have you? Well, it isn't your call. It's mine. You work for me, remember?"

The professor gave her a hard look. "If that's the

way you feel, I've no choice. I resign. But I'll stay here, and the dig becomes mine."

"The Chinese will never allow it."

"I'm willing to take that chance. I'd think they'd want someone with an archaeological background on-site while they deal with this. I suspect there'll be no defeating the dragon without at least some knowledge of the worship that went on here."

Anger simmered in her, even worse because on that point, Anastasia knew he was right. The Chinese would want someone to remain. She wondered if the BPRD would be allowed to help, to consult on the matter. And then she saw the end of this conversation.

"They'll keep Hellboy and the other people from the BPRD around. This is their sort of disaster, isn't it? I doubt they'll need your advice, Han. Particularly as they'll have mine."

"You can't keep me from staying, Stacie."

"You arrogant, self-serving bastard. You'd just abandon your daughter in the midst of this, after the trauma she's been through?"

Fury erupted on his face. His cheeks reddened, and when he spoke, nearly spitting, his hair fell across his eyes. "That will be enough insults. This is for Kora. Everything I do is my legacy for her. My career will be assured for the rest of my days based on this expedition. Lectures alone will support us. I'll write a book, and she'll have the proceeds long after I'm gone. The whole world will know us, Stacie, if you'd only be logical."

Disgust rippled through her. "The whole world. Fame, eh? That's what you're really after? I thought I knew you, Han. I thought we were friends. But you stand here with the dead and the dying around you, and you want to feed more victims to the dragon, throw your own life away on a gamble."

She sighed. "You're right. If Ellie will take Kora, there's nothing I can do to force you to leave. Your resignation is accepted."

Triumphant, he nodded. "Thank you."

"Don't thank me. This dig is still being run by the British Museum in conjunction with Beijing. You're banned from participating in the dig or going anywhere near the site until I or the Chinese government says otherwise."

He stared at her. "You wouldn't."

"I have. We'll be moving everyone not on the first helicopter out of here to the old monastery east of here. You're welcome to come along. Otherwise, take one of the undamaged tents and stay here. Just don't go anywhere near the dig."

Anastasia spun on her heel and strode away from him without another moment's hesitation. More than anything, she felt sad for Kora Kyichu, to have a father who cared so much more about a chance at fame than his own daughter's well-being.

The dead had been wrapped in scraps of charred tent. The first evacuation flight to Lhasa had to carry the injured. As she walked toward the black chopper, she saw them being loaded onboard. Frank Danovich—broken arm in a sling—was supervising the process with Ellie Morris, shouting to those who were helping, including the three ordinary BPRD field operatives, and the pilot, Redfield.

Hellboy, Abe, and Professor Bruttenholm, meanwhile, stood twenty feet away from the helicopter with Mr. Lao, having a very loud conversation. Koh was with the group, but hung back, just listening.

Anastasia marched toward them. Her talk with Han Kyichu had primed her for a fight, and nobody deserved her ire right now more than Mr. Lao.

Ordinary people—solid citizens—would have seen the lightning on the horizon and been heartened by the knowledge that dawn was on the way. The monsters came out at night, after all, and truly bad things don't happen with the sun high in the sky.

Hellboy didn't buy into any of that crap. He'd seen way too much evidence to the contrary. Government flunkies like Mr. Lao, for instance, did all of their best work during the daylight hours.

"You are entitled to make any complaint you wish to my superiors," Mr. Lao said, standing stiffly on the rough lakeshore, where the ground began to slope upward toward the ruined ridge above them. "Through proper channels, of course."

Hellboy crossed his arms, glaring at the insidious, pompous little bastard. Crossing his arms was good—

it helped him fight the urge to pop Lao's head off like a black-suited Pez dispenser.

Abe stood on Hellboy's left and glanced at him from time to time as though afraid he might have to stop Hellboy from doing that very thing. Koh lingered behind them, slinking angrily back and forth like a guard dog waiting for the command to kill.

Professor Bruttenholm didn't hang back at all. He was the field leader of this investigation, and right about now Hellboy felt pretty pleased about that. The old man looked furious. For a moment, Lao seemed like his feathers were getting ruffled. Hellboy liked that. If they could rattle his cage, that would be a good start.

"Those helicopters should be back here, Mister Lao," Professor Bruttenholm said. With his white hair wild, the man looked a bit crazed and even more formidable than ever. He held his burned, bandaged arm down at his side.

"That is not their purpose, Professor," the man from Beijing replied.

Bruttenholm glared. "With those additional helicopters, we could evacuate almost everyone to Lhasa in a single trip, not only the injured. Every moment these people remain here, they are in danger. Rather than oppressing the local populace, your troops ought to be here keeping an eye on the ruins and preparing to battle the dragon when it surfaces."

"We're going to need weapons to destroy the big

worm," Hellboy said, as if he were speaking to a child. He couldn't help himself. "Much as I'd like to just knock it unconscious, I don't think it's going to be that easy."

As he spoke, Stasia walked up, and he saw his own anger reflected in her expression. She stood beside him, her hand brushing his, but they didn't bother with any other greeting. They were unified in their disgust with Lao.

"There will be weapons. I have already reported these new developments to my superiors. More soldiers will arrive with the other representatives from your own organization. Your expertise will be utilized and appreciated—"

"Would you listen to yourself talk," Hellboy interrupted. "You're like a robot out of some lame sixties sci-fi show."

Lao flinched, and his expression hardened. Hellboy liked that.

"Your people are doing an admirable job evacuating the injured," Lao said. "At this time, the peacekeepers I brought from Lhasa must make Nakchu village their first priority."

"Peacekeepers!" Stasia sneered.

"We follow the Western example from time to time," Lao replied.

Abe put one hand on the butt of the gun he'd started carrying ever since surfacing from the lake.

"The village is already destroyed, you idiot."

Hellboy put up a cautionary hand. "Come on, Abe. Don't call the jackass names."

But there wasn't even time for the insult to sink in before he saw motion out of the corner of his eye. Stasia saw it too, and started to turn. But the dragon-men were swift. Koh lunged past her, transforming in midleap, crocodile jaws gnashing and fire spitting from his eyes as he reached for Mr. Lao.

Lao screamed.

Hellboy liked it.

But he knew that Lao dead would only mean some other heartless prick in his place. He snatched Koh out of the air, turned, and hurled him back the way he'd come.

The dragon-man hit the ground rolling and came up almost instantly, hissing and advancing again. He ignored Hellboy and the others, focused solely on Lao, speaking rapidly, spitting venom with each word.

"What's he saying?" Hellboy snapped at Lao.

The man from Beijing smoothed his suit, staring at the advancing Koh warily. "He says there are only forty-two left alive in his village. Keep him away from me, or there will be only forty-one."

Professor Bruttenholm moved toward Koh, his hands raised. "Be calm, my friend. We have only one enemy here."

Stasia laughed softly. "Right. Just not quite certain if it's the dragon or the snake here in front of us."

"No harm will come to the villagers," Mr. Lao said.

"They will be held at Nakchu while an investigation takes place. Your friend, Koh, will have to return there as well and await the results of our investigation."

Abe stepped up beside Koh. "That's not going to happen."

Hellboy glared at Mr. Lao. "Come on, even you don't believe we'll go for that. You want an international incident, and all the worldwide media coverage that comes with it? Push us. Let's see how that works out for you."

Mr. Lao smiled thinly, but before he could reply, Professor Bruttenholm cleared his throat.

"What you fail to realize, Mister Lao," the old man said, "is that if you want to defeat the dragon, we are going to need Koh's cooperation. You said yourself that you needed the expertise of the Bureau for Paranormal Research and Defense. You do. Of course, if you'd prefer we leave you and your 'peacekeepers' to deal with the Dragon King yourselves, we'd be happy to do that."

The smile left Lao's face. "You have a plan to destroy the creature?"

Hellboy glared at him. "Yeah, well, some of us are actually thinking straight."

Stasia shot him a sidelong glance, one corner of her mouth curled up in a smile. Koh moved nearer to Lao, but Abe put a gentle hand on him, and the dragon-man allowed himself to be held back.

The BPRD chopper, with Redfield in the pilot's

seat, lifted off with all of the injured onboard. The downdraft kicked up a cloud of dust, but Hellboy and the others did not turn their gazes away from Mr. Lao.

"We do, indeed, have a plan," Professor Bruttenholm replied. "Until the additional BPRD agents arrive to aid us against the dragon, however, our first priority is the safety of these people. Evacuating them as quickly as possible would speed us along to our goal of dealing with the Dragon King. We cannot wait hours for our pilot to return. Instead, a small team will escort the rest of the expedition to the ancient monastery to the east and hope that the Dragon King will not find them there, or, if he does, that its walls and cellars will protect them. Redfield will make as many trips as necessary to get everyone out of here."

Lao hesitated a moment, then lifted his chin and let out a long breath. He nodded magnanimously.

"I will bring one of my helicopters from Nakchu to aid in the evacuation effort, and half of my soldiers—"

"I thought they were peacekeepers," Abe muttered.

Professor Bruttenholm shot him a withering glance, but Hellboy smiled. Abe only got a chance to say it because Hellboy hadn't spoken up first.

"Half of my peacekeeping unit will be stationed here along with whatever BPRD agents remain to watch over the lake and guard against the creature's return."

"Mighty big of you," Hellboy said.

Stasia glanced at him. "Do you notice he can't say the word 'dragon?'"

Mr. Lao straightened his tie, ignoring them. He stared at Professor Bruttenholm. "If you insist on keeping custody of Koh, you will be held responsible for his actions. I do not think he can be trusted."

Abe cocked his head, studying Lao as though he were an insect. "Then we're even. None of us think that you can be trusted."

"Enough!" the professor said. He nodded to Lao. "I accept full responsibility for Koh's participation in this operation. I do this for your sake, sir. The young man may be our only hope."

Mr. Lao nodded in return, then turned and strode away, toward what remained of the camp. Hellboy, Abe, Stasia, Professor Bruttenholm, and Koh watched him go in silence. For a moment, Hellboy didn't know what the man was up to, but then Lao fished through equipment that had obviously come from his own tent and withdrew a long, black radio. He tested it a moment, then held it up and began to speak in Chinese. The language sounded melodic, even from the lips of this uninspired man.

Beyond him, in the camp, Hellboy spotted Tenzin next to one of the few remaining tents and felt grim satisfaction at knowing Lao would be overheard by someone who spoke his own language.

"Right, then, let's get on with it," Stasia said. She

took her Yankees cap from her back pocket, perched it on her head, and pulled her ponytail through the opening in the back. Her face was streaked with soot, but her eyes were bright and intense.

"Abe, what were you saying about the lake when Lao interrupted us?" Professor Bruttenholm said.

The fins on his neck rippled as though he were underwater, and he glanced at Koh before focusing on the others.

"The water is heating up. And not just a little. It's getting hotter and hotter with every passing minute. Since this is no natural occurrence, there's no way to know how hot it will get, but most of the fish and plant life in the water will be dead soon."

"You were able to follow the dragon?" Stasia asked.

Abe nodded. "I followed it to the far southern end of the lake basin. There's an opening there, where the sandy bottom meets the more solid wall that comes down from the shore. That's where the Dragon King went in. I could still see the fire burning in there when I swam back.

"It gets worse, though. You'll recall I said the soil at the lake bottom was oddly loose. I believe that somehow, it is only a layer of detritus that covers the true bottom of the lake. There are hollows down there. Caverns, perhaps. I am less concerned about the lake's temperature than I am about what lies under it."

"You're thinking more dragons?" Hellboy said.

Professor Bruttenholm ran a hand over his goatee.

"The legend does say that the Dragon King had many dragons who served him."

Stasia touched Hellboy's arm. A dreadful suspicion crept into her eyes.

"Perhaps we've been wrong," she said. "Perhaps the Dragon King's temple has been under the lake all along, flooded and covered over all those years ago."

"That's a pleasant thought," Hellboy said.

Koh hovered around them. He had reverted to his human face at some point, and he wore a frown as he tried to decipher their English. Hellboy glanced across the camp at Tenzin, realizing they'd need the guide to come along if they were going to be able to communicate with Koh.

"Here's an even uglier possibility," Abe said. "What if the one we saw is just one of the worker bees? What if it wasn't the king at all?"

"No," the professor said, "it's much too large to be a servant. Think how vast the caverns beneath the lake would have to be if this was only a small dragon, and the king had yet to be seen. I feel certain this is indeed the Dragon King. The legend suggests it, if nothing else. Still, no doubt we must accept that there could be others down there.

"Abe," he said, turning to the amphibious man, "did you discover anything else?"

"No, Professor."

The old man nodded. "Very well, then. You and I will remain here with what volunteers we might have from Dr. Bransfield's expedition, and however many soldiers Mr. Lao deigns to assign to this detail. Hellboy and Anastasia will take Koh and the guide, Tenzin, with them, and lead the rest of the expedition to the monastery."

Hellboy stretched his back, muscles and bones popping. He felt stiff. A walk would do him good. "Right. And then we go find the grave of the warrior midget."

"Monk," Anastasia corrected.

"Dwarf monk," Hellboy replied.

Professor Bruttenholm sighed. "Yes. The grave of Dwenjue. We'll fight legend with legend. And if that doesn't work—"

"We'll pummel it until it cries for its mommy," Hellboy finished.

"Something like that, yes."

It was late morning when Abe and a visibly exhausted Professor Bruttenholm stood just beyond the scorched remains of the expedition's camp and watched as Hellboy and Anastasia led nearly all of the survivors of the Dragon King's attack along the shore of Lake Tashi, toward the hills to the east and the mountain range beyond. Agent Meaney and Agent Rhys-Howard had gone along to help keep the evacuees organized.

Of the BPRD contingent, only Abe, the professor, and Neil Pinborough remained behind, along with Mr. Lao, Professor Kyichu, and three other members of the archaeologists' team. Those in the exodus carried most of the supplies salvaged from camp. The rest of them waited at the site of the attack for someone to come—BPRD reinforcements, Lao's peacekeepers, or the Dragon King himself.

Abe wondered which would arrive first.

"I do hope they'll be all right," Professor Bruttenholm said, his voice a low, thoughtful rasp.

"They'll be fine," Abe replied. "Hellboy's nothing if not durable. And he won't let any harm come to Anastasia."

The professor cast a brief glance at Abe. "It isn't physical harm that concerns me. It's this thing between them."

Abe blinked, about to speak, then he thought better of it. Instead, he just stood by Professor Bruttenholm, and the two of them watched as Hellboy, Anastasia, Koh, and Tenzin shepherded the frightened and lost away from the scene of the greatest horror of their lives. Hellboy and Anastasia walked close together, linked by some invisible bond.

One way or another, this whole thing was going to end eventually. They had no way of knowing how, or what would happen, but watching the two of them together, Abe understood the professor's concern. The Dragon King might be a threat to all of their lives, but there were graver dangers here than that.

CHAPTER 11

Hellboy felt like a pack mule. He carried backpacks full of food and radio equipment slung over his shoulders, as well as a canvas tent rigged up like a gigantic quiver—but instead of arrows, it was full of shovels and surveying equipment. He gritted his teeth at the weight of the burden but didn't complain. These people had seen their friends burned alive. They were looking to him to protect them. Hellboy wasn't entirely certain he could do that, but he'd try his damnedest, and in the meantime, he had no intention of letting on that he had any doubts.

So he lugged all their crap up the mountain and didn't say a word.

Anastasia was ahead of him on the switchback trail that had been worn into the steep hillside through millennia of footsteps. More than likely, they'd used horses and yaks up here as well, but the archaeological team didn't have any beasts of burden to carry their supplies. They just had their own hands, and Hellboy.

Koh and Tenzin were at the lead of this sorry parade, the dozens of expedition members following them, with Stasia, Sarah Rhys-Howard, and Tim Meaney bringing up the rear. Hellboy came last. He didn't mind. He put the weight of his burden out of his mind just by watching Stasia. She spoke to Sarah from time to time, and the two women were alternately grim, then smiling. He wondered if they were talking about him.

High on the mountainside—it was only a hill in comparison to the white-capped mountain ridges in the distance all around the circumference of the plateau—they continued their climb. Many times they had to rest. Most of the expedition were in excellent physical condition from all the time spent working on digs and traveling, but even they were not prepared for a three-hour hike across such mountainous country. Hellboy didn't like the idea of delaying a moment longer than necessary. He could picture in his mind's eye the infernal horror that would ensue if the Dragon King were to surface again and catch them on the switchback trail, and had to force the image away.

They rested, but he didn't allow them to rest for very long.

Above, he could see the end of the trail, the crest of the hill. Anastasia saw him glancing upward and smiled, dropping back to walk just ahead of him.

"Hello, handsome. You need help with your kit, there?"

"Yeah. Thanks for the offer, now that we're nearly at the top."

Stasia grinned. "I was socializing."

"You two were like a couple of hens."

"Girl talk," she confirmed. The thin air did not seem to bother her at all. The sun shone on her hair, still bright copper red despite the passing years. With all the death and horror around them, she'd never looked more alive.

Hellboy forced himself to turn his gaze away from her.

"What do you think is going to happen now?" Stasia asked.

He looked up, confused for a moment about what she was asking. "We're going to get these people out of here."

"And then?"

With all that he was carrying, it would be too much work to shrug. Instead, he cocked his head. "We cork the hole the Dragon King came out of, or kill it, if that's what it comes to, and if we can."

Anastasia stumbled on the path but caught herself. She took a few more steps before glancing back again.

"What about Dwenjue? You think we're going to find anything?"

Hellboy paused, the exertion getting to him at last. The muscles in his legs ached. His tail dragged on the ground. His hooves kicked up dust, and sometimes the wind eddied it around so he couldn't help breathing it in. Beating up monsters was less work, any day.

"You know better than anyone. No telling what you're going to find when you start digging up old tombs. Story of my life."

As they reached the final switchback, the trail widened enough that they could walk side by side. They'd fallen behind quite a bit. From up above, Hellboy heard Frank Danovich calling down that they'd reached the monastery. The muscles in Hellboy's legs sagged a bit in relief. Almost there.

Stasia walked beside him in silence for several steps. It felt nice—it felt right—having her there, and he let himself enjoy her presence without questioning it or complicating it with too much thought, the way he'd been doing pretty much ever since they'd arrived. For the moment, it was just right.

"When I was a little girl—"

"In pigtails?"

She shot him a comically angry look. "Shush."

"Shushing."

"Just about to say, when I was a girl I thought so much of legend and mythology must have been real, somehow. That there was truth to it. I learned about God in school, and the set of legends that makes up modern religion, which tells us there's nothing to all those old stories. They're rubbish, we're told. But I liked the magic of legend, as a girl. I didn't want to believe in God if it meant I couldn't believe in Zeus and Odin and Kali.

"I grew out of it, of course. Became very serious,

didn't I? Legends must have a source. That much, I knew. So I took it upon myself to discover the origins of legends. Archaeology was my only ambition. I wanted to know what the ancients dreamed about, what they fought about, what they feared. I wanted to know where the legends came from. There'd be weather patterns and great warriors and eclipses and cautionary tales at the genesis of legends, the template that creates a story that is altered by centuries of telling and retelling. The process fascinated me.

"But when I learned, at last, that the little girl I'd been wasn't entirely wrong—that some legends are not only stories, not variations, but *history*—everything changed for me. I love the idea of proving the zealots wrong. Not that God doesn't exist, but that their beliefs aren't the only ones with truth to them."

They reached the top of the trail. Back the way they'd come, the mountainside seemed incredibly steep. Hellboy took thin, reedy breaths. The thin air wouldn't bother him so much once he'd had a moment to rest. At the top of the climb, the members of the expedition were spreading out, dropping down to rest on their packs or their butts or their knees. Nearly all of them were gazing at the astonishing views all around them.

"So close to heaven, up here," Sarah Rhys-Howard said, catching her breath. The woman had to be hard and sharp in her work for the BPRD, but her eyes were wide with wonder and awe.

"The roof of the world," Anastasia replied.

Sarah nodded. Others began to wander the hilltop, getting a better look at the mountain ranges in the distance all around them. Only a handful had even taken note of the ancient monastery a hundred yards from where they stood. It was a squat brown building, well over a thousand years old. In the sun it was the pale color of an adobe hut, with blank, windowless walls that sloped upward from a foundation of wide, ancient brick.

"Not much to look at," Hellboy muttered.

Agent Rhys-Howard glanced at him. "It's shelter. For now, it will have to do."

Stasia slid her arm into Hellboy's smoothly, as if it was the most natural thing in the world. "Don't worry. If Lao is as good as his word, we'll have your man Redfield in his chopper and one of Lao's helicopters up here before the afternoon's half-over. Two trips, and we'll have everyone away from here."

Hellboy didn't reply. The idea of relying on Lao's word didn't sit well with him, but they had no choice.

Sarah and Meaney began to bark orders, prodding and guiding the archaeologists, engineers, and diggers as though they were lost sheep. Frank Danovich started to help out, and the people started moving. They trusted the engineer, who'd stuck around in spite of his broken arm, maybe because he sensed that. With all they'd seen, these people needed someone to trust.

Hellboy stepped away from Anastasia and set down the gear he'd been carrying. Hopefully, the expedition members would retrieve it once they decided where they wanted to set up camp inside the old monastery. If not, he'd carry it inside. For now, he rested, arching his back, stretching his legs and neck.

"You all right?" Stasia asked.

"Fine. You?"

With a groan she set down her pack. "Just need a few minutes before we start grave-hunting."

"Me too." He looked at her, his arm still feeling her touch. "You were right, you know, about legends."

Stasia furrowed her brow. "How so?"

"Seems to me pretty much everything is true, in some fashion. Legends and myths and monsters . . . I run across the real thing all the time. Yeah. Everything is true. Which means it oughta be chaos, right? So how come it always seems to me like there's some kind of order to it all?"

She slid down to the ground and lay back against the pack like she was on her living room floor, watching TV. "Design, you mean? Some kind of divine influence?"

Hellboy cleared his throat—recognizing it as a trait he'd picked up from his father—and shook his head. "Didn't say anything about divine, did I? Yeah, maybe I think there's a design to it all, some kind of answer at the bottom of all these mysteries, if we could just dig down far enough."

Anastasia took off her Yankees cap and pulled out the elastic she'd used to hold her hair in a ponytail. She shook it out and stared at him, troubled.

"I wonder if you're right. If you are, I wonder if anyone could ever decipher that design, if it exists."

Again, Hellboy stretched. He watched Sarah and Meaney checking out the entrance to the monastery, weapons drawn. Meaney went in alone, leaving Sarah with the civilians. He'd be checking the place out for animals or people, though Koh said the place had been empty for centuries, and it looked it.

"Makes my head hurt to think about it," he said.

"You know, you're a legend yourself, now. Or you will be."

Meaney reappeared, and the evacuees started carrying their gear inside the monastery. Hellboy noticed that Koh and Tenzin hung around the entrance. That was good. It was best they not get too comfortable. Tenzin turned and watched him, waiting.

"I don't know. People know I exist. I was on the cover of *Life* way back when. I'm no mystery."

"To a lot of people you are. A big part of the world's population thinks you're a hoax or just a story."

"I'm the bogeyman," Hellboy said.

"Only to the bogeymen," Stasia said, propped on her elbows, her hair spilling around her. In another life, they would've been on a picnic or something. The way she lay there, he could almost imagine it—sandwiches and glasses of wine. Another life.

"So I'm a legend, huh? Guess that means someday, some archaeologist will come along and dig up my bones, try to make sense of what they find."

Stasia stood, brushing off the seat of her trousers, and picked up her pack. She slid it over her shoulder, and when she looked at him, there was a terrible melancholy in her eyes.

"No one will be around to dig you up. You'll probably outlive all of humanity, and archaeology. You'll be the only archaeologist left."

Hellboy stared at her, a terrible weight on his heart. "Wow. You sure know how to cheer a guy up."

She laughed softly. "It's a gift."

Together, they walked toward the monastery, where Tenzin and Koh waited. The time had come to discover whether Dwenjue was more than just a legend.

Clouds had begun to roll across the sky by midafternoon. At first they seemed harmless enough, but soon white wisps gave way to low-slung, ominous black clouds, and it seemed certain a storm would soon arrive. For the moment, however, there was only that electric frisson in the air that preceded a thunderstorm.

Professors Bruttenholm and Kyichu, Agent Pinborough, Mr. Lao, an archaeology student named Corriveau, and a digger called Gibson had created a makeshift camp a few hundred yards from the ravages of the original. The hillside to the north was not quite so steep, here, which provided the illusion that they might make some kind of escape if the Dragon King emerged and set after them.

Absurd, of course. The swiftness of the worm would not allow any escape. If it came after them, their choices were to fight or to die.

Abe Sapien glanced over his shoulder at the men who'd remained behind to watch for the return of the Dragon King. The glance was instinctive—he tried to remain aware of his surroundings at all times. The entire plateau seemed strangely silent to him. Even the wind seemed to have died. The loudest thing he could hear was the sound of his own breathing.

The surface of Lake Tashi reflected the dark, pregnant clouds, the water a depthless stone gray. It ought to have been silver or blue, but Abe imagined it turning red or orange, glowing with fire below. He was not prone to such fancy, but the lake seemed so placid and ordinary that its very calm disturbed him.

At the shore, he paused. Only up close could he see the bit of mist that had begun to rise from the water. His eyes narrowed. Not mist—steam. The heat emanating from the water felt oppressive. A few inches from shore, two dead fish floated and bobbed as the water gently lapped the edge of the lake.

Abe surveyed the surface of the lake again, searching for some ripple in the water that would indicate the presence of something large moving beneath the still water. Images filled his mind of the Dragon King surging upward to snatch him in its jaws, there on the shore. Abe felt grateful that Hellboy had insisted he wear his heavy belt, for there might be something in one of its pouches that could have saved him. The pistol never felt right to him, weighing him down, throwing off his balance—and it wouldn't do him a damn bit of good against the flying serpent they'd all seen during the night—but it might buy him a moment or two. Sometimes a moment was enough.

He crouched by the water. The sulfurous, chemical smell that wafted up from the lake made him wrinkle his nose and gag. Abe cupped a hand over his nose and mouth to try to limit how much of that odor got through. With the other, he reached out to dip his fingers into the water.

Hissing through his teeth, Abe pulled back his hand. It might not be hot enough to boil, but the lake water had seared his fingers. For the first time, he realized that it was not impossible that it would come to a boil, if nothing was done. Already the fish were dying—were probably all dead. Soon what vegetation remained underwater would also be destroyed by the superheating of the lake.

He brought his stinging fingers to his nostrils and inhaled. The power of the scent made his eyes water. Abe blinked and stood up, backing away. He wiped his fingers on the bottom of his jacket and stepped back. When his boot hit a patch of soft soil on the shore, his heel sunk in deeply. Some of the sandy earth slipped away, spilling toward the water, and a small channel formed. Water rushed in to fill the depression.

Abe stared down at the tiny rivulet he'd made with that one step, collapsing part of the shore. The soil seemed to be spilling downward into the lake, like the tiniest avalanche. There had been no further tremors since the one that had harbingered the appearance of the Dragon King, but the lake bottom remained unsteady. Judging by the loose soil on the shore, the situation had worsened.

He backed away, pulse racing. He shook his head and turned, striding quickly toward the half dozen others who'd remained behind with him. Corriveau and Gibson were bent over a map of the region, talking with each other and gesturing from time to time to the ridge where the excavated ruins had been buried once more. Neil Pinborough sat with an assault rifle slung across his shoulder, gripped in both hands, staring at the surface of the lake with total vigilance.

Nearby, Professor Bruttenholm and Professor Kyichu were conducting a conversation with Mr. Lao. The black-suited man showed no sign that their words were even reaching him.

Abe strode over to them.

"Excuse me, Professor," he said to Bruttenholm. "You asked for an update."

"I did. Proceed, Abraham."

Abe glanced at Lao and Kyichu. He'd liked the

linguistics expert at first, but now he wondered. As for Lao, Abe worked with one government agency and didn't trust it overmuch. He certainly wasn't going to trust the secretive, hard-edged lackey of an oppressive government. But Bruttenholm had asked for his report.

So he gave them all an estimate of the water temperature and its probable toxicity.

"I don't think the rising heat is our most significant problem, though," he added.

Professor Bruttenholm frowned at that, reaching up to stroke his goatee. "Elaborate, please."

"The lake bottom is unstable. We know that. I believe it's getting worse. I noticed a strange phenomenon on the shore, soil pouring into the water. I've postulated massive hollows under the lake. What concerns me is the possibility of a sinkhole of some kind. If the ground shifts, the entire plateau could collapse into the earth."

Mr. Lao stared at him, expressionless. Abe knew such things troubled many people, but he could not be intimidated by such tactics. He was virtually expressionless himself.

"You are suggesting a major geological event," Lao said.

"Yeah. That's what I'm suggesting."

Professor Kyichu laughed softly. "You've guessed this by watching a bit of the shore erode into the lake, a natural process that is constant."

"What I saw was not natural. I'm sorry to say it, but the Dragon King may not be the worst fate in store for us. If we stay here, we could be swallowed by the earth itself. Or buried alive by some kind of rockfall."

Kyichu glanced over at the other two remaining members of the archaeological team. "We're not going. We're staying right here until the excavation can be reopened. I'm not allowing anyone else to take credit for finding what I've already discovered."

"You?" Professor Bruttenholm said, alarm lighting his eyes. "Don't you mean your team? Dr. Bransfield is the leader of our expedition. You cannot think to take all of the credit yourself."

"That's not it at all," Kyichu scowled. "I want the credit to remain where it belongs, with those of us who made the discovery, not whoever shows up to scour the land of dangers and lays claim to the artifacts and history that will be found here."

Mr. Lao stared at him, eyes narrowing slightly, betraying the tiniest concern. "Credit where it is due, Professor Kyichu. As long as the artifacts in question remain in the hands of their rightful custodians."

Professor Bruttenholm arched an eyebrow. Abe thought for a moment that he might challenge Lao's ideas about what constituted the rightful custodianship of artifacts from an ancient Tibetan excavation, but then the old man turned his focus to Kyichu.

"Han, I won't attempt to convince you to leave the dig site again—"

"Excellent. It's becoming tiresome," Professor Kyichu replied.

Bruttenholm's nostrils flared in irritation. Abe had studied the man's facial expressions for years. It was one of the reasons he found himself troubled by Lao's almost total lack of such expression.

"I'll only remind you," Professor Bruttenholm went on, "that Kora has suffered a terrible trauma, and now she's been separated from her father so soon afterward. To lose you at this point would be a blow from which she might never recover."

Hatred flashed in Han Kyichu's eyes. "Don't trouble yourself, Trevor. Kora understands what must be done here."

That was when Abe knew that the professor had become truly irrational. He had seemed to love his daughter very much, and been terrified for her, but from the moment the Dragon King had shown himself, Professor Kyichu's priorities had shifted drastically. Abe could not be certain if it was fame or simply the lifelong dream of an archaeologist to discover something significant, but the man had obviously subordinated all other concerns to his need to be associated with this project. His personal safety, and his daughter's well-being, were secondary. Abe had never been accused of callousness but began to feel that Han Kyichu deserved whatever would come next.

"Gentlemen, I think you might not be getting how

much danger we're in with every moment we stay here," Abe told them.

"We're not fools, *creature,*" Lao said dismissively.

Abe bristled. He thought about decking the man. If Hellboy had been there, he probably would have held Lao upside down by one ankle and shaken him, just for amusement.

Professor Bruttenholm flinched as if he'd been slapped. He stepped between them. "You may refer to my associate as Agent Sapien or Mr. Sapien or even Abe—"

"Actually, Mr. Sapien would be fine," Abe interrupted.

Lao held his hands up in apology. "I am sorry. I did not realize the word would offend you. But the sentiment remains. We're well aware of the danger."

Abe had his doubts. Did Lao truly understand that whatever geological changes were taking place might be far more perilous than the Dragon King? But he had issued the warning. As long as the British Museum expedition members were evacuated before anything worse happened, the job was done.

Professor Kyichu, perhaps fuming over the words exchanged with Bruttenholm and the suggestion that he did not have his daughter's best interests at heart, turned and walked over to the student, Corriveau, and the digger, Gibson—the only two foolish enough to stay behind with him.

Abe lost track of the conversation for a moment,

and when he tried to catch up, he found Professor Bruttenholm and Mr. Lao discussing weapons.

"—realize that bullets and even mortar fire will probably not be sufficient to destroy the Dragon King?" Bruttenholm said.

Lao nodded. "Let us hope that your Hellboy is successful in discovering how the beast was defeated the last time it emerged. I have given it some thought, however. There are other sorts of helicopters I could summon if they become necessary. But it would take time to get them here. While we wait, I have another idea, a way that perhaps we might at least slow the serpent down. On the next evacuation trip that our pilots make to Lhasa, I will have them retrieve something that will help us. That is, if you'll allow me to instruct your pilot."

Abe stiffened. He didn't like the sound of that.

But Professor Bruttenholm nodded. "As long as your request doesn't interfere with getting those people out of here, we'll cooperate fully."

Lao smiled. "I thought you might."

Moments later, they heard the rhythmic chop of a helicopter and looked up to see one of the two under Lao's command speeding toward them from the west. Twelve commandos—for that's what they truly were—leaped from the chopper as it set down and rushed toward Lao. They lined up, at attention, until he barked at them in Chinese as though he was embarrassed by their deference. The commandos took up a position in a scattered pattern along the lakeshore, on guard. As if they would do more than annoy the Dragon King.

Lao went to speak to the pilot of the helicopter, presumably about retrieving the British Museum expedition members from the monastery on the eastern hill.

Less than twenty minutes later, Redfield returned from Lhasa, ready for another evacuation run. Abe briefed him on the monastery and the professor's agreement with Lao before Bruttenholm brought the man from Beijing over to speak with the burly, bearded pilot.

Redfield didn't seem to like working with Lao any more than Abe did, but he didn't balk. Abe noticed that the pilot's eyes wandered to the surface of the lake several times while Lao spoke to him. The fourth time, Abe frowned and glanced over to see what kept Redfield so distracted.

The steam off the lake had altered. This was no low mist, but a fogbank of steam in the cold air.

And beneath the surface lurked an orange glow. The fire under the lake had grown, and spread.

Paris, France, 28 February, 1981

Hellboy could never have imagined a more perfect day. Winter had seemed to retreat for the day, and there'd been a hint of spring in the air. Stasia was still bundled up in a thick coat, but several times the sun had shone so strongly down upon them that he had carried it for her, over his arm, like a true gentleman. It felt odd, but also nice.

With Stasia on his arm, he drew longer stares than usual, but somehow found himself better able to ignore them. Together they had sat inside a café along the Seine and gazed alternately at one another and out the window at the river flowing by. The coffee had been heavenly, and the Parisian discourse had gone on around them, talk of politics and art, talk of studies at the Sorbonne and the latest films. Hellboy didn't think he'd ever seen a people who loved to talk more than the French.

Curiously, they seemed unwilling to talk about him while he was in the room. The French had always seemed to welcome him. As he and Anastasia strolled along the river and stopped in dress shops and hat shops for her, people reacted with surprise at the sight of him. Yet they did not look frightened, only fascinated.

This time of year, the street performers and vendors were mostly absent from Paris, even on a day that flirted with spring. Hellboy didn't mind. Wandering along the river and along the boulevards of Paris when so few people were out and about gave the city an intimacy he had only dreamed of. Late in the afternoon, when it grew dark, they stopped in a restaurant, only to find that neither of them was very hungry. Their dinner consisted almost entirely of bread, cheese, and wine.

When they emerged, the City of Light had blossomed into full illumination. The colors were breathtaking along the Boulevard Saint Germain, and the bright lights in the darkness along the river seemed to transport them back to a simpler time. Together, they had ranged around the world for nearly two years, with few opportunities to simply wander. They'd seen some of the most beautiful vistas the planet had to offer, after hard days of work or travel, but rarely with the time to do nothing but soak it in.

Paris had been peaceful for them today, and tonight would be the perfect culmination. The results of Anastasia's most recent archaeological dig would be unveiled as part of a new exhibit at the Louvre. Hellboy could tell she was a bit nervous, but the city provided a wonderful distraction.

Meandering along the Seine as the night came on and the winter chill returned, Stasia seemed giddy from the wine. She halted on the sidewalk and tugged his hand, turning him around to face her. Grinning up at him, she stood on her toes and reached up to caress his granite features. Hellboy bent to kiss her, her lips so soft on his. Somewhere, distant music played, a tinny sort of melody that he imagined piping from the windows of some World-War-II-era nightclub. The lights of Paris glittered all around them, the river sparkling with reflection.

The perfect night. He'd seen such bliss a thousand times in old movies but never imagined it to be more than fiction. Even if it had been true for ordinary guys, it couldn't be real for him.

Or so he'd thought.

In public with Anastasia, he always felt vaguely absurd and clumsy. It helped to focus on her. The previous day, upon their arrival in Paris, she'd convinced him to shed his well-worn duster. Together they'd shopped for a new coat, and Hellboy had settled on a charcoal gray greatcoat that had a similar cut to his duster but would not be quite so out of place at the Louvre.

Now the time had come.

They stood hand in hand at the entrance to the sprawling museum.

"Excited?" Hellboy asked.

Stasia turned to look at him, reached up to smooth the lapels of his wool coat. People passed them on the steps up toward the grand façade of the Louvre, a structure worthy of inclusion within its own exhibits.

"Aren't you?" she asked.

"It's your accomplishments they're celebrating tonight."

She took his massive right hand in both of hers and ran her fingers over it almost as though the rough, hard texture of it was her own personal worry stone.

"*Our* accomplishments," Stasia said quietly. "You're part of this. A big part."

Hellboy smiled. Museum patrons entering the unveiling of the exhibit probably saw his expression and thought him angry. It was a common misconception. His features weren't made to smile. But Stasia knew his face well, and she smiled in return.

They'd spent much of the winter at the Chateau de Chaumont at Loir-et-Cher, France. The castle had once been owned by Catherine de Medici, who had entertained sorcerers and astrologers there, among them the great Nostradamus. In 1613, archaeologists had discovered the skeleton of a giant buried beneath the castle, a man twenty-five and a half feet in height. Believers claimed the creature was one of the nephilim, gigantic creations that God had put on the Earth before he'd thought up mankind. Others said it was a hoax or an anomaly.

When restoration at the castle had revealed a previously undiscovered chamber—in which the stones of the floor had partially collapsed—it had at first been only an interesting aside. But when several of the stones had been removed and a gigantic human skull discovered under the floor, work had been suspended while archaeologists were summoned. Eventually, Anastasia had received a call asking her to join the dig. From the moment she began to tell him of the seventeenth-century discovery, Hellboy had understood why they wanted her. There wasn't an archaeologist in the world with more experience dealing with unexplained phenomena.

The skeletal remains of three giants had been discovered beneath the secret chamber under the Chateau de Chaumont. The shortest had stood at least twenty-seven feet in height during life.

"Interesting," Hellboy said, as they strode up to the entrance together, and stepped through the doors.

"What is?" Stasia asked.

Hellboy gave a small shrug. "The Louvre's got its rep as one of the most sophisticated places on Earth, but today it feels more like a carnival sideshow."

The moment he said it, he worried that he'd offended her. The exhibit focused on her work, after all. But Stasia only laughed.

"This is what happens when you find physical evidence of the existence of giants."

They followed signs and the gestures of finely dressed men and women positioned at intervals within the museum to point out the way to the gala. The corridors seemed endless to Hellboy, the museum a labyrinth.

When they reached the exhibit hall, they found a line outside the door. A dapper-suited man stood to one side, obviously security. For a moment, Stasia stepped away to talk to him. Hellboy figured she wanted to make sure they were in the right place, that as participants in the dig, they weren't supposed to be somewhere else.

Two thirtyish men were in front of him in line, silently shuffling forward as the crowd squeezed into the exhibit hall. In front of them were an older couple, both extremely well dressed. The woman wore a gown fit for a royal ball and the man an expensively tailored suit that clashed with his eccentric features, his gray-white, unruly beard, and his thick glasses.

"C'est elle," the woman said, nose turning up snidely as she gestured toward Anastasia.

Hellboy frowned, glaring at the old couple. They didn't register his presence at all.

"Dégout," said the old man. *"Ils la prodiguent avec l'éloge si meilleurs les hommes passent inapperçus."*

His wife wrinkled her nose further. *"C'est une culture de célébrité. Ils récompensent sa renommée, au lieu de ses capacités. Il est tout en raison de sa mascotte. Il y a une telle fascination pour ce rouge, singe de cirque."*

A cold rage came over Hellboy. He wanted to shove the quiet young men aside and challenge the old couple to support their slanderous bile or retract the comments and apologize. The old man must have had something to do with the Parisian Archaeological Society. His bitterness and jealousy about the attention Anastasia received were obvious. But for them to suggest that her success was due more to the media attention their relationship had received than her own intelligence and abilities . . . it made him want to break something. Or someone.

Stasia strolled back to him and linked her arm through his, blissfully unaware of the way she'd been insulted. The old woman watched her with a wary, judgmental eye, and as she turned to follow Stasia's progress, she saw Hellboy standing close behind her in the line.

Realization dawned upon her with horror. Pale, she faced forward, tugging her husband hurriedly toward the entrance to the exhibit hall, though there were still others in front of them, and they were crowding the line.

Hellboy's rage subsided, and a different emotion took its place. The words echoed again and again in his mind. He knew Anastasia had achieved all that she had at such a young age because of her dedication, motivation, and skill. But if the world had begun to dismiss all of those things and attribute her skyrocketing career to her association with him . . . he couldn't have that.

It got him thinking clearly for the first time. All this time, his only concern had been the way people perceived him. A monster. Something frightening. How selfish he'd been, never to wonder how his presence would change the world's perception of her.

He'd been willing to endure the disdain, the *Beauty and the Beast* headlines, and the looks on the faces of those around them, even when they made him feel less than human. Hellboy hated the way they got under his skin, reminded him of the circumstances of his arrival in the world. But he could endure that forever if he could make Anastasia happy.

But if being with him might destroy her career, interfere with the passions of her life . . .

He couldn't be a part of that.

Anastasia squeezed his arm and smiled up at him. It had been their most perfect day together. In his heart, it had become the most terrible.

They made it into the exhibit hall. In moments, people began to approach them, congratulating Anastasia and eyeing Hellboy warily. Some shook his hand good-naturedly.

The old couple who had such venomous jealousy in their hearts stood off to one side, glaring daggers at Stasia as she gracefully fielded the compliments of her peers.

Hellboy strode over to them. Eyes slitted and lips drawn back, he glared down. He thought the old man might wet himself, but the old woman sniffed as though he were some filthy hound in need of a bath.

"Je parle français couramment," he said.

The old woman took her husband's hand, and he meekly allowed her to lead him away.

Hellboy turned and watched as Anastasia chatted with her well-wishers and colleagues. To him, she had never looked more radiantly beautiful. But he knew now what the future would hold for them, and just looking at her broke his heart.

CHAPTER 12

Hellboy didn't like the idea of leaving the monastery behind. Two BPRD agents were on-site—Sarah Rhys-Howard and Tim Meaney—and even with a broken arm, Danovich could take care of himself, but he felt reluctant to leave them within the strange plain walls of that structure. Anastasia shared his trepidation. She'd suggested they wait for the helicopters to arrive. Two choppers would carry most of the refugees from the dig site, then they'd all breathe a sigh of relief. But there was no way to know when the helicopters were coming, and every moment that passed was another tick of the clock closer to the Dragon King's return.

There were a lot of things Hellboy wasn't sure about, but on that score, he was confident—the Dragon King was coming back. Maybe it'd be an hour, or a week, or at sundown, but now that it had been reawakened, it wasn't going to just go away. Especially not without its tasty human morsel as a sacrifice.

Koh and Tenzin led the way north from the monastery. They trudged down the hill on the opposite side from where they'd ascended, across a narrow valley, and started up a steeper slope. The peak that rose above them was not quite as high as that upon which the monastery stood, but the way was difficult, almost treacherous. Hellboy found himself reaching out for Anastasia again and again, fearful that she might fall and be lost to him.

It troubled him. He would not have wished away the fondness he felt for her, but they could not afford to let what they were feeling interfere with the job that needed to be done. Hellboy made an effort to focus on Tenzin and Koh, who seemed to have no trouble at all scaling the rough terrain of the hillside.

"They've cozied up pretty quick," he said, low enough that only Anastasia would hear him.

She steadied herself on an outcropping of rock, then continued her scramble upward. "They speak the same language. It's a bond we don't share."

"You don't think Tenzin's from Nakchu village?"

"I don't think he's one of them, if that's what you mean," Stasia replied. She'd put sunglasses on, and her eyes were hidden behind the dark lenses and under the brim of her Yankees cap. Hellboy thought maybe that was for the best.

"Nah. Me either." When they visited Nakchu, Tenzin had been just as much a target of the villagers' anger as the rest of them. "Just making an observation. It's probably for the best. If things turn ugly, I wanna make sure Koh knows what side he's on."

"Why would things turn ugly?"

Hellboy shot her a dark look but didn't reply. As if they had ever been in a situation that didn't turn ugly, at least for a little while. But he couldn't say that.

"You have any idea what we're looking for, exactly? The grave of Dwenjue, sure. But what's it look like?"

Stasia paused, taking a breather, and studied him through her dark lenses. "I don't know. Koh apparently knows exactly what he's looking for. What puzzles me is the fact that there's a grave at all."

She started climbing again. Hellboy nearly offered her his hand, as if to help her up the hillside, but he thought better of it.

"What do you mean? You think Dwenjue's just a story?"

"Doubtful. No, that's not what I meant. You don't know this?"

Hellboy shifted his belt to keep his pistol from banging against his hip as he mounted the steep slope. "Obviously. If I knew, would I look all confused?"

"It's your perpetual look."

"Funny. Talk."

Koh and Tenzin had lengthened the distance between them. The guide and the dragon-man had been on these mountains their entire lives. They were used to climbing, and did it with the ease of San Franciscans striding up Telegraph Hill.

"You really don't know this?"

Hellboy fixed her with a withering glare.

Stasia laughed and held up a hand in surrender, using the other to keep her balance. "All right. Don't get your knickers in a twist. I'm just surprised, is all. There's an excellent reason why there aren't any tombs or catacombs back at the monastery. The people of Nakchu village are unusual for this region. The most common method of disposing of the dead is sky burial."

"Sky burial? They shoot them off in rockets? Float them on balloons?"

"It's fascinating, actually. The dead are brought to the monastery—unless of course the deceased is a monk, which would mean he's already there. There's a ritual, quite beautiful, in which the body is prepared. Then it's carried away from the monastery to a nearby hilltop meadow. They light incense to draw the birds—vultures, crows, and hawks—then they cut open the body and remove the organs, which they dispose of later.

"The men step back, and the vultures cover the entire corpse. In ten or fifteen minutes, they've picked it clean, and fly off. The monks use huge mallets to reduce the bones to powder and shards, then mix it with barley flour and feed it to the hawks and crows. When they're done, not a trace of the corpse is left behind."

Hellboy felt rocks give way beneath one hoof, and he grabbed fistfuls of hillside to keep from slipping. His left hand closed around tall grass that grew in patches.

Brow furrowed, he glanced at her. "That's pretty hideous."

"Actually, I think there's a kind of beauty to it."

"But that's why you're surprised there's a grave for Dwenjue, right? I mean, this ancient sky burial thing, he was a monk, they would've fed him to the birds?"

"It isn't only an ancient custom. It's still the most prevalent method of disposal of the dead."

Hellboy started up the hill again, and Anastasia fell in beside him. They were nearing the top. Above them, Koh and Tenzin had paused on the highest ridge. The guide carried his rifle over his shoulder. Koh wore a hat that made Hellboy think of Genghis Khan. He'd chosen not to mention this.

"You're telling me they still do that? Cut their dead open and feed them to birds?"

"It's sacred."

Hellboy shook his head but said nothing more. Odd and gruesome as sky burial seemed to him, he found he liked the idea that there were still places in the world with customs so strange to him, places where McDonald's and Hollywood hadn't completely taken over.

The incline grew easier and the terrain more pleasant as they neared the top. The grass filled in, and the entire hilltop was one large meadow, now. It wasn't Julie Andrews at the beginning of *The Sound of Music*, but the beauty of the place was undeniable.

Until he saw Stasia glancing up, followed her gaze, and saw the vultures circling.

"It's my best day ever," Hellboy muttered.

Koh and Tenzin waited for them at the edge of a large, fenced meadow. There were two small temples, one at the northwest corner and one at the southeast. At the center of the meadow was a circle of stones where the grass seemed to grow taller and thicker than elsewhere. Hellboy tried not to imagine what kind of fertilizer had helped the grass along.

"This is a *durtro?*" Stasia asked.

Tenzin repeated the question to Koh in the dragon-man's language.

Koh nodded.

"I'm guessing that's where they do sky burials," Hellboy said.

"What gave it away, the vultures?"

He said nothing, only strode off to the right, toward the small temple there. Koh shouted something after him, but Hellboy ignored him.

"Wait!" Tenzin called.

Hellboy ignored him, too. But by the time he reached the door to the temple, Tenzin had caught up. Koh hung back, eyes narrowed. The morning had been sunny, but now, in midafternoon, the sky had become gray and ominous with storm clouds. Against that dark backdrop, the flames that had begun to lick from the corners of Koh's eyes were vivid and bright.

"This is a holy place," Tenzin said. "You must allow Koh to enter first."

Hellboy looked at them, then stepped aside and gestured with a flourish. "Be my guest."

Koh hesitated at the door, then entered. Hellboy followed him in, leaving Stasia and Tenzin outside in the meadow. The shadows were deep inside the temple, but he could tell by the scent of the place—its damp, rich aroma—that no one had been inside in a very long time. Not until they'd violated its peace, just as they had with the Dragon King. That was archaeology, though, a series of disinterments and violations. All for the greater good, of course.

Once upon a time, there might have been something of interest inside that temple. If so, the time had passed. Hellboy walked the narrow confines of the place, reminding himself that it actually might be possible that a legend about a dwarf warrior monk fighting the king of dragons to a standstill could be true.

They left the temple. The look of disappointment on Stasia's face made him smile softly. He pointed across the hilltop with a massive finger.

"Let's try that one."

All four of them started across the meadow. Other than the circle of stones, the vultures above, and that second temple, they could see nothing but grass on top of that hill. When they reached the stone circle, Koh and Tenzin skirted its edges, apparently not wanting to walk across the place where some of their ancestors might have been stripped of their flesh by vultures and had their bones pounded to dust.

No. Not Koh's ancestors. They kept their dead in those caves, a tomb of dragons and their offspring.

"Tenzin," Hellboy said. "Ask Koh why Dwenjue didn't get a sky burial. Ask why he has a grave."

The guide began to translate, but then Hellboy saw that Stasia had stopped to study the circle of stones.

"What?" he asked.

She glanced at him, then back at the stones. Her finger traced the circle in the air. "Something odd about this. It's a bit different from the others I've seen. At least what I've seen in pictures."

"You've only ever seen one of these in pictures?"

"It's not the sort of thing they invite Westerners to."

Tenzin and Koh paused to watch them. The guide wore a curious expression. Koh started back toward the circle of stones.

Hellboy stepped between two of the waist-high markers. He studied them, searching for engravings or any trace of ancient images, but to no avail. He turned in a circle, taking in the locations of the two temples and the stones, wondering if there was significance to their placement or number.

"This is where Dwenjue's grave is supposed to be?" he asked, looking toward Koh.

Tenzin translated, and Koh nodded, staring at the ground at the center of the circle.

Hellboy's hoof struck stone, and he froze. It hadn't

been a rock underfoot. He took two steps and kicked at the dirt several times until, once more, there came the clack of stone.

When he looked down, he caught the gleam of metal. The clouds were still thick and dark, hanging low, but enough light sifted through to glint off the iron ring set into the massive stone tablet, laid into the earth at the center of that stone circle.

It began, quite lightly, to rain. Droplets dampened the earth his hooves had disturbed.

Hellboy glanced up at Stasia. She'd removed her sunglasses and tucked them into the collar of her shirt. Her eyes were bright despite the growing storm.

"What do you want to bet?" he asked.

She crouched down and began to work her fingers around the edges of the round tablet, clearing some of the dirt away, defining its circumference.

"I never bet against you."

Koh started talking excitedly. Tiny hissing noises were made each time raindrops struck the fire that flickered from his eyes. Hellboy glanced over at Tenzin.

"What's he up in arms about?"

The guide dropped down to help Stasia clear off the edges of the slab. "Koh has never been here before. He has only heard about it from his father. The legend says that Dwenjue is buried on this hill, but he wasn't sure he believed it."

"And now he does?" Stasia asked.

Koh strode around the edges of the stone slab, nodding with satisfaction. Tenzin asked him the question, and the dragon-man looked up, his face still human though his eyes were on fire. When Koh replied, Tenzin translated.

"He's never seen anything quite like this," the guide said. "A *durtro* isn't supposed to have anything like this. He's right about that. It's nothing I'm familiar with, either. Koh believes that the iron handle is there because whatever this is—Dwenjue's tomb or something else—it is meant to be opened by one with strength far greater than any ordinary man. Even one of his own people couldn't do it alone."

All three of them were watching Hellboy in anticipation.

"What makes you think I can open it?" he asked.

"Come on, then, old bugger," Stasia teased. "Only one way to find out."

Hellboy stepped off the tablet, braced himself, and reached out to grasp the iron ring in his massive right hand. That hand wasn't made of stone, but the texture of it seemed strangely like that of the round slab in the ground. He gripped the iron ring tightly.

Koh and Tenzin looked on with rapt attention, obviously curious to know what was beneath that tablet and wondering if he could really lift it. Hellboy wondered the same things. Only Stasia seemed weighted with the true gravity of the situation. If they were wrong about Dwenjue, Hellboy was going to have to fight the Dragon King on his own. Lao's peacekeepers weren't going to be much help.

"Here goes."

Hellboy took a breath, clamped his teeth, and pulled. For long seconds nothing happened. His tendons stood out like cables on his arms. With a great exhalation, he relaxed his grip. Frustrated, he glanced up at Stasia. She nodded once, urging him on.

Again, he pulled. The weight of the stone would be tremendous, but something else held the slab in place. It had been sealed shut, he felt sure. A single grunt escaped him. Jaws grinding, he threw himself backward, putting his entire body into the effort.

The round slab shifted, stone grinding against stone. Dust rose from its edges, then it lifted. A gasp of ancient air came from the darkness beneath. The rain spattered Hellboy's head, wet droplets running down his sawed-off horns and sliding down the back of his neck. The coolness felt good. He took another breath, then braced the stone against his body and repositioned his hands, releasing the iron ring and gripping the bottom of the slab.

With a low roar, he upended the massive slab, pushing it away. It started to roll like a wheel and crashed to the ground. Hellboy could feel the impact. Stasia was beside him in an instant. Now that there was no danger of being crushed by the stone, Tenzin and Koh stepped nearer.

The four of them stared down into the grave at the

still, lifeless form of Dwenjue, the warrior monk. The dwarf lay clad in simple, rough, brown clothing. He had a long mustache that drooped on either side of his face, but not a hair on his gleaming pate. In his hands, the monk held a sword that had been buried with him. It pointed downward, toward his feet. The sword seemed nearly as tall as the monk himself.

Koh muttered something in an awestruck voice.

"How is it possible?" Stasia asked. She knelt at the side of the grave.

Hellboy understood her confusion. Dwenjue might have died centuries earlier, but he looked as though he'd been laid in the ground hours ago. If anything, he appeared far healthier than any of Hellboy's companions.

"Tenzin?" Hellboy asked.

The guide listened to Koh's mutterings a moment, then gestured into the grave. "He thinks the sword has mystical properties. That may be what has kept the body preserved."

Hellboy dropped to his knees and reached his huge right hand down into the pit.

"You're not going to disturb the site," Stasia said, the admonishment sharp.

He glanced up at her. "You can't be serious. This isn't a museum gig, babe. We may need to kill the Dragon King ourselves. If we can't have the monk who offed him the first time, the mystical sword is a decent runner-up prize. Anything will help, at this point."

Anastasia hesitated. He saw it in her eyes. The idea of disturbing an ancient grave, or any site of historical value, was anathema to her. But he spoke the truth, and she recognized that as well. She sighed and rolled her eyes, averting her gaze so she wouldn't have to see him desecrating the grave of Dwenjue.

Hellboy wrapped his hand around the blade.

Dwenjue's nostrils flared, and he breathed in. His features contorted as though he'd caught the scent of something that disgusted him. His eyes opened—small yellow eyes—and he stared at Hellboy for a moment.

"Crap," Hellboy muttered.

The dwarf monk's gaze shifted past him. True hatred engraved itself upon his face, and perhaps a bit of madness, and the monk let out a cry and thrust himself up from the grave. The rain fell harder, spattering off his bald head and the glistening sword.

Hellboy backed off, raising his hands. "Whoa, Tattoo. Hold on. Tenzin, tell him we're friends. Tell him!"

The guide had scrambled backward in terror, but now started talking to the yellow-eyed warrior in hard, sharp words. Hellboy moved in front of Anastasia protectively.

But Dwenjue had no interest in Anastasia. He sniffed the air, the rain pounding the ground all around them, and spun to glare at Koh. He screamed one word, and lunged.

Koh shifted instantly, his face elongating, his skin

altering to the rough scale of dragons. The fire bloomed from his eyes, and he lowered himself into a defensive crouch. When the sword whickered through the air and the rain, Koh managed to dart out of the way. He did not try to attack, shouting at Dwenjue instead, trying to explain.

"We don't have time for this," Hellboy muttered. He shot a glare at Tenzin. "What's he doing?"

The guide shook his head. "He smells dragon! What do you think he's doing?"

Anastasia moved past Hellboy at a run. Dwenjue brought his sword back for another swing, and she grabbed hold of his wrist. Dwenjue glared at her with those yellow eyes and started to shake her off. Then Hellboy was there beside her. He picked up the little warrior by the wrists, keeping the sword far away from him.

"You wake up nasty," Hellboy said.

Tenzin and Koh continued to shout at him.

Dwenjue blinked, and soon the hatred and madness seemed to lift from his eyes. All the tension went out of him, and the warrior monk replied, quietly, staring at Koh.

"What's he saying?" Stasia asked.

"He wants to know how long he's slept. And he wants to know how long the Dragon King has been awake," Tenzin replied.

Hellboy nodded toward Dwenjue. "Ask him how he knows the worm's awake."

The monk, the guide, and the dragon-man conversed a few moments, then Tenzin glanced at Hellboy and Anastasia again.

"He thought he had been victorious against the Dragon King, but the rest of the monks were not certain. They asked him to sleep here in eternal peace, never to be disturbed unless the Dragon King returned. We woke him. The scent of dragons is in the air. All he wants is to fulfill his destiny, to destroy the Dragon King forever, and return to his rest. Or to die."

Hellboy looked down at the diminutive monk with the fierce eyes. "I like his style."

"Right, then," Anastasia said. "Tell him what he needs to know, and let's get to work."

By dusk, Redfield and Lao's pilot had taken most of the evacuees to Lhasa on board their two helicopters. A small handful of evacuees were left at the monastery, but it had been decided that those few would have to take shelter there for the night. The consensus seemed to be that the Dragon King was likely to come after dark, and Bruttenholm and Lao agreed that they ought to be at full strength when that happened. If the dragon hadn't emerged by dawn, the last group of evacuees would be airlifted from the monastery shortly thereafter and returned to Lhasa.

For tonight, they would have to fend for themselves.

Redfield and Lao's pilot had returned from their

latest trip to Lhasa well armed, and with the surprises that the man from Beijing had promised. There were handheld antitank missiles with infrared guidance systems, at least two dozen American-made M47s, ironically called "Dragons." The black helicopter guided by Lao's pilot had delivered several portable surface-to-air missile systems whose make Abe didn't recognize. It reminded him of some European model he'd seen—the stand and gyrostabilizers were similar—but it had to be a Chinese model. There'd been no time to outfit the helicopters with missiles, but he thought these would do just as well. If the Dragon King could be brought down with flying explosives, they would do the trick.

Besides, the choppers would be otherwise engaged delivering Lao's real surprise. Half a dozen enormous, electrified nets had been procured from some strange black box Chinese government warehouse in Lhasa. Abe had asked him what their purpose was and why they were in Lhasa to begin with.

"What are nets for, Mr. Sapien, but to capture things?"

Lao would not elaborate further, though Abe pressed him. He wondered how many things happened around the world—how many odd, dangerous, perhaps unnatural things—that the BPRD never caught wind of. The nets certainly implied that the Chinese government had needed to capture something huge and deadly before. Abe wondered if it had worked, but since the BPRD had never learned of it, he could only presume it had.

Some kind of monster, or demon, he figured. His big question, though, was what the Chinese had done with the beast after they'd caught it. Abe decided he didn't want to know.

The mist of steam had grown thicker atop the lake, but the glow of fire beneath the water had only brightened. The stink of sulfur rose from the water, and where the wind rippled the surface, the lake foamed. Abe stared at the water, scanned the lake from end to end, then turned from the shore to join Professor Bruttenholm. Idly, barely aware of it, he kept his right hand on the grip of his sidearm.

The professor stood in the lee of the rocky hillside with Mr. Lao and his commandos. The night sky had been obscured by clouds since early afternoon, but now only a soft drizzle fell around them. Dim moonlight diffused by the gauzy cloud cover provided enough illumination to see by, but Professor Bruttenholm had forbidden them to use lantern, torch, or spotlight if they didn't have to. Drawing the attention of the Dragon King would be foolish, and probably fatal.

But the old man was working on that.

The commandos lined up in front of Professor Bruttenholm and stood calmly as he painted their faces with ocher, inscribing sigils with his index finger. Lao had gone first, as if to set an example for his men, to make certain that they cooperated. Abe joined them and waited patiently for Professor Bruttenholm to finish his work. As he drew on their foreheads and cheeks and around their eyes, he muttered a quiet incantation again and again.

When the professor had finished, Lao barked orders at his men. All of their calm dissipated, and they scrambled to obey, taking their places behind what cover they had found—tumbled-down rocks and ditches dug with the help of the few members of the archaeological team—with assault rifles, rocket launchers, and the other weapons the pilots had brought back from Lhasa. Lao followed his commandos to their posts, issuing further orders, still looking like nothing so much as a dour businessman or politician.

Abe watched them, glancing at the water every few moments, even as Professor Bruttenholm dipped his finger into the ocher paint he'd mixed in a small tin bowl. The old man began to trace the same sigils upon his own face.

"When I'm through, Abe, I'd like you to check my handiwork and make certain I've done the work properly. I haven't a mirror."

"Of course, Professor."

"You're certain you don't want me to paint you with the ward as well?"

Abe cocked his head, scrutinizing the man's work. The sigils looked perfectly fine to him. "I'll be in the chopper with Redfield. There'll be no hiding a helicopter from the dragon. Whether it can see us inside won't matter very much."

"True enough," the old man said, finishing the lines around his eyes and dipping his finger into the paint again.

"Do you really think this will work?" Abe asked.

Professor Bruttenholm frowned, brow wrinkling.

"With the proper incantation, which I've recited, these sigils ought to make anyone temporarily invisible to the senses of the dragons."

A chill mountain wind blew across the plateau, momentarily eclipsing the heat emanating from the lake and stirring the steam above the water. Abe glanced around, unable to escape the dreadful knowledge that they were woefully unprepared.

"When do you think our reinforcements will arrive?" he asked.

Professor Bruttenholm glanced at the southwestern sky as if expecting a phalanx of helicopters to appear at that very moment. "I wish I knew. We've got to presume that we're on our own, at least for tonight. If the Dragon King will only stay submerged another day, our odds will be much improved."

Abe frowned. Without a child sacrifice, he doubted the Dragon King would content itself to remain under the lake. Kora Kyichu had been taken away to Lhasa with the other evacuees, and half the complement of Mr. Lao's commandos were in Nakchu village, keeping the survivors of the dragon burning there captive. That might not save them from a return of the dragon, but it ought to keep any of the dragonmen from returning to Lake Tashi to sacrifice one of their own children.

The Dragon King had not been appeased. The fire beneath the lake provided proof enough of that.

"What of Professor Kyichu and the others from the dig?" he asked.

A troubled expression crossed Professor Bruttenholm's features. "They're digging, believe it or not. Kyichu has them attempting to excavate the preparatory chamber for the third time to retrieve the bodies of their colleagues buried there. An admirable effort, but damned foolhardy timing."

"They're not going to fight off the dragon with shovels," Abe said, shaking his head in wonder. "What about the wards? Have you painted their faces yet?"

Weighted with regret, the professor glanced up at the ridge where the ruins of the city of the Dragon King had been ravaged. "Professor Kyichu was the first person I approached. He declined the offer of the protective ward."

Bruttenholm gave a sad laugh. "Apparently, he doesn't believe in magic."

Abe stared at him in horror. Professor Kyichu, Corriveau, and Gibson were as good as dead if the Dragon King set his sights on them.

"All we can do is our best, Abe," Professor Bruttenholm said, laying a paternal hand on his shoulder. "It is always hardest to save people from themselves."

A dusting of rock and loose soil slid down the hill behind them. Abe glanced up to see Neil Pinborough clambering toward them. The agent dropped the last seven or eight feet and landed in a crouch. In the dark, he seemed made of the night. Across his back were slung a long bow of simple design and a leather quiver containing perhaps half a dozen arrows of similar rustic quality.

"You spoke to them?" Professor Bruttenholm asked.

Pinborough nodded. "If the worm comes back, they're not going to sit about and wait to die with Kyichu. They'll be right along."

The old man sighed. "Foolish, even so. They ought not to wait. They should come now."

Abe cocked his head again and stared at the professor in admiration. He'd had Pinborough talking to Corriveau and Gibson behind Professor Kyichu's back and didn't even think to mention it.

"They're being careful," Abe said. "If Kyichu's gamble pays off without getting them killed, they'll be able to take credit for helping him save the dig."

"Silly sods," Pinborough muttered.

"Agreed," Professor Bruttenholm replied.

Abe studied Pinborough's bow. "What do you plan to do with that? If the guns aren't going to help—"

"One of the little treasures we brought along at the

start of this whole mess," Pinborough replied, glancing at Professor Bruttenholm before looking back to Abe. "The brief indicated something to do with dragons, but really, we had no idea what we'd be up against, so we threw a few things into our kit. Ancient Chinese alchemist named Gui Xian—said he was immortal, but time proved him wrong—made a compound that would turn anything it touched to silver. One of his enemies took his spells and put them to new use, made these arrows, tipped with the compound, and killed him with one."

Abe stared at him. "You did see the size of the Dragon King?"

Pinborough shrugged. "We use what's on hand."

"True enough," Abe replied. He'd grown to like Neil Pinborough. The man had been trained to be brutal, but it didn't seem to have gotten into his psyche as much as it had with Meaney.

"Abe," Professor Bruttenholm said. His voice had gone cold.

Filled with dread, Abe followed the professor's gaze to the lake. The water had begun to churn, perhaps even to boil. In places, the surface seemed to be on fire.

"Choppers!" Pinborough shouted.

"Watch yourselves," Professor Bruttenholm said.

Abe called to him to do the same, already in motion. He and Pinborough ran side by side. Abe shouted to Redfield and Lao's pilot, whipping his arm in the air in a signal for them to get the rotors turning. He could only imagine how exhausted both pilots must have been given the flights they'd made back and forth to Lhasa in the past day and a half. But both men were alert.

The rotors came to life, whipping the air.

Abe and Pinborough ducked low and rushed to the helicopters. Each had the electrified nets attached to their undercarriages. Pinborough reached the black chopper and jumped into the back. Each chopper had only a pilot and a single one of Lao's commandos, plus one BPRD agent. Abe hauled himself into the back of Redfield's helicopter. The bearded pilot didn't even wait for him to slide the door closed before bringing them aloft.

The black-clad commando beside Abe muttered something in Chinese and gripped his assault rifle in both hands like a security blanket. Abe wanted to tell him it wouldn't provide any security, but he didn't speak Chinese. Plus, he'd been touching his own pistol like a lucky charm, so he couldn't really talk.

As they rose into the air—the other chopper taking flight beside them—the lake erupted with fire and water in a replay of the previous night's explosion. Yellow scales glowed in the firelight. The lake water mixed with the falling rain and showered back down again.

The Dragon King slithered into the sky.

Lao's commandos attacked immediately. Surface-to-air missiles whisked from their ground positions and seared across the sky. Two struck the huge worm in quick succession, one striking its long, whipping tail and glancing harmlessly away. The second embedded itself into the red scales of the dragon's belly and exploded in a small burst of flesh and scale and blood.

The Dragon King screamed, not in pain, but in fury. It thrashed in the air, throwing its antlered head back as though trying to buck a rider. Flames erupted from its gullet and sprayed the dark, cloudy night sky.

"Redfield, move it!" Abe cried. "This may be our only shot!"

"I'm on it!" the pilot barked.

The commando chopper rose to the west. Redfield navigated east, riding an updraft. In seconds, both of the helicopters were above the Dragon King. It twisted in the air, barely paying any attention to them. The great serpent seemed to be searching for something. Another missile hit its ridged back, but it exploded without doing any real damage. That was when Abe understood that Professor Bruttenholm's wards were working. The dragon couldn't see the professor, Lao, or his commandos on the ground.

A fresh gout of fire bursting from its nostrils, the Dragon King whipped its head around to glare at the ridge where the excavation had been. Abe cursed aloud. It had sensed, smelled, or seen someone up there on the ridge. Kyichu would still be hiding, but now Abe realized that it had been a huge mistake for

Pinborough to ask Corriveau and Gibson to run for the professor's help when the dragon appeared.

"Hurry! It's seen them!" Abe shouted.

Redfield gritted his teeth but didn't reply. The Chinese commando said nothing. The pilot pulled the stick, and the chopper rose higher.

"Get ready!" Redfield called.

Abe took a breath, grabbed the door on his side, and glanced over to see his commando partner do the same. The commando nodded and simultaneously they slid open the doors. Abe could barely breathe. The altitude of the plateau itself was high enough to thin the air, but they were much higher now. He worried how high the chopper could go before it ran out of airspace, before the air wouldn't hold them aloft anymore, and then he chided himself for worrying about things he couldn't control.

"Set?" Redfield called back.

"Wait!" Abe replied, dropping to the floor of the chopper. He reached an arm out, searched with his hand and found the release that'd been jury-rigged to the undercarriage. Halfway down would release the first net. All the way would release the second.

Abe glanced back at the commando and saw that he was in position as well. The two levers had to be released at precisely the same time if they wanted to be on target with the net. The thing would electrify the second that something pulled against it, trying to break free.

"Set!" Abe called.

As he glanced back out into the rainy night above Lake Tashi, he saw the other chopper release its first net. He thought he could see Pinborough and a commando in the back, lying down just like him. The net seemed almost to float on the air, like a man-o'-war on the water. But it caught the lower half of the Dragon King's body and tangled around the beast instantly. The worm tried to rake it off with the eagle talons of its rear legs, and the moment it did so, the entire net sizzled and smoked.

Again, the dragon bucked at the air and screamed. The fire that gouted from its maw burned past the helicopter. Redfield shouted and jerked the stick to the left. Seconds later, they were hovering just above the Dragon King in the air.

"Now!" Redfield shouted.

Abe pressed the lever halfway with a loud clank, and the first net dropped away. It landed on the Dragon King's head, strung like cobwebs in its antlers. The sizzling and smoking began again, and the Dragon King kept screaming and bucking.

The other chopper started to maneuver to get back into place. Abe saw Neil Pinborough kneeling just inside the open side door of the combat helicopter. He was shouting something, probably telling the pilot to hold her steady, and he had the bow in his hands. Quickly, he drew from the quiver one of the arrows that had killed Gui Xian and nocked it.

Even as the two helicopters danced away from one another, Abe caught one last glimpse of Pinborough loosing the arrow. He could barely track its flight, but then saw a black streak across one of the dragon's eyes. The arrow struck the gigantic, writhing sky serpent, and it squealed with a pain Abe had not heard from it before.

The dragon's left eye turned to silver.

It thrashed in pain and fury, tearing the electrified nets, reaching up to claw at its dead, silver eye. With a roar, it opened its jaws and spewed fire in a wide arc that caught the other helicopter in a tidal wave of flames.

Abe shouted some denial of what his eyes had seen. In the open rear compartment of the chopper, Pinborough and the commando were ablaze like some wicker effigies of men.

Then the chopper's fuel tank exploded. A conflagration of flame and metal careened from the sky and crashed into the steep mountain slope to the south of the lake.

Abe stared in horror. The dragon tore free of the net that covered the lower half of its body, and the entire length of the serpent whipped the air. It struck the tail of the chopper, dashing it from the sky.

Metal tore. Redfield swore as he tried to get the helicopter under control, but it hurtled toward the lake.

Abe fell.

The chopper spun away from him, and he tumbled end over end, down into the steaming, searing, sulfurous waters of Lake Tashi. He plunged into the water. The heat embraced him, and Abe cried out soundlessly as it rushed through his gills.

The impact had dulled his thoughts. He hung there, swaying in the water like a dead man, sure that the dragon's fire would boil him alive.

His vision blurred. Darkness encroached at the corners of his eyes. Then he saw something moving in the water. Small and gray-blue, translucent and swift. This was no dragon.

Barely conscious, he tried to focus his eyes . . . and saw the ghost of a child staring back at him. The girl smiled sweetly and waved at him as though they'd passed one another on the street. The spirit reached out and touched him, and Abe felt an electric jolt that brought him fully awake.

The little girl's ghost wasn't alone. Behind her were two boys, gray-blue shades of death, perfect and beautiful and innocent. Farther back in the water that still glowed with dragon fire from the depths of the lake, he saw so many others. Dozens. Perhaps hundreds. The children of the Nyenchen Tanghla mountain range.

And he knew.

These were the ghosts of all of those children who had been sacrificed to the Dragon King. Lost souls, lingering, waiting in this world for someone to release them at last, to destroy the worm.

Their presence soothed Abe. The heat of the water did not burn so terribly. The sulfurous taint in the lake did not choke him. They were lending him the strength of their spirits. The ghosts of those children had saved him.

He reached out, and his fingers passed through the little girl's hand, but the covenant was made. Abe would do whatever he could to aid them in return.

Chapter 13

Hellboy couldn't understand a word Dwenjue said, but he liked the grim little warrior. The dwarf monk had a deadly serious disposition, a disdain for everything but getting his job done, and yellow eyes that glowed in the dark. He carried his long, mystical sword over his shoulder because if he'd put it into a scabbard, it would have dragged on the ground. Dwenjue wouldn't have been any fun at a pub, but on a mission to kill a monster that burned and ate people and demanded the sacrifice of small children in exchange for mercy, he was just the kind of guy Hellboy wanted along.

They'd gone back to the monastery to find only ten people remaining, including Sarah and Meaney. Apparently evacuating the rest at night had been deemed too dangerous. A helicopter would return for the last group at first light. Meanwhile, they had to hunker down for the night in the monastery. Hellboy had suggested that Tenzin and Stasia stay there, but neither of them would hear of it. The suggestion pissed

Stasia off. The guide, on the other hand, just knew he was needed and had a job to do.

The five of them had trekked down from the monastery and turned west. Now they could see Lake Tashi ahead. Not a single light gave away the presence of BPRD agents or Chinese government forces on the northern shore. Hellboy picked up his pace. He knew worrying made little sense. Professor Bruttenholm would have insisted they move in darkness to avoid drawing the dragon's attention if it came up after dark. The only illumination came from the lake itself, which seemed to have caught fire far below the surface.

"It's beautiful," Stasia said.

"That's one way to look at it," Hellboy replied.

"It's terrible, too."

He only nodded. Both descriptions were correct. Whatever happened in the next twenty-four hours or so, there was a kind of breathtaking magic to it, and a brutal ugliness as well.

Koh marched on his left and Dwenjue on his right, that sword over his shoulder. Tenzin and Stasia followed close behind them. Hellboy felt like he was trudging with cement blocks around his legs. He could endure just about anything, but that didn't stop him from getting tired. How Stasia and the guide were managing to keep walking was a mystery to him.

They followed the lakeshore to the right. Hellboy figured they had three-quarters of a mile or so before they'd get to the location of the original camp, just below the dig on the ridge.

Dwenjue muttered something.

"What'd he say?" Hellboy asked, glancing back at Tenzin.

"He smells dragon. And it isn't Koh."

From the look of the water, with that firelit mist swirling on the surface, Hellboy wasn't surprised.

"Something's going on down there," Stasia said, and he could hear uncharacteristic fear in her voice.

Koh picked up the pace, nearly breaking into a run. As he moved, his body changed again, his dragon features coming out, the fire starting in his eyes again. Hellboy made to shout after him, but then he saw the way the water had begun to churn.

"Stasia," he said.

"Run!" she shouted.

They sprinted along the shore toward the place where they knew the remainder of the camp lay. Hellboy heard shouting, then the roar of helicopters whirring to life.

The lake exploded with fire and a fountain of scalding water. The Dragon King snaked into the sky, and the helicopters were in pursuit. As he ran, leaving Stasia and Tenzin behind, only Koh and—amazingly—Dwenjue able to keep pace with him, he watched as the choppers flanked the dragon in the sky, watched them drop their nets.

When the dragon shrieked its pain, Koh cried out

as well, though whether in triumph or sympathy, Hellboy could not tell. Gunfire and rocket fire came from the darkness ahead, and Hellboy followed the tracers back to their launch point. They trampled the spot where the original camp had been burned.

The dragon shrieked again. It writhed in the air, beginning to tear free of the nets, which crackled with electricity and smoked as it struggled against them. Shouts came from the ridge to the right, and Hellboy looked up to see the archaeologists who'd been stupid enough to stick around with Han Kyichu sliding and practically crashing down the rocky slope of the hill toward them.

"Go!" Stasia snapped. "I'll deal with them."

"Keep them quiet!" Hellboy barked at her.

He ran on, though he felt part of him tethered to Stasia as he left her behind, wondering if those were the last words they'd ever exchange. Dwenjue barreled along beside him, somehow fleet of foot in spite of his size and the massive sword. The yellow eyes weren't the only magic in the little monk. Koh had bent low to the ground and ran with a strange, reptilian smoothness.

Ahead, the commandos Lao had brought in were using both shoulder-launched rockets and others on portable stands. As Hellboy watched, one struck the red underbelly of the Dragon King and exploded, blowing a bloody wound in the thing's scaly hide. Another wound showed a previous strike. A second missile went off right at the serpent's neck as it thrashed in those electrified nets, the helicopters buzzing around it. That explosion didn't harm it at all.

"The red stripe!" Hellboy shouted as he thundered toward the commandos, forgetting that they could not understand him. As with so many other armored creatures, the dragon's belly was vulnerable.

Assault weapons fire punctured the night in staccato bursts. Hellboy ran, now leaving even Koh and Dwenjue behind. Up ahead, behind the commandos, exhorting them on, he saw his father and Lao. Professor Bruttenholm had some kind of war paint on his face. It took Hellboy a second to realize that Lao and the commandos had it as well, then another second to figure out that these were wards.

"Crap," he snarled. If the wards were working, keeping the dragon from seeing them, then his arrival and that of his companions would draw the big worm's attention right here.

Professor Bruttenholm shouted at Lao over the weapons fire. He gestured toward the helicopters, then to the commandos. Hellboy felt a spark of pride seeing the old man taking command in the field. Whatever danger they were in, Trevor Bruttenholm had it under control.

The dragon screamed.

Hellboy spun around just in time to see dragon fire strafe one of the helicopters. Men were set ablaze as the chopper was engulfed in flames. The fuel tank exploded, and Hellboy slid to a halt, staring in horror as the helicopter careened into the southern cliff face, leaving nothing but burning metal shrapnel to fall into the lake.

He sensed rather than saw Stasia, Tenzin, and the two expedition members who'd been with the absent Kyichu come up behind him, staggered by the sight. Koh hissed low in his throat. Dwenjue took a step toward the shore, those yellow eyes gleaming.

Professor Bruttenholm called to him, but Hellboy could not tear his gaze from the Dragon King. The serpent thrashed hard enough to tear itself loose from the nets. Its body whipped in the air, and Hellboy shouted in fury and anguish as it struck the second chopper.

The helicopter's engine whined as it spun through the air. Redfield might have been the best pilot Hellboy had ever seen. He'd be struggling to get the thing under control. But even as the chopper twisted away at a dangerous angle from the Dragon King, a lone figure tumbled out of the chopper's open side door, dropping like a stone into the lake.

"Abe!" Hellboy roared.

The engine of Redfield's chopper shrieked. The pilot managed to right it, but it fell too quickly. Smoke came from the engine. Something broke off, and the net came loose, but now it swept upward instead of down, tangling itself in the chopper's undercarriage. Fifty feet off of the ground, it seemed to pull up a moment, as Redfield saved himself from crashing.

Electricity surged through the chopper, killing all of its operational systems. It crashed; then, glass shattering and metal screeching as it tore, but the main body of the helicopter remained intact. Redfield and whoever else was on board might still be alive if they were extremely lucky.

In pain, the Dragon King writhed back and forth in the air above the lake for several seconds, as though the sky and the ground were one and the same to the creature, despite its lack of wings. Then the worm twisted in the air and dived back into the fiery water, slipped under the surface, and was gone, save for the flames that burned in places right on top of the water, and the waves splashed up by its dive.

Hellboy ran for the water. Spindly fingers gripped his wrist and he turned, brows knitted in fury. His anger dissipated when he saw that it was his father who'd grabbed him.

"What do you think you're doing?" Professor Bruttenholm demanded.

Hellboy shook his hand off. "Going after Abe. He's still alive, but down there in the water, he might not be for much longer. You need to get some people over to the chopper, see if Redfield's alive, and whoever's with him—"

"Wait," the old man said. His damp, aged eyes gleamed with the reflection of the fire on the water.

"I'm the leader of this investigation. You're not going anywhere."

"What are you talking about?" Anastasia demanded, whipping off her Yankees cap and marching up beside Hellboy to glare at the professor. "Abe's down there. You saw him fall. You can't imagine Hellboy's just going to stand here!"

Professor Bruttenholm stared at her. "You're not a part of this team, Dr. Bransfield. I am responsible for Abe Sapien, just as I'm responsible for all of you. The water is his natural element—"

"Not water like this!" Hellboy snapped.

Beyond his father, Hellboy saw Professor Kyichu scrambling down the rocky slope. He'd been hiding somewhere, but with the Dragon King gone again, he'd reared his crazy head.

"We've got to figure out how to destroy this creature before others die," Professor Bruttenholm said, his gaze shifting from Hellboy to Stasia and back again. He completely ignored the presence of Koh, Dwenjue, and Tenzin, and the quick approach of Lao and Kyichu. "Abe knows the risks of the mission. He will find his way out of the lake."

"If his brains aren't scrambled from the fall," Hellboy said, glaring at his father. "Besides, we know how to destroy the damned worm." He reached down and clapped a hand on Dwenjue's back. "Meet the warrior monk. Professional dragon killer. Now I'm going to save my friend."

He turned and started toward the water. Stasia stayed with him, walking down to the shore at his side, not trying to talk him out of it but just wanting to be with him every moment now, when the unimaginable could happen at any time. Hellboy knew his father would look after Redfield, and work with Dwenjue to figure out how to finish off the Dragon King. The professor was in charge, and he was good at it. That left Hellboy to do what had to be done. Abe would never have left him on his own. No way would he abandon his best friend.

More shouting filled the night behind him; this time it wasn't in English. Then Tenzin called his name. Hellboy turned to see the guide running after him, with Koh and Dwenjue on either side of him. The dragon-man moved low to the ground, as though the more time he spent around the Dragon King, the more like a full-blooded dragon he became.

"What's up?"

"Dwenjue says there's a better way to do this," Tenzin told him.

Hellboy stared into the warrior monk's yellow eyes. "Talk to me."

Without translation, Dwenjue muttered something in reply and pointed to the water.

"He says the lake did not always look like this," Tenzin explained. "Once, the temple was here."

Anastasia put a hand on Hellboy's arm to steady herself. "I knew it."

"Dwenjue says the temple is still here. He keeps saying there is an easier way to save your friend."

"Well, tell him to get on with it, then."

Tenzin translated for Dwenjue, and the dwarf smiled for the first time since they had woken him from his centuries of sleep. He held the sword in both hands, blade pointed up at the night. The rain hissed as it touched the metal. It pattered the ground all around them and plinked at the surface of the steaming lake.

Dwenjue began to chant, and the sword glowed the same yellow as his eyes.

The ground rumbled beneath their feet. Hellboy grabbed hold of Stasia. Several of the commandos shouted, but already Professor Bruttenholm had four of them racing along the lakeshore toward the downed helicopter. The ground shook harder, and Tenzin went on one knee. Hellboy saw his father grab one of the missile launchers to keep himself upright.

A crack like the loudest thunder boomed across Lake Tashi. The water seemed to surge upward a moment, the mist of steam beginning to clear, then all went still.

Only the rain and the gleam of that mystic blade remained.

But, staring at the edge of the lake only a few feet away, Hellboy felt sure that what he saw was no hallucination.

The water had begun to recede.

The lake began to churn around Abe. It tugged at his limbs with such force that at first he thought the ghost children of Lake Tashi were pulling at him, attempting to drag him in a dozen different directions. But the ghosts—the lost spirits of those beautiful children—only swayed in the water like reeds, watching him.

Powerful currents plucked at Abe and yanked him back and forth, spun him around. A whirlpool formed, and he twisted into a funnel that sucked him down, down, into the depths of the lake. The ghost children darted through the water, unaffected by the pull of the currents.

Abe's mind swirled as though with the tug of the water. Already disoriented, he tried to pull his thoughts together, to build understanding from fragments of the moment. What was happening to him? To the lake? The water churned, but this couldn't be only the motion of the Dragon King passing under the surface. This was far more than that.

Draining.

The suction of the currents that pulled at him meant the water in the lake had to be flowing somewhere else, and it could only be into deep trenches and crevices, into freshly opened hollows in the earth beneath the mountain plateau—beneath the water. Lake Tashi was draining away.

Calm.

Abe tried to find a calm place within himself, the way he entered a meditative state sometimes when he had first been discovered and awoken in the custody of the BPRD, floating in a glass tube, a subject of scientific study. He'd gone into himself to combat the boredom and the invasive inquisitiveness of his doctors.

The water rushed around him so quickly that his gills could barely breathe. He closed his eyes to fight the vertigo and pulled his arms and legs tight to his body to lessen his body's drag on the water—reducing the speed with which the whirlpool spun him down and down.

The ghost children were little more than blurs at the edges of his vision. Whatever soothing effect their presence had had upon him vanished, and the water seared his flesh, the taint of it seeping in through his gills. Abe felt himself on the verge of losing consciousness again as a terrible nausea tore at his guts.

Through the membrane that covered his eyes he saw a bright flash. Abe opened them and saw a pillar of fire erupting from below, coming up from the soft lake bottom. He beat his arms and legs against the terrible current, trying to slow himself enough that he could see the bottom clearly.

It, too, was spilling away. The loose soil, he understood at last, had not been soil at all. Only one substance shifted so easily, even more fluid than sand. The entire bottom of the lake was comprised of ash—the burned remnants of ancient peoples, ancient cities, ancient terrain. Somehow the Dragon King had turned the whole lake bottom into a nest of ashes.

The ash drained away with the water.

Another powerful current tore at him and Abe was pulled deeper. He glanced around and realized that he could no longer see the ghost children of the sacrifices to the Dragon King. They had helped him, given him succor and spirit when he needed it most, and now they had withdrawn, leaving him indebted. Someone had to get vengeance for those children.

Fighting the maelstrom exhausted him. Abe felt his strength diminishing with every passing second. Jets of fire erupted below him at odd intervals, but the water did not seem to grow any hotter. Or perhaps his seared flesh had grown numb.

Got to stop, he thought. Soon, he would lose consciousness completely, and the thought of waking up in some subterranean cavern—if he woke at all—did not appeal to him. He would never be able to break the grip of the twisting currents by swimming upward or trying to slip from the whirlpool. Abe's only choice was to submit. He swam downward, spinning with the draining lake water. If he could just find an outcropping of rock or anything to grab hold of or wedge himself against, he could rest. He could fight the inexorable pull of the water.

Something flashed in the light of dragon fire, off to his right. For a moment, Abe thought that the ghost children had returned. As he spun, he fought the current a moment to get a better look, and what he saw made him surrender completely for a moment.

A row of short spires atop a curved, sloping roof, windows and carved columns and level upon level of those stone-tiled roofs—the most enormous temple he had ever laid eyes upon, too large for human occupation. The windows alone were a dozen feet high. The ashes that had made up the false bottom of the lake were sifting away from the temple, revealing it by inches, falling through into the subterranean hollows like sand through an hourglass. The lake water rushed down, the level dropping with every passing moment, and then Abe knew that the temple of the Dragon King—for surely that was what it was, what Anastasia had been searching for—might be his only hope.

With all the strength left in him, he struck out from the maelstrom, fighting it, and it swept him around, away from the temple. But the whirlpool kept spinning, and he rode it until it carried him closer than ever to those spires and that curved tile roof.

Abe kicked out, pulling toward it, knifing through the water. He reached out both arms to grab hold of one of those short, thick spires. The current slammed him into the spire, and he felt bones in his chest crack, but he held on. His arms and legs wrapped around the spire, tiles under him, and he latched himself there, refusing to let go. It felt as though that scalding water might scour the flesh from his bones, but Abe held on past the point of any conscious effort. If he'd died in that moment, they'd never have been able to unwrap his arms from that perch.

The water drained, rushing around him, and within minutes, the heat and drag of it lessened; then it dropped below the level of the roof. The cool night air swept over him. Gasping for breath, allowing his lungs to fill, feeling like he was coming awake from a dreadful slumber, Abe stared down at the temple of the Dragon King.

The sprawling, gigantic structure had been built on a slab of bedrock in the midst of the lake. The water seemed to be settling now at a level just below that bedrock, and he imagined that this was the original depth of the lake, back in those ancient times when the Dragon King had reigned.

On the bedrock island around the base of the temple, the yellow-and-red serpentine body of the Dragon King lay coiled. Fire jetted from its nostrils like twin furnaces.

Yet there were other flames as well, guttering like torchlight from the glassless windows of the temple. Things shifted and lumbered inside the structure beneath him. Abe felt their presence, felt the stones of the temple—for it had been built entirely of stone—settling and groaning with the motion of whatever monsters slithered in and out of the great halls of that place of worship.

First one, then two others, emerged from within, gliding out of the windows and through the air as though water still surrounded the temple. One had a small beard scruff like a billy goat, and the other two had small sets of antlers. The color of their scales differed, with two varying shades of red and orange and one almost black. The largest couldn't have been longer than fifteen feet, the smallest less than ten.

Hatchling dragons, the worshippers of the Dragon King. One of these things had bred with a human woman, and the half-breeds of Nakchu village had been the result.

They had been dead for hundreds upon hundreds of years. They had rotting holes where their eyes should have been, and their scaly hides were dry and cracked when they flew through the air or slid in through a window of the temple.

Undead dragon hatchlings. They had returned at last to a world lost to them. Their king slumbered, perhaps injured or simply resting, at the base of his temple. Soon, Abe felt sure, they would emerge from that island in what was left of Lake Tashi. They would want to create living dragons, to begin again the Dragon King's reign of fire. The mountains would be scoured of life, but they wouldn't stop there. He felt confident of that. Lhasa was not so far away, after all. There were many children there, and many people to give the Dragon King the fear and obedience he required.

With an awful whistle, a missile tore down into the sunken lake and struck the sleeping Dragon King. It woke and raised its head, growling deep in its chest.

Abe stared into the eyes of the dragon, even as more of his dead hatchlings stirred, sliding like worms from the temple windows. One of them took flight, whipping back and forth in the air, small eagle talons clutching at the sky. It banked around, prowling; and then it turned toward Abe.

The rotting, withered dragon thing flew toward him. Abe clung to the roof of the temple and wished he were anywhere else.

Hellboy stood at the edge of what had once been the lakeshore. The water level had dropped by a hundred feet or more. Beside him, Anastasia clung to one arm, weak with her astonishment.

"It's beautiful," she said.

"Aside from the zombie dragons on fire, you mean?"

She ignored the sarcasm. "It's like nothing I've ever seen before. I'd only imagined how huge it must have been. It never occurred to me that the temple might have been the true home of the dragons, that it wouldn't be part of the city itself."

Dwenjue lowered his sword, and the yellow glow of the blade cooled. The warrior monk's eyes retained their color. Rain sprinkled his bald pate, drizzling upon them all, now. The fire from Koh's eyes seemed to dance around, trying to avoid the droplets. Tenzin had his rifle in his hands, as if he might be thinking about taking some potshots at the sleeping Dragon King or his undead clan.

"Nice trick," Hellboy told Dwenjue.

The dwarf looked up, confused, until Tenzin translated. Dwenjue replied, and the guide smiled and glanced at Hellboy.

"He says it isn't a trick. It's the purity of his spirit that allows him to touch the world."

Hellboy nodded. "Clean living. I keep meaning to take that up."

His father had taken some of Lao's commandos along the shore to see if Redfield and his passenger were still alive. The other black-garbed soldiers had been shaken from their aggression by surprise and perhaps a bit of awe. Even Mr. Lao stared, unsure what to do. Their weapons were not going to solve this problem.

Corriveau and Gibson had found the ocher paint Professor Bruttenholm had used to dab wards on the faces of the others and were trying to copy the sigils. It wouldn't do a damn bit of good, since they didn't know the incantation involved, but Hellboy didn't bother to tell them that. They'd only panic more.

Professor Kyichu ignored them. He pushed his way between two commandos and staggered to the edge of the steep drop-off down to the water, where the temple stood upon an island in the midst of what had once been called the Dragon King Pool.

"So many," Han Kyichu whispered.

Hellboy turned to look at him. He could feel his

mouth twisting into a sneer and could not help it.

"Guess you wish you'd left with your daughter, now."

The white-haired man stared at the rotting, burning dragons that kept spilling out of the temple as if he hadn't heard a word.

"So many," he whispered again.

"Stasia," Hellboy said, turning to her. "Get him out of here."

She frowned, a storm brewing in her eyes. "I'm bloody well coming down there with you. I've been up against monsters before, and I'm a better shot than you by half."

"More than half," he replied, one corner of his mouth lifting. Hellboy reached out and touched a lock of hair that had escaped both her ponytail and her baseball cap and tucked it behind her ear. "You're a way better shot than I am. But we've been through this. Take a look down there, Stasia. The odds aren't great. Lao's people, they're soldiers. You're not. Me? I'm damn hard to kill. I'm thinking Dwenjue's pretty durable as well, living as long as he has. Koh may be easily breakable, but he's not—"

Hellboy closed his mouth so hard his teeth clacked.

Neither of them needed to hear him say the next word that would have come from his lips. Once again, here it was. Anastasia might be intelligent and courageous, but she had the fatal flaw of being human. Hellboy didn't have that problem, no matter how much effort he spent pretending to himself that that wasn't the case.

Fiercely, almost as if she were striking him, Stasia reached up and grabbed his head with both hands, pulling him down to kiss him hard. Hellboy liked it. It hurt his heart how much he liked it.

"Go get Abe," she said. When she released his face, she practically pushed him away. In a whisper so low he could not hear it, she added something else. Three words. If he'd been any good at reading lips, he thought maybe it would have been almost impossible for him to walk away from her.

"Tenzin," Hellboy said, "you're staying here. Tell Koh and Dwenjue we're just gonna have to go without communication from this point."

The guide translated quickly, his disappointment over not joining them obvious in his tone. Hellboy admired him for that. While Tenzin spoke, Dwenjue and Koh nodded. The warrior monk laid his mystic blade across his shoulder again, ready to attack.

Koh opened his long, dragon jaws and for the first time, when he spoke, Hellboy thought he could see a flicker of flames in his throat. He snarled something.

"He says that the time for talk is over. There will be no more worship for the Dragon King."

"Took the words right out of my mouth," Hellboy said.

Some of the rotting dragons had begun to fly around the temple. Hellboy saw Abe clinging to a post on top of the roof. Others of the dead things nuzzled their sleeping king, while still more began to slither skyward, toward the upper rim, where Hellboy stood waiting. Lao barked orders, and his remaining soldiers took up positions behind Hellboy.

He cast one last glance at Anastasia, then stepped off the edge of the shore, hooves digging into the damp slope of the lake basin that had been underwater only minutes before. Dwenjue and Koh descended the slope with him, the commandos following close behind, silent and grim.

As they neared the new shore of the diminished lake—of the Dragon King Pool—nighttime shadows thrown by the burning worms in the air, a noise like machine-gun fire filled the air. Hellboy flinched, but a second later, he knew what he'd heard.

He looked to the southwest and saw black helicopters whirring through the curtains of rain and hanging storm clouds. There must have been nine or ten, and perhaps some were so cloaked in darkness that there were even more. Reinforcements had arrived, both Chinese government and BPRD.

He wondered how much difference they would make.

With the Dragon King, he figured very little. The battle against the lord of them all wasn't going to come down to helicopters and explosives. This was a place of legends, and the end would be the stuff of such legends, not of men and guns.

On the other hand, as they waded into what was left of the lake, Hellboy sort of wished he'd brought along a missile launcher, or maybe a box of grenades. Something that would blow up dead, squirming, burning things that might otherwise want to eat him.

Chapter 14

The withered dragon slid through the air toward Abe. Abe held on to the spire atop the temple of the Dragon King, trying to think of some other way to fight the worm besides hand to hand. Fire churned up from its nostrils and eyes and mouth and from all the tears in its rotting flesh. Whatever it was—some remnant of an ancient species, now resurrected, or a thing that had lived far too long under the bottom of Lake Tashi with its fire eating away at it from within—Abe didn't care much.

He pulled his sidearm, raised the pistol, and squeezed off three shots. The bullets took the thing dead center in the face, which tore with the dry, brittle texture of a piñata. The dragon didn't slow down.

So much for that.

Abe turned and slid down the curving, sloped roof of the temple. The tiles clacked beneath him but did not break or collapse. He caught himself on a small ridge at the edge of the roof and managed not to shoot right off the side. Below was another roof level, but he had no interest in falling.

The dragon didn't care. It slunk down after him, not touching the roof, flying without wings—only the twisting of its serpent's body propelled it through the air. Not fair at all, by Abe's judgment. Especially since the thing darted toward him, most of its face torn away, fire guttering up from the gaping hole in its head.

A buzzing noise filled his ears. The rain felt good on his skin, but the heat of all of the dragons only added to the damage the scalding water had done.

Abe stared at the dragon, and he knew he didn't have a choice. He fell to the roof, rolled off the edge, and plummeted to the next level down. His shoulder flared with pain as he struck the tiles. His gun flew from his hand and went over the side—no great loss, all things considered. The worm slithered across the night sky above him and started to circle around for another pass. He'd been hoping that, like some kind of hornet, it might pass him by and lose interest, but it was persistent.

The thought of hornets brought the buzzing back to his ears, but this was more than a buzz. Abe spun and saw the black helicopters sweeping down across the diminished lake toward the temple. He felt like cheering, but the urge passed when he realized he didn't know what difference more guns were going to make.

He stood on the west side of the temple's roof. From that vantage, he couldn't see up to the shore, couldn't know what Professor Bruttenholm might be planning. All he could do was keep himself alive and see if he could take some of the undead dragon hatchlings out of the game. Many more of them slithered through the air, now, twenty or more, as though they were merely waiting for the Dragon King to awaken.

Except for one.

The thing intent upon eating him, likely charred, slipped down through the night toward him, speeding up as it drew nearer. Abe crouched on the edge of the roof. A third level lay below him, maybe thirty feet, and forty or fifty feet below that, the slick yellow scales of the enormous body of the Dragon King covered most of the stone island around the base of the temple. The master of dragons remained coiled about the place of his worship, the home of his followers, or kin, or children, or whatever they were. Beyond the Dragon King was the water. Abe thought about just taking a dive, but not even a strong breeze would carry him far enough to hit the water. He'd end up landing on that lowest roof level at best, or on top of the Dragon King at worst.

Not much choice.

The burning dragon corpse swept down upon him. Abe faced it, crouched low. Its jaws opened wide, unhinged like a snake's, and he saw the fire ballooning up from inside, about to erupt toward him.

Abe leaped at it. He twisted sideways even as the flames began to vomit forth, and he plunged the fingers of his right hand into the gaping, burning eye socket of the dragon. With all his strength, he twisted its head away from him, and the fire scorched the night air, instead of his flesh.

His fingers, though . . . his fingers burned.

Abe shouted as he pulled his hand back. Furious, the dragon whipped its serpent body back and forth. Its eagle talons raked at the air as though it wished they were sunk into his flesh. Twisting, it came back on him again.

The roar of a helicopter filled his ears, close enough that the downdraft from its rotors pummeled him. Abe looked up and shielded his eyes as the chopper dropped toward the roof of the temple. Shouts came from within. He saw only silhouettes of figures through the open door at the side of the helicopter—and the barrels of guns. The dragon with its broken jack-o'-lantern head, twisted in the air, its attention on the chopper now instead of Abe. In the light from the burning dead thing's fire, he caught a glimpse of a patch on a jumpsuit inside the chopper.

BPRD.

The dragon darted toward the helicopter. Gunfire punctured the air, riddling the dragon and knocking it backward a few feet, interrupting its attack. But that parchment, withered skin only tore, letting more fire out.

New shouts from inside the chopper. Someone calling his name.

With a noise like the rush of hydraulics, something erupted from inside the chopper. A grenade launcher. It had to be; firing a rocket launcher in that confined space would have been disastrous.

The projectile struck the dragon, tore right through its papery skin . . . and did nothing. The worm stared at the chopper for a second, then turned to gnash its massive jaws at Abe, tossing its head up, antlers charred but gleaming in the firelight. Then something exploded inside the withered dragon. The fire went out, snuffed in an instant, and the monster froze as blue-white ice crystals formed on its skin.

Abe could only stare at it as fresh gunfire erupted from inside the helicopter. This time, the bullets struck the dead, frozen flesh of the dragon and it shattered like glass, pieces of its dead flesh skittering across the tile roof with a tinkling like wind chimes.

"Agent Sapien!" a voice shouted from the chopper, barely audible over the sound of the rotors. "Let's go!"

The helicopter dipped closer to the roof. Abe didn't hesitate. He ran to the edge and leaped into the air. His belly hit the bottom of the door frame and he scrambled for purchase, reaching inside the helicopter for something to grab hold of as his legs kicked in the air.

Then strong hands grabbed him and hauled him into the chopper, and he looked up to see faces, some familiar and some not. All of them wore jackets emblazoned with the insignia of the BPRD. The nearest agent to him, one of the men who'd hauled Abe into the chopper, was Gawaine Johnson, who'd been there for one of Abe's first solo missions with the BPRD, back in the early eighties.

"I see someone has a plan," Abe said.

Gawaine smiled and lit a cigarette. As the chopper rose up into the darkness, he took a drag. His words were smoke. "Liquid nitrogen."

"You think it'll work on the Dragon King?" Abe shouted over the roar of the helicopter.

"One thing at a time."

Abe looked out through the open door of the chopper and saw that the rain had stopped. In the night sky, some of the storm clouds had begun to break up, and he could see glimmers of moon and starlight peeking through.

In the sky above Lake Tashi, above the temple of the Dragon King, helicopters buzzed toward withered, corpse-dragons nearly as large as the helicopters themselves. The dragons were easy to track—they were all on fire, like beacons in the sky.

One by one, he saw them begin to fall, their fire extinguished, ruined, icy flesh disappearing into the darkness of the lake water below or crashing into the temple and shattering.

And at the base of that ancient structure, the Dragon King began to stir once more.

Redfield would live.

Professor Bruttenholm knelt by the injured pilot

and checked him over for broken bones. Blood streaked his forehead from a cut on his scalp and ran down into his beard. There were a dozen other small gashes on his face and arms, and there would be terrible bruising where his restraint belt had pulled taut against his body during the violent landing of the chopper. The bird was ruined, but it was a lot easier to replace than a pilot with the loyalty and skills of a man like Redfield.

The pilot's breathing seemed shallow, and his eyes were a bit too dilated. Bruttenholm figured him for bruised or cracked ribs and a minor concussion. His spidery hands moved over Redfield's limbs, and the man hissed in pain when the professor touched his left forearm. A broken bone, for sure.

Even so, Redfield would live.

The professor told him as much, speaking low comfort to the man, even as he rose, his old knees paining him terribly. A dozen feet away, Lao's commandos were seeing to the body of their comrade, the soldier who'd been aboard the helicopter with Redfield. The commando had been unrestrained, probably even standing in the back of the chopper when it went down. The cranial trauma had been too much. Bruttenholm figured he'd been killed on impact, but didn't speak enough Chinese to offer this small comfort to the other black-garbed soldiers.

Worry wrinkled his brow as he turned to watch the helicopters in combat with flaming dragons above the ancient temple and the lake. He couldn't see Hellboy and his odd companions down in the water, or on the shore of the rocky island at the lake's heart.

The Dragon King had begun to stir. It raised its head and slowly slid in a circle around the base of the temple.

Hurry, son, he thought.

The radio on his hip crackled. "Professor?"

He knew the voice immediately. Snatching the radio from his belt, he lifted it and thumbed the button on the side.

"Abe? You're all right?"

"Debatable. But I'm alive," he said. The roar of a helicopter distorted his voice, and Bruttenholm knew he was aboard one of the birds. "Gawaine Johnson's leading the reinforcements, but you're field leader. What are your orders?"

A shiver went through Trevor Bruttenholm, but he did not hesitate. "You're using liquid nitrogen?"

"Johnson's idea," Abe confirmed.

"Tell Gawaine to get a chopper to my location ASAP. Redfield's injured and needs attention and evac. The rest of you, destroy as many of the dragonlings as you can. If you must engage the Dragon King, try for the eyes, throat, or the red scales of its underbelly. The liquid nitrogen grenades will not puncture the yellow scales of its hide."

The radio crackled. Abe's voice nearly drowned in the chopper's thrum. "What about the king, then?"

Bruttenholm watched as the Dragon King slithered up into the sky, fire issuing from its nostrils and the corners of its mouth, streaking back along its body. The worm's serpentine body was at least one hundred feet long, five times the largest of its withered followers. It soared into the sky and began to twist in on itself, surveying the conflict that churned around it.

How anyone could reach it from the ground—even his son and a mystic warrior who'd defeated it once before—Bruttenholm didn't know. He tried not even to think about the size of the thing.

"Hellboy's on it," he said.

"Yes, sir," Abe replied, as if that was all the explanation he needed.

Professor Bruttenholm realized that it was. Helicopters, guns, and liquid nitrogen were all well and good, but once again it had come down to the inevitable—Hellboy was their best chance at destroying the Dragon King and getting off that Tibetan plateau alive.

What had once been the shore of the lake was now a ridge atop a long slope that led down to the Dragon King Pool more than two hundred feet below. Anastasia stood on the edge and felt a wave of vertigo wash over her. Behind her, Lao's remaining commandos had begun firing at the Dragon King once more. The gigantic serpent swam across the sky, and missile after missile arced above the lake and the temple.

Some struck the ancient myth—most of those bursting harmlessly on the thick yellow scales of its back and sides—but others went wide. One projectile struck its antlers and exploded, splintering a branch and sending that shard tumbling down into the water far, far below.

At the center of what remained of the lake, she saw Hellboy, Koh, and Dwenjue climbing out of the water. With the Dragon King now airborne, a stone ledge perhaps twenty-five feet wide had been left unguarded around the temple. The smaller dragons—servants of the king, she presumed—were in combat with the BPRD and Chinese government helicopters that had arrived with such fortuitous timing. More than half of them had already been destroyed, and she'd seen only one of the choppers spinning out of the sky in a flaming ball of wreckage. Anastasia did not have a callous heart, but she could not help thinking of this as an acceptable loss.

It meant they were winning.

At least, the others would see it that way. Behind her, she could hear Lao exhorting his soldiers. Some of the commandos cheered when two of the dragonlings crashed down onto the temple roof and shattered into fragments. They were exultant, and why not? To them, the tide had turned. But Anastasia knew that their real problem remained. If they could not destroy the Dragon King, it would all be for naught.

Hellboy, Koh, and Dwenjue seemed to pause a moment. Then Koh pointed toward the temple of the Dragon King, and Anastasia squinted to study the flicker, burning windows of the place. Shadows moved there, and she understood that there were still some of those dead-looking dragonlings inside.

Koh started for the front of the temple, leaving Hellboy and Dwenjue behind. She wished she had field glasses so she could get a better look at Hellboy's face, perhaps read his lips, something at which she had only a little bit of practice.

Dwenjue raised his mystical blade again. Hellboy stood behind him, glancing around as though protecting the dwarf while he performed this task. The blade began to glow that eerie yellow once more.

"Do you think they'll be able to kill it?" a voice said beside her, loudly enough to be heard over the firing of the missiles and the roar of the helicopters.

Anastasia flinched and turned to find the digger, Gibson, and Alan Corriveau just a few feet away, staring down into the lake below with twin expressions of dreadful uncertainty. Though they had worked for her on this dig, she didn't know either of them very well.

"It's Hellboy," she replied, as though that were answer enough. For her, it was. They didn't look convinced.

Motion on her left made her turn, and she saw Professor Kyichu walk tentatively to the edge. He gazed in open wonder at the Dragon King flowing through the air and the choppers in combat with its burning kindred.

"Extraordinary!" the man cried, almost jovial. He turned to look at Anastasia, the thrill in his eyes repugnant. He'd sent his daughter away in the hands of strangers after she'd been through trauma unimaginable for a child.

"We're making history, Stacie!" the man said, hardly seeing her, intoxicated with the horror all around them. "Think of it. We'll be legends ourselves, now. All of this . . . they'll be teaching our names at universities for centuries, if your ex can just kill the beast so we can get back to work."

A shiver of disgust went through her, and she cocked back her fist and swung. The crunch of her knuckles on the side of Han Kyichu's face resulted in a pain that was awful and satisfying, all at once. The man staggered back and fell to the ground, staring up at her in fury and humiliation.

"Who do you think—" the professor began.

"Shut your gob, you bloody git!" Anastasia roared at him, knowing she sounded like some nutter in the stands at a football match, and not caring.

Applause sounded behind her. She spun to see Corriveau and Gibson clapping for her.

"Well done, you," Gibson cheered.

She ignored them, and turned to watch Hellboy and Dwenjue. They were all behaving as though the worst was over, but for Anastasia, the worst had just begun.

Koh left Dwenjue and the demon behind and raced toward the temple of the Dragon King. This close, his transformation had somehow been affected. He felt more the dragon than ever. Liquid fire burbled in his throat and flickered from his nostrils. He crouched low to the ground as he ran, and in the back of his mind was the fanciful idea that if he could just let go of his humanity, he might take to the air and fly like his ancestors.

But that was something that Koh would never do. He might not be entirely human, but within him existed enough spirit to feel hatred toward the Dragon King and all of his servants. They were the scourge of humanity, and of the children of Nakchu village. No more would die. Koh would stand with the humans and the strange beings that had come with them and see the Dragon King destroyed, or die himself.

Within the tall windows of the temple he could see the resurrected dragons moving like worms driven up from the earth by heavy rains. They burned with internal fire, casting hideous shadows. Koh hurried toward the nearest window and paused to gauge the height of the frame, wondering if he could jump and grab hold to pull himself in.

The *whump-whump* of helicopter rotors filled the

air above him, driving the air down, pummeling him with it. As he spun, the helicopter set down on the island, fifty feet from Koh. The side door had been opened, and through it he could see the strange fish-man the others called Abe grabbing hold of the barrels of a pair of heavy, wide-mouthed guns and pushing them upward to prevent the soldiers within from firing at Koh. Abe shouted at them until they had all put up their weapons.

Then the fish-man signaled for the soldiers to follow him and jumped out of the helicopter. They followed, leaping to the ground and running across the stone toward him.

A flash of fire glinted in the corner of Koh's eye, and he turned to see one of the burning dragons slither from a window. It darted toward the soldiers and Abe, who didn't seem to have noticed it over the chop of the helicopter blades.

Koh shouted, knowing they would not understand him. He ran at Abe, pointing at the dragon as it arced down at them, fire beginning to erupt from its maw. Only then did the soldiers turn. They raised their weapons and several of them fired. With loud pops, dark projectiles burst from the barrels and struck the dragon, even as fire started to fall. Koh reached Abe, grabbed the fish-man, and twisted around so that the flames cascaded across his own back. Where the fire struck, his clothes incinerated, but he kept Abe safe.

The dragon fell, its internal flame extinguished,

and shattered into huge shards of ice-crusted, dead flesh. One soldier cried out as he burned, but the others were far enough back that the dragon fire never reached them.

Koh's clothes were smoking and still burning in places. He tore the remnants of his shirt off. The soldiers stared at him—at his scaly flesh and fiery eyes—and he knew they had to resist the urge to kill him as well. They saw only the dragon in him, not the man.

Abe clapped him on the shoulder and said something that Koh presumed was gratitude. Yet even the fish-man wore a dubious expression that Koh had no trouble reading. *Why are you doing this?* that expression said. Even if he'd been able to speak the fish-man's language, he was not sure he would have tried to explain. Was it so hard for Abe to understand that the village of Nakchu had been peaceful before all of this, that they were not savage people? All Koh and his father and the rest of his kin had wanted was to be left alone.

Or perhaps Abe had trouble understanding why Koh would help after what had happened to his village. If they survived this night, he would explain to the fish-man that—though the archaeologists had disturbed the Dragon King—they were not responsible for what the great ancestor had done to Nakchu.

Regardless of whether his motives were understood, though, Koh would fight at the side of these intruders. Once upon a time, the whole mountain range had lived in terror of the Dragon King. Koh was not going to let that happen again.

Two soldiers were tending to the one who had fallen. Another helicopter was landing, disgorging more troops, all armed with the same weapons that were freezing the dragons from the inside. Miraculous, terrible things.

Abe picked up the fallen soldier's weapon and looked at Koh. He gestured toward the temple, and Koh nodded.

Side by side, they ran along the front of the temple until they found a window low enough to leap to. Another dragon emerged, but the soldiers were ready this time, and they all had to stand aside to avoid being struck by its frozen corpse as it fell. Then they were all up and inside the temple, and the ancient dragons swarmed within, burning, fluttering with fire.

The weapons boomed.

One of them lunged at Koh, and he ran straight toward it and leaped, claws and jaws tearing into flesh and fire.

Hellboy didn't bother with the gun. It wasn't going to do him a damn bit of good. He flexed the fingers of his right hand, the only weapon that he knew he could rely on. Maybe the guys in the choppers could fill the Dragon King full of liquid nitrogen, but he didn't think the pilots could get close enough for enough direct hits on the gigantic worm's belly or mouth to take it down, and no way were those grenades going to puncture its hide anywhere else.

No, this thing had to be up close and personal. That worked fine for Hellboy, and he figured Dwenjue wouldn't have it any other way.

Heat rose up from the lake and blew out of the temple on the wind, buffeting them where they stood on the rocky ledge of that island. In the sky only a handful of the smaller dragons remained, but far above them all, the Dragon King whipped through the air, twisting in upon itself. The fire that guttered from its maw and eyes streaked along beside its coiling body.

It prowled the night sky like a predator, considering what it wanted to kill next.

Dwenjue held his sword before him, point straight up—so much taller than he was—and chanted in a low, nasal cadence. The yellow light that emanated from the mystic blade grew brighter, so that Hellboy had to squint to look down at the dwarf monk. Dwenjue did not return his gaze. The ancient warrior only glared up at the darkness, at the vanishing storm clouds and the celestial ebony beyond, and performed that incantation.

A ripple of light ran up the length of the sword. In that moment, Hellboy felt a pulse of some kind emanate from the blade—power, energy, magic.

In the sky, the Dragon King ceased its coiling. It darted across the air far above the lake, nearly to the southern ridge that had once been the shore, and turned around. Dwenjue broke off his chant and glanced at Hellboy, muttering some warning. But Hellboy did not need to be warned. Somehow, the sword had drawn its attention, and now the Dragon King swept down toward them—coming for them. One of its eyes burned with fire, but the other glinted silver in the moonlight.

He risked a quick look at Dwenjue and saw the anticipation on the ancient one's face. Hellboy understood. The monk had started a job many centuries ago and never finished it. Maybe he wouldn't have been able to finish it on his own—Hellboy figured either one of them, alone, might not have been able to do the job. But this time, Dwenjue had help. One way or the other, this was the warrior's second chance, and there wouldn't be a third.

The Dragon King slithered down from the sky. The size of the thing, up close, made Hellboy catch his breath. It dropped toward them, a hundred feet away, then seventy, then forty, and it opened its jaws wide. The wind of its momentum sucked some of the fire from its gullet, but Hellboy stared into the inferno of its throat, and he braced himself for the pain to come.

Dwenjue held his mystic blade up in front of him and did not move.

The Dragon King shook its antlers like a bull about to charge, then it straightened out. Bright red-

and-yellow flames erupted from the dragon's maw with such force that it burned the air that separated it from them—the distance from the worm to the ground.

Hellboy set his hooves firmly, and the fire engulfed him, blasting around him, scorching the clothes from his body. He grunted in pain as the flames seared him, but his flesh did not char or burn. The ammunition in the gun at his hip exploded and knocked him sideways, nearly causing him to lose his balance. He shouted in surprise and pain. Dressed only in burning rags, he crouched and readied himself.

Dwenjue held up his blade, and the flames washed around him, as though some invisible shield protected him. The fire swept past him like a river around a large stone in its midst. Hellboy kept glancing at him, waiting for him to do something, but the warrior only stood there, motionless, blade in his hands.

Then the dragon was upon them. Hellboy couldn't wait for Dwenjue any longer. The Dragon King darted its head down, jaws wide, the fire ceasing as it tried to snap them up in its teeth.

Hellboy sprang with all of his strength, crimson flesh smoking with the heat of the dragon fire, the last tatters of his clothing still burning. He slammed one hoof down onto the giant worm's skull and reached out for the Dragon King's antlers. His hands clutched at them, but he missed and instead slammed into the tangle of sharp antlers. The impact knocked the breath from him, but he managed to get a grip on one of the bony protrusions, the size of a small tree.

As he did, he glanced down and saw the Dragon King snatch Dwenjue up in its jaws.

The dragon lanced skyward, shaking its head back and forth as its jaws worked on chewing the dwarf monk and swallowing him. Hellboy swore loudly as he tried desperately to hold on to the bucking, thrashing, coiling dragon. It twisted, even as it flew higher and higher. Fire gusted from its eyes, but he ignored it, using all of his strength just to hang on.

What had Dwenjue been thinking? Did he want to rest so badly that he'd just let the Dragon King eat him? No. No way. Hellboy had seen the intensity in the warrior's face when he'd talked about his destiny. Getting himself down the dragon's throat might not be the smartest move ever, but Hellboy had to believe that Dwenjue had some kind of clever scheme in mind.

Meanwhile, Hellboy's plan was not to die. At the moment, his focus was how to bring the Dragon King down without getting killed himself. They were high. As the worm slithered across the sky, Hellboy glanced down, but he could barely make out the soldiers near the helicopters that had landed beside the temple. The choppers in the air were visible. He scanned the original lakeshore, but the dragon whipped him around so fast he couldn't catch a glimpse of the camp where Stasia and the others were.

The Dragon King rolled.

"Son of a bitch!" Hellboy roared.

He held on tightly as his legs dangled beneath him. A second later the worm righted itself, then snaked across the sky back toward the temple . . . and a black chopper headed their way.

"No," Hellboy said, the wind sucking away his words. "Don't be stupid."

Too late. He didn't know if it was a BPRD chopper or the Chinese military, but the Dragon King opened its jaws, and fire strafed the helicopter in huge gusts. The chopper blew backward, spinning out of control, bathed in fire that was almost liquid. Then it exploded.

"That's it!" Hellboy shouted.

Forget about the distance to the ground and forget about falling and forget about waiting for Dwenjue to do something. As far as Hellboy knew, the little monk had already been digested.

"No more burning!" he bellowed, and he punctuated each word with a sledgehammer blow from his stony right fist. "No more villages! No more worship! And no more dead kids!"

With each blow, the Dragon King flinched, and jerked, and tried to twist away from his assault. But Hellboy wasn't going anywhere. He struck the worm's skull over and over, felt bone and thick hide and scale giving way as he hammered at it. Blood began to leak from the corner of the Dragon King's intact eye, and finally Hellboy knew he had done some damage.

The gigantic sky serpent began to glide lower.

Hellboy held on tightly to one antler with his left hand and shouted with the effort as, with that oversize right, he cracked off a prong from the other antler. The Dragon King darted downward. Hellboy slid down, clutching the antler between his left arm and chest, barely hanging on. He raised the broken prong, and, with all the strength he could muster, he drove it through the skull of the Dragon King.

Fire erupted from its maw in a scream. Its body twisted and whipped in the air. It soared downward, no longer gliding but crashing. The Dragon King speared toward the rocky hills to the west of Lake Tashi, the foothills of the mountains, one hundred feet of streaming fire and scales.

It struck the ground at an angle, tearing up the earth as its huge body tangled up in itself, twisting and careening across ridges and rocks. Hellboy tried to hang on to the Dragon King's antlers, but the worm's head canted sideways, prongs stuck in hard earth, and the resultant snapping of the dragon's body bucked him away. He tumbled through the air, end over end, slamming to the ground twenty feet away, flipping several times; and then he came to rest on the slope of a low hill.

Darkness dragged him down.

Hellboy's eyes snapped open, and he drew a deep, ragged breath, blinking and looking around. His body ached as though he'd been beaten by a gang of trolls carrying baseball bats, which he'd experienced once firsthand. A spike of pain went down the back of his neck as he started to rise, and then full awareness returned, and he cursed under his breath and glanced around, expecting to be burned or eaten.

No attack came. The Dragon King lay unmoving, its length contorted in a sprawl all along the hillside that had once been the western rim of Lake Tashi.

Grunting in annoyance at the bruises he'd acquired in the crash, Hellboy stared warily at the still form of the dragon. It couldn't be dead. That much he knew. Maybe it had been injured enough to go into some kind of catatonic state, or revert to whatever weird undeath it had existed in before the preparatory chamber had been opened, stirring its consciousness to wakefulness. But no way would he take anything for granted.

His hooves slipped on the grassy hill, so different from the rockier slopes to the north. Hellboy got his footing and continued on, crouched low, watching the motionless worm. This close and unmoving, its bulk seemed even more enormous. He picked up his pace, wanting to get to the head of the Dragon King to see if the fire still churned inside it, and to be at the spot where he thought he could do the most damage if it should suddenly awaken.

The Dragon King's body had been twisted around on impact, so that as he moved past it, yellow scales gave way to the softer red scales of its underbelly.

Hellboy eyed the worm, and as he hurried, he gritted his teeth against the discomfort of his injuries.

The dragon twitched. Hellboy froze, twenty feet away, and stared at the spot on its red belly that had moved. It might have been involuntary, some kind of muscle pulse, but he didn't want to take any chances. He started walking again, hustling toward the massive head of the beast with its broken antlers. The prong he'd jammed through its softened skull still jutted there, black blood crusting around it.

Again, the belly twitched. Hellboy tensed.

Something punctured the Dragon King's red-scaled stomach from within. Coated in blood and viscera, still the tip of the mystic sword glistened in the light of the moon and stars that showed through the remnants of the storm clouds above.

Dwenjue.

As Hellboy watched, the blade tugged against the scaly flesh and began to slice. In a jerking, staggered motion, that mystic sword slit the Dragon King's belly open, exposing black blood and thick yellow fluid and releasing a stench of sulfur and rot that made Hellboy gag. He put a hand to his mouth as bile rose up the back of his throat and managed to avoid vomiting. He started breathing through his mouth, trying to diminish the smell.

The sword split the red scales, lengthening the split, steaming innards spilling out onto the tall grass. Seven feet. Twelve. Eighteen feet.

Then it ceased. The sword stopped moving, jerked once, then went completely still, lodged in the flesh of the dragon's gut.

"Crap," Hellboy muttered. The Dragon King hadn't moved at all while Dwenjue had been slicing it open. Whether that meant it was really dead or not, he didn't know, but he couldn't just leave Dwenjue in there.

Hellboy climbed up the hill to the Dragon King's gutted remains. The worm's body was so thick that on its side, it was taller than he was. The heat from its insides radiated outward as though he were standing much too close to a fire. He reached up and grabbed hold of the flaps of scaly flesh on either side of the slit that Dwenjue had cut in its belly and began to tear.

The dragon's underside tore with a wet, slippery noise, and more of that stink wafted out at him. Hellboy gagged but did not turn away. He took a better stance, improved his grip, and tore again, ripping another five of six feet of red scales in two.

Dwenjue spilled out with coils of the dragon's viscera, wet with its blood and bodily fluids, sword still clutched in his hands. The dwarf had never seemed so small as he did, lying there on the hillside, that sword so much longer than his own body.

The warrior monk's eyes fluttered open, mucuslike fluid gumming his eyelids together. Weakly, he spoke to Hellboy, gesturing with one hand back into the Dragon King's belly. The words did not register, but their meaning was evident. He'd been trying to get to something inside the dragon, trying to cut his way to revealing some vulnerable spot.

Dwenjue's eyes fluttered weakly. His flesh beneath the blood had been burned, but there were also blisters all over his skin and areas where the skin seemed to have been eaten away. He'd been partially digested in the Dragon King's belly.

"Don't worry, pal. We'll get you some help," Hellboy said. "But first, I'm guessing what you really need is to get this job done."

Hellboy reached down and took the sword from Dwenjue's hand. The dwarf released the blade to him, pain and hope alternating in his eyes. He said something else, his voice a rasp, but of course Hellboy could not understand him.

The mystic sword felt like ice in Hellboy's grip. He switched hands, and the moment he put the blade in his right hand, it began to glow once more with the vibrant yellow of Dwenjue's eyes.

A frown creased Hellboy's forehead. He glanced down and saw that the dwarf's eyes were now flat, ordinary black. Regret struck Hellboy, but he knew there could be no hesitation now. This thing hadn't turned out the way legends should, but he needed to get it done.

Leaving Dwenjue, he thrust the shining blade into the dragon's belly and put all of his strength into it, enlarging the slit that the monk had begun. The red scales blossomed apart. Hellboy dragged the sword up toward the dragon's head. As he did, he reached a place where the red scales became more difficult to cut. It took all of his strength to split the skin there, and when he did, nothing spilled out.

Inside, a small fire burned. The object was oval, more than a foot long, and it burned with red-and-yellow flames that somehow raged there without consuming the object itself. Hellboy stared a moment, thinking that if this thing still burned, the Dragon King couldn't truly be dead, no matter how much damage they did to it. This thing—this was what made it immortal, this eternal fire.

Then he knew what it was. The Dragon King's heart. It all made sense to him now. Dwenjue had been trying to reach the heart, to kill his ancient enemy once and for all.

Hellboy raised the sword. Its yellow glow became so bright he had to squint. He felt none of the deep satisfaction he would have imagined in killing this thing. It had to be stopped, but there were too few ancient things, too few legends still in the world, and there was a bitterness in its destruction.

"All over, now," he muttered.

He brought the sword down . . . but stopped himself before the blade could strike the burning heart of the dragon. Hellboy glanced back at Dwenjue, taking in the ruins of the warrior's face. The dwarf's body had been ravaged; he was dying.

This isn't how it's supposed to be, he thought. *This legend isn't mine.*

Grimly, Hellboy strode back to Dwenjue, reached down, and picked the diminutive monk up under his arm. He carried the ancient warrior back to the place where he had revealed the dragon's heart and set him down as gently as he could.

"Dwenjue," Hellboy said.

The monk blinked, gaze clearing a moment before he started to drift again. Hellboy shouted his name, and this time, the dwarf's eyes went wide, and his nostrils flared with anger or surprise.

Hellboy took his hands and closed them around the grip of the mystic sword that had rested with him in the ground for so many centuries. The glow diminished slightly, but as it did, Dwenjue's eyes took on their former yellow gleam.

"Up," Hellboy said, gripping him under the arms. He lifted the monk bodily and set him on his feet.

Dwenjue stumbled, nearly collapsed, but Hellboy caught him.

The sword pulsed with light and magic. Dwenjue stood up a bit straighter, still swaying but not about to fall. His back went rigid as he stared down at the burning heart of the dragon.

The sword fell. It flared yellow the instant it struck the Dragon King's heart. The fire went out of the worm's core, and it cleaved in half.

Dwenjue collapsed, sliding to the ground, then

tumbling over onto his back. As he stared up at the night sky, the illumination went out of his eyes, and they turned black once more. A single, shuddering breath came from the warrior, and he fell still.

The ancient enemies lay dead, side by side.

Hellboy sat down beside Dwenjue, leaning against the dead Dragon King. He glanced at the sword still clutched in the monk's hand, but did not attempt to retrieve it. That blade belonged with Dwenjue and would return with him to his grave.

A strange satisfaction filled Hellboy, mixed with profound envy. He'd helped Dwenjue fulfill his destiny, and now the warrior could rest.

Rest.

The word tasted bittersweet, even in his thoughts.

Epilogue

Upon the death of the Dragon King, those few of his dragonlings that had not already been killed simply ceased, the fire snuffed out within them. Their flesh became brittle, and within hours, had begun to decompose.

Now, the cleanup was under way.

Redfield had been medevacked to Lhasa along with other wounded. The last of Dr. Bransfield's team had been retrieved from the monastery on the eastern hill. Only three members of her original expedition had agreed to stay on with her at the site of the temple of the Dragon King. The British Museum would organize a new team. To everyone's surprise, Professor Kyichu had been on the first helicopter headed for Lhasa, determined to reunited with his daughter even as he nursed a dark bruise on his face.

According to the digger, Gibson, Dr. Bransfield had knocked some sense into him.

Meanwhile, Anastasia would see to it that the Chinese government would do nothing to hide or damage the dig site or attempt to deny the events that had transpired here.

Abe thought it evident that Lao would have liked to do just that, but there had been too many killed and too many international observers on the ground and in the air during the event. Barring the possibility of secrecy, however, Abe figured they would be working far more closely with the British Museum's efforts than they had before. Anastasia and Mr. Lao were going to be spending a great deal of time together. The BPRD would also be keeping a small team on-site for the duration of the archaeological efforts, in case anything else unusual came up and also as an impartial observer.

Crews would have to be brought in to remove the wreckage of the downed choppers. Someone would have to decide what to do with the corpse of the Dragon King. But those were all issues to be examined over the days ahead.

At the moment, only one issue remained on Abe's mind.

He stood with Koh and Tenzin in the scorched ruins of what had once been the archaeologists' camp. The sun had begun to rise, and it shone brightly up on the ridge where the preparatory chamber had twice been opened, and where digging would soon commence once more.

Not a trace of the dragon could be seen in Koh.

They had all agreed it would be safer that way. He seemed like just an ordinary man, now.

Together, the three of them watched the argument going on between Professor Bruttenholm and Mr. Lao in the shadow of one of the black military helicopters that the man from Beijing had summoned. The normally emotionless Lao appeared angry. Bruttenholm, on the other hand, had fallen back on his English reserve. He kept his face expressionless, his chin slightly lifted, gazing at Lao with all the moral authority he could muster.

When Lao took a breath, the professor spoke calmly.

Lao stared at him for several long seconds, then threw up his hand and turned on one foot to march over to the helicopter and lift himself into the cockpit. He glared at Bruttenholm again as he slid on the communications headset, apparently needing to conference with his superiors, then slammed the door closed.

Professor Bruttenholm walked away as though the scene had not troubled him at all. He strode over to where Abe, Koh, and Tenzin awaited him.

"What did he say?" Abe asked.

The professor stroked his white goatee a moment in thought, then gave the smallest of shrugs. "He said that what happens to the people of Nakchu village is not our concern, that they are being detained while the question of whether or not they present a danger to humanity is evaluated."

Tenzin quickly translated this to Koh. Fire flickered in the dragon-man's eyes, and he sneered something in anger, jaw clenched.

Abe held up a hand to calm him, even as Tenzin put a hand on Koh's arm and spoke some words of comfort.

"And what was your reply?" Abe asked the professor.

Bruttenholm's eyes brightened and he arched an eyebrow. "I patiently explained that the people of Nakchu village have suffered a terrible loss and should be allowed to mourn, then left alone. Given their unique nature, I told Mister Lao that the villagers are most certainly the concern of the BPRD, and that if he disagreed, he could feel free to take it up with our United Nations sponsors. I told him that the BPRD agents who remain here with Dr. Bransfield will be visiting Nakchu several times a week and making regular reports, and that any attempt to interfere with those visits would be frowned upon by the world community."

As he spoke, Tenzin rattled off the translation to Koh, who began to smile. The dragon-man grabbed Professor Bruttenholm's hand and clasped it in gratitude.

"You're pretty good at this stuff," Abe told the old man.

Bruttenholm waved a hand. "The wisdom of age. And the bludgeon of diplomacy." The professor studied Tenzin and Koh a moment. "Have you had that conversation with Koh that we discussed?"

Abe nodded. “I have.”

“And?”

“He hasn’t given me an answer.”

Professor Bruttenholm studied the dragon-man. “Right, then. What do you think, Koh? Could I convince you to return to the States with us and work with our organization?”

Tenzin smiled and asked the question.

Koh stood up a bit straighter and replied with profound dignity.

“I’m sorry, Professor,” Tenzin said. “Koh cannot leave the plateau. With his father dead, he knows that his people will need someone to lead them, to care for them. And he wishes to offer Dr. Bransfield as much help as he can in her efforts here at the temple.”

Abe put out a hand, and Koh shook it, after the fashion he had observed among the other Westerners. “I’m sorry you won’t be joining us,” Abe said. “I’m honored to have met you, and I owe you one for saving my bacon down there.”

Koh nodded, smiling.

“Ah, well,” Professor Bruttenholm said. “All is as it should be, I suppose.”

Hellboy and Anastasia stood on the stone island surrounding the temple of the Dragon King, bathed in the glow of the rising sun. Their hands were clasped between them, and he gazed at her with a terrible longing and a strange nostalgia. He knew he shouldn't feel nostalgic for someone who stood right in front of him, but could not help it. They'd come to the end of things, and yet it felt to him so much like a new beginning.

The aftermath unfolded all around them. Soldiers and BPRD agents worked inside the temple, careful not to damage the structure itself even as they checked to be certain all of the dragons were dead. Helicopters buzzed overhead. Not far away, Corriveau and Gibson, two of Stasia's team who'd agreed to stay with her in the interim, were taking photographs of the façade of the temple.

"Going to get busy around here," Stasia said.

"Get busy?" Hellboy asked, eyebrows raised.

Stasia laughed softly. "I mean it. We'll be thick with soldiers and archaeologists once the word of all this gets out. I only hope the museum lets me stay on to lead the dig."

"They will. They'd be idiots not to."

"And all of the people you have to answer to are Rhodes scholars, I suppose?"

Hellboy frowned. "Not quite. But they'll keep you on. They'll realize no one else is suited to the work. This is your dig. I have faith in you."

She squeezed his fingers. "I know you do. I always know it. In the hard times, it helps. I just wish you didn't have to go."

The moment she said those words, Anastasia

blinked, and a tiny sound came from her lips, as though she'd surprised herself. Hellboy felt a tremor pass through him, and suddenly he didn't seem to be able to breathe right. He cursed himself inwardly for being a fool, tried not to speak his thoughts aloud, and failed.

"What if I didn't go? What if I stayed with you? The BPRD's going to assign a few agents to stick around for the duration. I could arrange to be one of them."

Her smile filled him with bittersweet tenderness. Anastasia reached up and touched his face. She rose up on her toes and pulled him down, and they shared a soft, brief kiss. Then Stasia laid her cheek against his chest. He heard her sigh.

"Do you have any idea how wonderful that sounds to me?"

"I think I've got an inkling, yeah."

Stasia hesitated, as Hellboy had known she would. They knew each other too well. Wistful, he took hold of her shoulders and moved her out to arm's length, gazing down at her.

"I feel a 'but' coming."

She nodded. "Yes. You are aware we're being watched, I presume?"

Hellboy glanced around, saw where Stasia was looking, and narrowed his eyes to focus on the lone figure standing far above them on the lake rim, staring down.

His father, no doubt with brow furrowed in concern.

"He's a little overprotective, huh?" Hellboy asked.

Stasia shook her head, gaze intensely sincere. "Not at all. He loves you. He's meant to look out for you, isn't he? Your father?"

Hellboy studied her face. "So, you were about to say?"

Her smile illuminated her entire face, but her eyes were full of sadness. "We've been down this route before, love. Those who do not learn from history . . ."

"Are doomed to repeat it," Hellboy finished for her. The truth of it settled in. She was right. If he stayed, they would be inseparable for a time—months, maybe years—but all of the old ghosts would still be there to haunt them, and eventually Hellboy would have to withdraw from Stasia, for her sake as well as his own.

"Do you remember that day in Paris?" Stasia asked, her eyes moist and her voice cracking.

Hellboy didn't have to ask her which day. "Of course I do."

"I've never stopped feeling the way I felt that day. I don't think I ever will. It's a gift you gave me, and I cherish it."

"Even though it hurts?" Hellboy asked, trying to memorize the way she looked at that moment.

"The pain's part of it. Comes with the territory, doesn't it?"

"Yeah," he said. "I guess it does."

The sun shone on her hair, the cool autumn mountain breeze whipping it around her face. "I'm going to miss you terribly."

Hellboy traced a finger along the line of her jaw, then he shrugged.

"No worries. I'll see you in another five years."

About the Author

Christopher Golden is the award-winning, bestselling author of such novels as *The Myth Hunters, Wildwood Road, The Boys Are Back in Town, The Ferryman, Strangewood, Of Saints and Shadows,* and the *Body of Evidence* series of teen thrillers. Working with actress/writer/director Amber Benson, he cocreated and cowrote *Ghosts of Albion,* an animated supernatural drama for BBC online, from which they created the book series of the same name.
(www.ghostsofalbion.net)

With Thomas E. Sniegoski, he is the coauthor of the dark fantasy series *The Menagerie* as well as the young readers fantasy series *OutCast,* which was recently acquired by Universal Pictures. Their comic book series *Talent* is also in development at Universal. Golden and Sniegoski wrote the graphic novel *BPRD: Hollow Earth,* a spinoff from the fan favorite comic book series *Hellboy.* Golden also authored the original Hellboy novels, *The Lost Army* and *The Bones of Giants,* and edited two Hellboy short story anthologies.

Golden was born and raised in Massachusetts, where he still lives with his family. He graduated from Tufts University. His latest novel is *The Borderkind,* part two of a dark fantasy trilogy for Bantam Books entitled *The Veil.* Most recently, he completed work on a lavishly illustrated gothic novel entitled *Baltimore, or, the Steadfast Tin Soldier and the Vampire,* a collaboration with Hellboy creator Mike Mignola. There are more than 8 million copies of his books in print. Please visit him at www.christophergolden.com